CW00498554

Brutal Retribution

To Janice
With Best Regards &
Kind wishes

Brutal Retribution

by

CLIVE OWEN BARRY

Clive Owen Barry

This book is dedicated to my darling wife,

Debbie Sue.

With all my love, now and forever more.

'Unaquivicably' of course.

Books by this Author

Middle Grade

'Granule Speck and the Ichkin'.

'Granule Speck, the Witch and the Princess'.

Adult Crime

'Brutal Retribution'.

CHAPTER ONE

Sally would never have believed what happened that morning. Everything was surreal and in slow motion, with a background of white sound.

The whole world had gone still as she stood up from the pine bench in the kitchen. There was, or at least there had seemed to have been a mist covering her eyes as she slowly walked over to the draining board, picking up the old four inch Sabatier paring knife, last used the night before to peel potatoes for making chips for the bairn's tea.

Silently, she walked the seven paces from the kitchen sink to where her husband was sitting in the living room. Then just as silently and with all the strength she possessed, she plunged the knife up to the hilt, deep into the back of his neck.

Charlie had been sat with his left leg tucked up underneath him in his favourite armchair facing away from the kitchen, leaving his large back fully exposed. The knife entered above shoulder level midway to the base of his skull, completely severing his spinal cord.

Charlie screamed. He had no idea of what had just happened, nor why there was such a sharp pain. Further to that, why he could neither turn nor move either his arms or his legs anymore.

Sally on the other hand had not finished. She was not functioning as Sally the mother of two small children, or even Sally the oppressed housewife. At this moment in time she hated Charlie with a passion she would never have believed possible. Seemingly she had finally found both her inner strength and determination.

She pulled with all her reserve and the slim bladed knife slowly sucked loose. She then stepped unhurriedly around to the front of him and while staring directly into his piggy little eyes, she plunged the knife deep into his throat.

It could be said that Sally was out of control. She was definitely in a state of total confusion and just couldn't understand why Charlie hadn't raised a hand to stop her.

She plunged the knife for the second, the third, the fourth and many, many, more times after. Severing skin, muscle, sinew, veins and arteries. Charlie's head eventually rolled back. He gurgled, he choked, he bled profusely, then whilst sat in his favourite armchair, watching one of his favourite programmes on the television, Charlie died.

CHAPTER TWO

This day, like far too many days before it, hadn't really started out too well. Earlier that morning, Sally Oldham had woken from a very sporadic sleep clutching her torn pyjamas and fleecy bathrobe tightly round her slim body. She was cold and shivering from an extremely uncomfortable night spent in the foetal position on the hard bedroom floor.

She'd been roused by the overpowering stench of sour beer, vomit and blood. The blood was hers, it was up her nose, it was in her mouth, it had congealed on her teeth, it was smeared across her face and it was splattered down the front of her pyjamas.

The sour beer, vomit together with the distinctive odour of shit on the other hand belonged to Charlie her husband. He was laid fast asleep on his back, snoring loudly while sprawled diagonally across the big soft bed. Far too drunk the night before to remove the remainder of his clothes when he'd come upstairs. First making sure of course, that the unreasonable demands he'd bestowed upon Sally his young wife were fulfilled, thus satisfying any animal cravings he might have had. Sally lay still on the floor, she didn't dare move, Charlie had told her not to.

It was nearly time for the kids to wake up and she desperately needed to get through the bathroom and clean herself before they saw the state of her face. She quietly rose and looked into the small magnifying mirror sat on the bathroom windowsill, realising there was no way on this God's earth could she possibly conceal the black eye, or the bruised and swollen torn lips. She also noted the throbbing pain in her rear passage as a result of being held face down by the neck across the back of Charlie's chair. Thankfully he was so pissed when he came in, it only lasted seconds. It didn't stop the good hiding she got after though, that lasted a lot longer than the buggering did.

Sally showered quickly, whilst noting that the discolouration against the pale white skin covering her ribs was rapidly turning into dark bruises. She dressed as fast as she could, grabbing a pair of worn tracky bottoms and a baggy sweatshirt out of the dirty wash basket.

Charlie had made it quite obvious during previous good hidings that he didn't like her wearing t-shirts or tight fitting tops. He said it drew far too much attention to her from other men. Her old pink Converse shoes were still in the corner of the bathroom where she'd kicked them off the night before, so she just slipped them back on without any socks.

Sally towel dried her hair and combed it straight back off her face with a simple side parting. There was no way she was going to chance using the hair dryer and disturb her snoring husband this morning. She didn't dare wake him before he'd had a chance to sleep off the painful thumping hangover she really hoped he was going to have when he eventually surfaced.

Little Charlie, named after his dad, was seven years old and tiny Georgia, named after Sally's dad was four. They were both already downstairs in the living room, sat in their pyjamas watching cbeebies on the telly when Sally came down from the bathroom.

The room was a mess from the night before. The table lamp was over on its side and the heavy wooden coffee table which it normally stood on, lay upside down.

There were remnants of half smoked, hand rolled cigarette butts scattered about the floor, having fallen from the upturned ashtray. These together with the empty beer cans that were strewn across the room as Charlie single handedly devoured the six pack he'd brought home. This after an already long afternoon, come evening session with his mates in the pub. The cans were all crumpled by Charlie showing off his so called vast masculine strength, missing the waste basket on the other side of the room with every throw whilst shouting in his best television announcers voice, 'one hundred and eighty.' He laughed thinking it was a huge joke, he was the only one in the room that had found it even remotely funny.

Sally quickly tidied up while the kids got dressed out of pyjamas and into school uniforms. She then gave them their Weetabix and cups of sweet milky tea at the pine kitchen table with the bench seats, whilst whispering softly for them both to be as quick as possible and not to wake their daddy. He was still sleeping and would be very angry with them if they woke him.

The children both nodded their heads in understanding. They'd received the wrath of Daddy many times in the past when he'd been roused too early and they really didn't want to go to school crying again.

Neither of them mentioned the distorted appearance,

11

bruising and swelling of their mam's face. They were far too used to that. It was sad, but they'd seen it all too many times before.

Sally now twenty four years old, had short brown hair, highlighted throughout with hints of blond. A fair complexion, hazel coloured eyes, with a small straight, slightly freckled nose and soft full lips that could produce the deadliest of smiles. Under normal circumstances this completed an extremely pretty face. She stood five feet seven inches tall in her size six bare feet and was a petite ten in a dress size.

Once regarded as 'well fit' by all the local lads, Sally had played on the school netball team throughout her high school years, but had given it all up when she'd met Charlie at the ripe old age of sixteen.

She was not quite as busty around the top as she had been in those earlier days, having lost quite a bit of the remaining youthful puppy fat that filled her out. What with running about after two small children and a fat idle husband who enjoyed nothing better than to sit watching daytime television, resulted in what could only be described as 'norra pickin' on 'er,' by the well covered, black legging adorned, fat arsed lasses of the same age group. This may have been fact, but more than likely it was just plain jealousy on their behalf.

Sally didn't wear much jewellery, in reality she couldn't afford any, however she did have a large pair of gold hoop earrings she wore in pierced ears that had been carried out at the Claires accessory shop in town when she'd turned thirteen. This had been part of a birthday present from Mam and Dad. She also had a pair of small gold sleepers put in at the same time, it was all part of the same deal.

Sally wore her cheap engagement ring of cut glass, real diamonds were totally out of the question. That together with a thin gold wedding band which had apparently once belonged to Charlies' now deceased gran. Charlie told Sally it had been a family heirloom and therefore very precious to him. In fact he'd stolen it along with some spare cash when he'd visited the old lady just prior to her death.

She wore no watch and told the time by the Samsung Galaxy S4 that her older brother Mike had given her after he'd upgraded to a two year contract with Vodafone. Sally thought she was very posh.

The family lived on the Westernside council housing estate, Eastscar by the Sea. It was a poor rundown area where the local council funding never seemed to reach the area, nor the people who voted for them.

Councillors were all there in their droves when it came to election time. Shaking hands with the out of work dads, made redundant years before from the local rolling mills and never been able to find any kind of work since. The tired, weary, downtrodden mams. Whilst from an arm's length, they gently stroked the heads of the constantly crying, snot nosed little baby's, whilst trying desperately to keep a distance from their greasy pasty covered, grubby little fingers, for fear they might get their bonny posh Marks and Sparks suits soiled.

There were always permanent smiles on their condescending bureaucratic faces, however after the elections win or lose, they were nowhere to be seen. Or at least not around this estate and certainly not before the next election when votes would once again be required to keep them safe, up in their comfortable little ivory towers.

Sally and her family had lived here all their lives. In reality, Sally had hardly ever been outside of the town limits except to go clothes shopping in the city of Seaborough eight miles away and before meeting Charlie, with friends every now and again for the occasional day trip.

The distance to the school was only a short one and Sally always insisted on walking the kids there and back herself. They both stayed for free school dinners, so it was only a short walk twice a day.

Little Charlie met up with his mates and walked half a dozen paces in front, laughing and joking about the latest episode of whatever it was they'd been watching on the telly the night before.

Sally, holding tiny Georgia's hand walked with her head down trying her hardest to become as small and inconspicuous as she possible could, while desperately hoping nobody would notice her. It was all futile, Jenny one of the older mams and a good friend of Sally's bustled directly over to her, reaching out and lifting Sally's chin to look her straight in the eye.

'Again!' She exclaimed, 'how many bloody times now? And how many more bloody times are yeh gonna lerrit happen wi' out doing summit about it? When he finally kills yeh, who d'yeh think's gonna look after them poor bloody bairns man?'

It was the same conversation as the one they shared after each and every one of Charlie's drunken bouts. The truth was, he wasn't always drunk, but Sally had decided a long time ago that it was better if they all believed he was. Who would understand a husband that could belt his wife for no reason at all? It was embarrassing, but it was also much easier all round to let them believe he just couldn't hold his ale.

The other mothers at the school smiled condescendingly as she walked past. It was a standing joke in the schoolyard on the morning after the local football team lost. All the mothers watching and looking to see who it was going to be wearing the proverbial black eyes.

Husbands, partners, boyfriends, they'd all congregated in the Ship and Anchor the day before to watch the live match on the big LCD wide screen in the back room. All the lads had been drinking heavily. Swearing and shouting at the millionaire Prima Donna's on the box who got paid far too much money to run about and kick a ball. Then roll about on the grass in agony only to jump up and sprint away after the referee had issued his red card to a totally somewhat bewildered opponent. It didn't really matter if they won or lost, the players were all multimillionaires either way. So who were the daft twats paying hard earned money to watch them?

The lads would all get one another pumped up and rattled, taking the piss out of each other and some could take it and others couldn't. Those that couldn't, were generally the ones that handed it out when they got home to the wife and bairns, Charlie fell into that second category.

Sally left the schoolyard, but rather than going directly home, she decided to call into the little convenience store around the corner and pick up a litre of milk. The kids hadn't left very much after their breakfast.

She was going to require an instant coffee fix when she got home and knew that Charlie would be waking soon. Needing at least two bowls of cornflakes and tea in his big, 'Best Dad in The World' mug that Sally had hypocritically bought on behalf of the kids last Father's Day. Better to be ready than to have Charlie going off on another one, she thought.

Mr. Patel the shop owner was his usual concerned self as she entered.

'What has happened to you this time Sally my dear? Have you been falling down the stairs? Or have you been banged on your head by the cupboard door again? Or maybe you just have another excuse that I haven't yet heard.'

He wasn't really asking, he was just voicing an open observation.

Sally looked up at him and smiled meekly, she didn't answer. Instead she paid for the milk and left without saying anything other than, 'thank you Mr Patel.'

Balraj Patel was an elderly, gentle speaking Hindi of seventy two years. He'd been born in Bombay (now Mumbai), India in 1944 whereby he, together with his parents and two older brothers had left not long after India's partition in 1947. His father strongly believed and had said on more than one occasion.

'India is doomed and will crumble quickly downhill once our beautiful and very strict departing British government leave.'

Maybe he was right, there again, maybe not.

Mr Patel was married by arrangement to the very pretty Aanya in 1967 and soon became besotted with her. She in turn presented him with five beautiful children, two girls and three boys. Aanya was now riddled with arthritis in both knees and far too old to be climbing up and down the stairs to serve in the shop from their small flat above. However, all their children and grandchildren took it in turns to come around on a daily basis to help out while catching up on all the local gossip.

Mr Patel had always been very kind and considerate to Sally, allowing her to pay later if she didn't have the readies available. He'd known her and her family since she was just a small girl living at home with Mam, Dad and her two older brothers Paul and Mike.

He was also aware of what the score was with Charlie and Sally knew that he knew, so there didn't really seem to be any point in arguing or trying to defend her husband. It always seemed as though the more she wanted to keep her home life private, the more everyone ended up knowing about it.

When Sally eventually arrived home, she went straight into the kitchen filled the electric kettle and switched it on. As it was coming to the boil, she could hear Charlie start to move about upstairs and her stomach began to churn. It felt as though a nest of spiders had just hatched and woken up inside her. Her legs started to give way and her hands began to sweat and tremble as she leaned against the draining board for support.

What was she going to do? More to the point, what was Charlie going to do? Or even say for that matter?

Downstairs, Sally was made aware of the loud revolting noises coming from the upstairs bathroom, as Charlie raked up last night's smoke filled phlegm from the back of his throat, coughed, spit, belched and farted. Then there was the inevitable tumultuous water fall as Niagara burst its banks into the toilet bowl.

Sally knew there would be as much on the outside of the bowl as there was ever likely to have gone in it. Another job for her later that day, mop up Charlie's piss from the bathroom floor, wash the puke soiled sheets and probably his shit stained boxers from a followed through wet fart. Sally loved it when Charlie had a good night out.

CHAPTER THREE

Charlie was a bit older than Sally at twenty seven. He'd never had a job, leaving school twelve years earlier with neither a completed education of any type, nor any qualifications whatsoever.

He was just below average height at five feet eight but what he lost in height, he now made up for in girth and weighed around eighteen stone.

Charlie had a premature receding hair line and therefore shaved his head as was popular in the area by a lot of the other lads. He had Charlie and Georgia tattooed on his right forearm in old English script and a Japanese Samurai sword on the left one. Charlie thought he looked dead hard, but to all the other lads that knew him, he looked like uncle Fester and was just a legend in his own mind.

Charlie had never been the athletic or animated sort, not even when they'd first met. Although he had been much thinner in those days. But Sally as a young lass had been both flattered by the attention of an older lad and quite taken in by his eloquent gift of the gab and supposedly at the time, his gentle, if not somewhat weird sense of humour.

One night not too long into their relationship Sally had, after much persuasion, succumbed to Charlie's passionate advances and thirty six weeks to the very day, little Charlie popped his head out. Mam and Dad had gone ballistic when they were told she was pregnant and Mike her brother had wanted to go around and have a quiet word with him. Older brother Paul was away at the time with the Royal Marines in Afghanistan, both brothers were well known in the area as a couple of handy lads.

Eventually everyone calmed down when she explained it had probably been as much her idea as it had been his. This had been far from true, but as tempers were already totally frayed, this wouldn't have been the best time to dispute it.

They were married at the local Registry office soon after. Sally however being under the age of consent at seventeen, was required to have signed permission from Mam and Dad. That done, nothing more was to be said. The saddest part of this whole travesty was, those were the good times, it all went downhill rather quickly after that.

Charlie walked into the kitchen rearranging his genitals through the vomit stained jeans he'd just slept in.

'What the fucks the matter wi' you?' He asked.

He was wearing neither a shirt nor socks and his immense white, blue veined belly protruded like a jelly type substance over the top of his unfastened jeans.

His breath smelt as though something evil had climbed inside his mouth and died and he had a week's growth of patchy beard with some very unpleasant looking yellow sleep encrusted in the corners of his swollen bloodshot piggy eyes.

'What happened to yeh fuckin' face then Sal? It's a

19

fuckin' improvement man.'

Charlie chuckled at his own little joke. Sally just looked down, she knew much better than to speak just yet. Charlie would need time to talk and find another pathetically lame excuse for what he'd done to her the night before and if he could, she knew he would blame it all on anyone and everyone, it was never going to be just his fault.

'Can't believe them last night,' was his opening rhetoric. It was almost as though nothing else in the world had either taken place or mattered.

'Lost three fuckin' goals to two and by a bloody penalty. What a bunch of fuckin' tossers. I coulda done better me fuckin' self and with me fuckin' eyes shut. I had a fuckin' tenner on that game.'

Charlie rambled on for the next few minutes about who did what and who should have done this, or who should have done that. Then who had said what to whom and eventually went onto the subject which had obviously been the one to upset him this time.

'That fuckin' Mark last night. He reckons you're too fuckin' good for me. He reckons you coulda had anyone yeh wanted, he even says you're a fuckin' good catch and I should take better fuckin' care of yeh. Well I fuckin' told him straight man, it does what it's fuckin' told mate. Have you been seeing him behind me back? Cos if I fuckin' find out yeh have, you're gonna get more than just a tiny fuckin' slap.'

So, that's what this was all about. Sally didn't even know which one of Charlies' cronies Mark was. She didn't know who any of the people Charlie mixed with were anymore. They were all loud, vulgar and enjoyed talking to each other in sentences containing numerous four letter expletives and wild hand gesticulations of the one and two finger variety.

'You deserve everything yeh get,' Charlie said, 'I'm a

fuckin' good husband and yeh just take fuckin' advantage of me good fuckin' nature. Yeh want for nowt around 'ere and that Mark needs to mind his own fuckin' business man.'

Charlie actually believed everything he said, but his insecurities were starting to show, and Sally was on the brink of feeling sorry for him yet again. She always did, he was so absurdly pathetic.

She put his bowl of cornflakes in front of him and his big mug of tea, then completed making the instant coffee she'd promised herself an hour earlier.

Once Charlie had completed eating the first bowl of cereal and was halfway through his tea, Sally plucked up enough courage to address the present situation and started by quietly saying.

'This has got to stop you know Charlie pet. You really hurt us again last night, an' I can't go on gettin' hurt like that anymore.'

'Not my fuckin' fault, is it?' Was his reply, 'if you'd a stayed fuckin' still and done what I'd fuckin' told yeh to do, we coulda all been playin' 'appy fuckin' families by now.'

'But it's happenin' all the time Charlie and I'm runnin' out of excuses and what to say to people about the state of us. I'm a human bein' and you're treatin' us worse than an animal,' Sally replied.

Sally's eyes started to brim with tears, she'd thought they'd dried out last night after he'd kicked her all over the bedroom floor and was now becoming angry with herself for allowing him to see her vulnerable all over again.

'Yeh are a fuckin' animal man!'

Charlie screamed at her, slobber, spit together with milky cornflakes spraying all over her face.

'You're me fuckin' pet wife man and I'll treat yeh any

fuckin' way I want and you'll do as I fuckin' say, won't ya?'

As bulky as Charlie was, Sally didn't even notice him stand up from his side of the table and walk around to her. The last thing she did notice when she looked up were the bright flashing lights, then miraculously everything went dark and quiet.

A little while later the lights flickered back on in Sally's pounding head. She could just about hear Charlie voice off in the distance. He was watching Jeremy Kyle on the television and laughing at the guests.

'Ow Sal, we should get on there. You could have that fuckin' lie detector test and confess all yeh fuckin' extra marital affairs?' He was saying, 'I find out either of those fuckin' kids aren't mine and you've been seein' that Mark behind me fuckin' back, you're fuckin' dead mate.'

Now Charlie was a total idle waste of space at the best of times, but one of his many brain numbing activities was to watch cookery programmes throughout the day.

This could be anything from the Great British Bake Off to Can't Cook, Won't Cook and although he himself was totally useless in the kitchen, other than the eating and drinking part, he firmly believed that every good cook should have sharp knives.

This was due in part to one of his daily television cook fests, when he'd heard the condescending words of wisdom uttered from Worrall Thompson saying, 'blunt knives were far more dangerous than the sharp variety,' and thus Charlie one quiet sunny afternoon had waddled out into the back yard and honed all the kitchen knives on an old whetstone he'd found years before. Taking each and every one of them to the very best surgical quality edge he could possibly attain.

The family didn't possess a full set of matching cutlery. They had a few odds and ends that friends and other members of the family had disposed of and donated to them over the years. Some of a reasonably good quality, but needless to say each and every one of them were all extremely sharp, because Charlie had actually successfully completed one of his very limited handyman jobs.

At the time Sally rose from the bench and walked to the kitchen sink, she hadn't even considered how sharp the paring knife had been. She hadn't considering anything, in fact she was totally oblivious to her surroundings. But for the next few short minutes of her young life, Sally Oldham nee Vickers felt as though she had total power against her long time oppressor.

For the second time that day, Sally came out of a dream like stupor covered in blood. The good thing was, this time it wasn't hers and she wasn't feeling any further physical pain than she already had when she'd woken earlier that morning.

She stood staring at what had at one time, not too long before, been her fat, violent, overbearing husband. Then she went quietly and sat on the soft leather look sofa facing him. Feet and knees clenched tightly together, with hands sat demurely on her lap.

After a while, the adrenalin rush subsided and reality started to slowly sink in. She found herself staring and wondered why Charlie's head was tilted so far back that he seemed to be smiling from his throat. She was still holding the blood stained knife in her hand and the smell of blood in the room was now far greater than it had been when she'd woken on the bedroom floor earlier that day.

The metallic iron stench was everywhere and not only the smell, the whole of Charlie's bare chest, the chair he was sat in, together with the shag pile rug covering the council house painted concrete floor was a deep crimson red. 'I don't remember that colour,' she sat thinking.

23

It wasn't long, maybe a few short minutes before Sally became aware of what she'd done. She felt nauseous and ran to the kitchen where she retched into the sink, unable to remove the yellow coloured plastic washing up bowl quickly enough.

Cautiously she stepped back into the living room and looked at the remains of Charlie. He was still sat with his eyes wide open, smiling and watching Jeremy Kyle, but now it was Jeremy who was doing all the shouting and Charlie was just sat very quiet, smiling, but very quiet.

The whole house was far too silent. There was hardly a sound to be heard anywhere other than Sally's jagged breathing and somewhere in the distance the voice of Jeremy. She was shaking uncontrollably now and seemed to be gasping for breath.

Sally wondered if she might be going into shock, so she ran again into the kitchen and completed drinking the coffee that she'd made so long before. It was still surprisingly warm. With the knife still clutched tightly in her right hand she stood covered from head to foot in her dead husband's blood, wondering if it was nearly time to pick the bairns up from school yet, 'what do I do?'

It wasn't so much a thought, more of a wide awake nightmare, a panic.

'What do I do? Who can I call? Don't let them take me bairns away from me. I need to pick them up from school soon and I can't bring them home to this. They're going to hate me when they see what I did to their dad.'

A million thoughts went through Sally's turmoiled mind in the space of a just few milliseconds, and at the end of it all she came to a very simple conclusion, phone our Paul.

CHAPTER FOUR

Paul Vickers was her eldest brother and next to Dad, was the closest thing Sally had to a guardian angel. He doted on his little sister, he loved her to big bits and would do just about anything for her. Sally knew this and had to be extremely careful about what she said in Paul's presence.

Mike, the younger brother however was far more laid back, but Paul could be almost psychotic about protecting her. She was still his little baby sister, irrespective of how old she was or how many kids she might have. She would call Paul.

He picked up on the third ring.

'Yeh, what you want?' He answered.

'It's me Sally,' she replied.

'Away man, I know who yeh are, I wanna know what yeh want?'

Sally wasn't sure how this was going to pan out so she became cautious.

'I need teh talk to yeh our Paul. No! I need teh see yeh, now, as soon as I can.'

Sally couldn't keep the fear and tremble out of her voice.

'Why what's up sweetheart?' Paul asked.

'I can't say over the phone our Paul, but I need teh see yeh now, at my place as soon as yeh can.

Paul, although the eldest sibling seemed to act quite immature at times and could sometimes appear on the surface, as though he was just not the brightest star in the sky. However, under that laid back, slow façade, he could be extremely subversive, so just to wind his little sister up a little bit more he asked again.

'Why what's up like?'

Sally was not generally the one to use expletives in her normal day to day vocabulary, but on this occasion felt the need to express herself with just a little bit more emphasise and therefore screamed down the phone at him.

'Just fuckin' get here now...please.'

There was a space of a second or two then she heard Paul's meek reply.

'Aye alright sweetheart, on me way, give us fifteen minutes. Hey, put the kettle on, I got our Mike with us, is that okay?'

'Aye,' she replied quietly, 'please, just get here.'

George Vickers, Sally's dad, was in his fifties, fifty six to be precise. He'd worked hard as a fisherman since leaving school at fifteen, first as a boy apprentice to his own father and then when his dad passed away after having a major heart attack, he took over the boat himself.

He bought the five metre Yorkshire coble, Bonny Doris, with a bank loan from Barclays in the late eighties and named her after his pretty young wife. They kept the boat on a trailer in a small lock up area with a few of the other fishermen's boats across the Eastscar Esplanade near the beach, always ready to be launched on any available tide.

George, due to poor health caused by chain smoking related emphysema didn't go out anymore now, but Paul and Mike were more than capable fishermen and had been going out with their dad as young lads of five or six years old, so now he just let them get on with it and take over the business of fishing.

When Paul got the call from his sister they'd just completed painting and weather proofing the small standing shelter on the boat. They'd been out in her earlier taking the morning tide, but the catch had been small, so they just turned around and came back ashore, in the end deciding to do some much needed maintenance instead.

They threw the remnants of the flask of tea they'd been sharing onto the sand covered tarmac, locked the boat up and wandered back to the old dark blue Ford Mondeo estate that was parked alongside the outer security fence.

Mike looked up at his older brother and asked.

'So, what's 'appenin' then?'

'Don't fuckin' know our kid,' Paul replied, shrugging his massive shoulders.

'Our Sal needs us, she sounded weird though, it's not like our Sal to bad talk like that. That fat bastard husband of hers better not a fuckin' touched her again cos I swear she won't be able to stop me rippin' his fat fuckin' head off his shoulders this time. He's a lazy idle twat and for the life of me I will never understand what she fuckin' saw in 'im.'

Mike looked at his big brother, smiled and said nothing, they got into the car and with Paul driving, left the beach and drove without talking the short distance to Sally's house.

The three siblings had always been close as children with both lads constantly looking out for their little baby sister.

They actually believed she was a real princess when Mam brought her home from the maternity hospital, she even looked like one, perfect in every minute and tiny detail.

As close as they were however, they all respected each other's privacy, so after parking the car outside Sally's small council house at number 35 Frazer Avenue and walking up the uneven broken concrete path, passing the overgrown weed filled lawn littered with kids brightly coloured moulded plastic ride on cars and bikes, they knocked on the front door and waited for someone to invite them in.

It was Mike who noticed the vertical blind at the front window move, seconds later the door slowly opened, but with nobody standing there they just stepped inside.

Sally had retreated further back away from the open front door in the small passage and was now standing in the kitchen doorway.

'Alright our Sal?' Paul said as he walked in, 'So what's so fuckin' urgent? Where's lard arse?'

Then he saw her.

'What's he fuckin' done to yeh? I'm gonna fuckin' kill him.'

Mike who'd been standing behind his older brother had seen nothing and had no idea as to what was going on. Paul took the few steps to his baby sister and gently took hold of her slim hands in his huge paws.

Sally was sobbing uncontrollably now that her brothers had arrived, but felt that everything would be alright. Her big brothers always made everything alright.

'He's in there.'

She extracted herself from Paul's grip, pointing with an uncontrolled, wildly shaking hand to the living room door on the left side of where she was standing. There was no sound emanating from inside the room. The television had turned itself off and an eerie silence prevailed.

For whatever reason, instinct made both Paul and Mike enter the living room cautiously, but when they finally stepped inside, nothing could have prepared them for what they saw.

'Holy bloody shit!' exclaimed Paul.

'Oh, my fuck!' was Mikes considered reply.

CHAPTER FIVE

'Who the fuck did that?' Questioned the big lad.

Mike said nothing, he was actually starting to turn a strange colour of green and although he could ride out a force nine in a coble, he was seriously struggling to keep his present stomach contents in place.

'I did,' whispered Sally.

'You fuckin' did? How the? Why the? Oh fuck!'

The stupid confused state just verbally poured out of Paul's gaping gob, while Mike forcibly kept his own clenched tightly shut, letting his big brother conduct the interrogation.

'Right, right.'

Paul muttered to himself, shaking his head in disbelief at the total carnage his baby sister had just introduced them both to.

'What am I going to do? Can yeh help us? What am I gonna tell me bairns when they get home? They can't see this, they're gonna hate me.' Sally continued to ramble incoherently.

It was Mike who seemed to be the first to regain his composure. Taking a dirty tea towel from the kitchen sink and from arm's length and a very safe distance, managed to throw it neatly across Charlie's face, covering it.

'What time is it?' Mike asked.

'Why? Where the fuck do yeh think yeh goin man?' exclaimed Paul in horror at the idea that he may be left alone to deal with the devastation all by himself.

'Nowhere man, it's cos we don't want the fuckin' kids walkin' in on this, do we?'

Mike was thinking positively and the other two were quite happy to let him.

'Half past two,' Sally finally replied, 'I have to go for the kids in ten minutes.'

'No yeh don't,' said Mike, 'what yeh have to do is get a bin bag and throw all those fuckin' clothes in it. But first is there anyone that can get the bairns and keep them for a while?'

'Well I could ask Jenny, she has a couple of kids herself in the same class as ours. She'll do it cos she knew we been fighting, I could tell her it's best if the kids don't come home just yet cos we're still at it.'

'Good, go do that then Sal and ask if she can keep them for a couple of hours so we can get some breathing space and sort this fuckin' mess out.'

Mike was sometimes brains, but with Paul, it was usually brains and brawn.

Sally went off and made the phone call to her friend whilst Mike and Paul discussed the game plan. She was back within a few minutes.

'She says she'll keep them overnight wi' her kid's cos it's not fair on our bairns listenin' to us goin' at it all night.'

Mike looked relieved.

'Thank fuck,' he said, 'so we got a bit of time to sort this fuckin' mess out then. Sal go open them back windows and get the stink out of here. He was a dirty, smelly fat bastard when he was alive but fuck he stinks worse than a bucket of pig shit now.'

Sally did as she was told while her two older brothers, their backs to her, unceremoniously lifted the body of her now lifeless husband onto the floor. Sally stripped where she stood, taking off all her outer clothing and shoes, placing everything on the blood covered living room rug and leaving on just her panties and bra. She then ran barefoot upstairs, removed the remaining under clothes and stepped under the shower for the second time in only a few hours.

When Sally came back downstairs a short while later, she was wearing cut off jeans and a big oversized pink sweatshirt. The body of her dear departed was laid naked with his arms crossed over on his chest, feet together on the living room rug.

The gaping wound of his neck seemed to have shut over while he was laid flat and his eyes had been closed, he looked quite calm and at peace.

'Where's his clothes? Why's he naked?'

Sally asked in surprise. Mike looked at Paul, then back to Sally before explaining.

'All clothes and owt with blood on that can be burned is goin' into plastic bags. We'll wrap fat boy up in the rug for now and take him for a drive during the night when there's no fucker 'round to watch.'

Paul continued to be busy while Mike explained the plan.

'Make sure yeh don't get owt on yeh again our Sal, in fact go in the kitchen and put the kettle on, I'm parched, I could do with a very strong drink about now and I'd really rather it wasn't fuckin' tea.'

It was dark when they eventually completed the

cleanup operation of the living room. They'd managed to roll Charlie up in the rug, although his feet had stuck out from the bottom, his head and face had been covered.

The lads always carried spare gear and tackle for the boat in the back of the car, so Mike had gone out earlier at Paul's instructions and brought back a small tarpaulin and a roll of nylon cord that they used for repairing the older lobster traps. Charlie and the rug were now rolled up in the tarp with both ends tied off looking like a very large blood sausage.

Sally and the boys had got busy once they managed to get Charlie tidied up and placed out of the way under the window at the back of the living room.

The painted concrete floor had been mopped and scrubbed a dozen times with a mixture of Domestos and then Detol. The silk emulsion painted walls were washed down to remove the remaining spray of congealed blood and the house now smelt like the emergency trauma unit of the general hospital.

There'd been a lot less blood than there could have, but as the first stab was to the back of the neck, Charlie had actually died before the severing of his throat and carotid arteries, consequently his heart had already stopped pumping.

They'd tried to remove the splattering of blood from Charlie's chair but to no avail, so whilst Sally and Mike carried on cleaning, Paul put the chair and all the soiled clothing together with the mop and cleaning rags into the back of the car, wrapped in plastic sheets. He then drove the short distance to behind the local shops where there were a couple of refuse skips kept.

All the rubbish was thrown into a skip and then Paul set fire to it. In this area, fires in skips were common place and always being lit by the local kids. No one was going to pay any untoward attention to this one.

He sat in the car a small distance away just to ensure everything was well lit and that the local fire brigade didn't turn up, then he drove back to Sally's house.

While Paul had gone off to set fire to the local skip, Sally phoned Jenny.

'Hya Jen, it's only me Sally, I just wondered if I could talk to me bairns?'

'Course yeh can pet I'll get 'em for yeh now. Are yeh alright? He hasn't hurt yeh again has he?'

'No, no, I'm fine, just a lotta shoutin' and stuff goin on. I just needed to talk to me kids before they went to bed.'

Sally could hear Jenny call in the background.

'Kids, away, yeh mam wants to talk to yeh and say night, night.'

Sally had trouble keeping the many emotions out of her voice as she spoke first to Georgia, then little Charlie. They were both happy, they'd eaten all their tea and were in clean borrowed pyjamas watching cartoons on the telly ready for bed.

Jenny told Sally that she would see them all to school the next day and that she didn't have to worry. Sally thanked her with a genuine gratitude, tears in her eyes and a sob in her voice and let her know that she would be there in the afternoon to pick them up straight after school. At least she hoped she was.

Sally and Mike were finishing a pot of tea when Paul arrived back, so he poured himself one and whilst they were all sat in the kitchen at the bench table, Paul gently probed.

'Sal, sweetheart, I gotta ask yeh, what the fuck 'appened? What brought this lot on? If anyone 'ad said teh me you did that, I'd a fuckin' laughed at them and said you were the last one in the world capable of what we saw in there.'

Sally, elbows on the table, cradling her mug in both hands spoke.

'I think I were just so fed up of bein' his punch bag our Paul. I guess I sorta lost the plot a bit. I don't actually remember a lot about what 'appened, I just sorta woke up and there it all was.'

Both lads just nodded, they thought maybe they understood. After a few silent moments in the kitchen, Sally then asked.

'What we gonna do with 'im?'

Considering a few hours previously she'd been a total wreck, Sally was now quite calm with her big brothers sat by her side.

'I think it best if yeh let us worry about that sis,' said Paul.

'Ya,' Mike replied, 'the less yeh know, the less yeh can worry or talk about. Yeh need to concentrate on you and them bairns now and we'll sort the rest out.'

Sally nodded her head in agreement.

'It's time to go,' Paul whispered much later, 'you ready bro'?'

Mike lifted his head from the kitchen table and tried to focus on his big brother's face. He'd been napping for a couple of hours with his head resting on his arms, waiting for a time when they could both leave the house carrying the large bundle to the car without being seen by anyone that might become suspicious.

Sally had gone upstairs earlier at their insistence. Removed the vomit covered bedding off the once matrimonial bed and put it in the washing machine downstairs on a setting of a very hot cotton wash. She then went to the airing cupboard at the top of the stairs, took out fresh bedding. Upon

35

completion of scrubbing it, she then turned the mattress over and made the bed up again.

After asking the lads downstairs if there was anything else they needed, she changed into clean pyjamas, climbed under the quilt totally exhausted from the previous twenty four hour's exertions. Sally was fast asleep almost before her head touched the pillow.

It was one thirty a.m. on a still and quiet spring morning, when Paul and Mike finally walked out the backdoor of the little council house that Sally would now share with just the two children.

Mike went first to ensure that no one was around, opened the back of the car, then returned inside to pick up the feet end of his once brother in law. Paul took the head end and together they both struggled with the heavy uncooperating lump of dead flesh. They dumped the corpse in the back of the car, shutting the door over as quietly as they could, then both looking around to ensure they weren't being observed.

People living in this part of town purposely didn't observe anything, certainly not if the local constabulary or anyone else representing authority might get involved. The majority of the local populace of this area all had something they didn't want to draw attention to.

CHAPTER SIX

Paul drove again and went straight to the boat compound. Mike got out and unlocked the padlock on the big gates, all the owners of the boats within the compound had keys for the lockup so they could get their boats in and out during unsocial hours.

After Paul reversed through and parked the car alongside the Bonny Doris, Mike then relocked the padlock on the front of the gates by putting his hands through from the inside.

The car lights turned off, the engine now silent with the only sound being that of the waves washing against the sea wall on the far side of the road and seagulls screaming under a street light as they fought over the remnants of a late night revellers discarded Big Mac and fries.

The brothers stood at the back of the car with the hatch door open. The body had not moved, and it became a bit of a struggle for the two of them to get a firm grip within such a confined space.

Charlie took up the whole area in the back of the car

and had wedged, but with a bit of pushing and shoving they managed to get a grip on his feet and pull him straight. It was just a matter of them now dragging together and with a few tugs and jerks, Charlie dropped heavily out of the back and onto the sand covered ground next to the boat and trailer.

Neither of the lads heard or saw the big car pull up outside the gates, but when the torch light caught Mikes eyes he automatically shaded them with his hand, blinded by the brightness.

'What you up to in there?' Came a male voice from the car.

'Stay where you are and keep your head down bro.'

Mike whispered to Paul as he walked towards the big BMW X5 police car.

'Alright mate?'

Mike replied standing on the inside of the compound. The police officer in the passenger side had his window down but made no move to get out.

'You're up late or is it early?' The officer asked.

'Early,' said Mike, 'tide'll be turnin' in a few hours so me brother'l be along soon and we'll be goin out for the day, see if we can make a bit of a livin' at this bloody game.'

The officer stared at Mike inquiringly, then asked.

'You're Mike Vickers, aren't yeh? Yeh got an older brother Paul and a younger pretty sister, what's her name Sandy?'

'Aye, that's right but her names Sally, Paul should be along soon. The boat used to be me dads but he's knackered wi' bad lungs now, so me and our lad are the registered operators.'

The officer looked him up and down slowly then said.

'You don't remember me do yeh? We were in the same year at Thornton's secondary, Dave Riley, we were on the same footy team.'

Mike smiled in recognition.

'Oh ya, I remember, how yeh keeping mate?'

'Good thanks, but I gotta ask, how come yer locked in the compound?'

Mike gave a short laugh and shook his head.

'I'm not locked in mate, I locked the gates me self cos we get a lotta drunks comin' out of the clubs at this time of night and I don't wanna get mugged or have to put up wi' the hassle of twattin' some shit faced little smack head while I'm tryin to get ready for work.'

Mike took the keys out of his pocket and showed them to the policeman.

Officer Riley laughed.

'Okay mate we'll leave yeh to it, we gotta go see if we can find some bad guys. You take care and be safe out there though, eh?'

Dave Riley gave Mike the thumbs up with his arm outstretched from the police car passenger window and waved as they drove off.

Mike breathed a sigh of relief as he slowly turned around to walk back to the Mondeo, his big brother and a very dead Charlie.

'I think I may have just shat me self,' he muttered out loud.

Paul was still crouched low behind the car when Mike returned.

'What the fuck was that all about man? I thought yeh was gonna invite him over for a fuckin' beer while yeh was reminiscing. They could at least of give us a hand to lift this fat twat into the boat cos we're gonna need a fuckin' crane to pick him up. If Charlie had been a tuna fish we'd be worth a fuckin' fortune by now.'

Paul was right, to lift the deadweight of Charlie's eighteen stone into the boat was going to take a superhuman effort, unless they could find some lifting gear. With the boat sitting on the trailer made it at least two and a half foot off the ground, that combined with a five foot of freeboard clearance required a lift of over seven foot.

Paul was a big lad at six foot one and Mike only slightly smaller at five eleven, but to lift Charlie above their heads was going to be hard to say the least and so they didn't. Instead, it was Paul that came up with the bright idea of putting Charlie in the boat, piece by piece.

'You are fuckin' jokin'? Oh please tell me your fuckin' jokin man.'

Mike had gone that strange colour of green again, he had only just got back his normal pallor after seeing Charlie sat in the arm chair, covered in his own blood with an extra gaping mouth in his neck.

'Nah, nah, listen,' said big brother Paul, 'I'll do all the cutting up cos I do most of the gutting an' cleaning anyway an' it really doesn't bother us. We can pack 'im in them spare cold boxes to take 'im out, then pack the parts into the lobster traps. The fuckin' crabs and lobsters'll do the rest. Them greedy little crustacean bastards'll eat owt. Then in a few days' time we can go back out an empty any of the remaining bones. Just think 'ow fat those fuckin' crabs'll be after 'avin dinner wi' our Charlie.'

'And 'ow long do yeh think this is gonna take? We're sat here in the middle of a fuckin' boat yard an' any one of the other lads could be coming in for their boats. Tide'll be turnin' in a few hours.'

'Well we best get fuckin' started then hadn't we our lad,' said Paul.

The brothers didn't carry anything larger than the

boning and filleting knives on board the boat. They had a small hatchet for cutting the lines in an emergency, but that had rusted so badly it was neither use nor ornament.

'Right up you go,' said Paul to his younger sibling, 'get up that fuckin' ladder and pass down those fuckin' cold boxes while I start trimming our Charlie down to size.'

Mike looked at him and shook his head.

'You're fuckin' sick you. I always thought it when we was kids, but now it's confirmed, you're a total sick fuck.'

Paul put on a pair of the industrial rubber gloves he used for fish handling, then started by removing the ropes holding the tarpaulin. He unwrapped Charlie naked onto the ground and with the sharpest knife he trimmed around Charlie's right wrist, slicing through skin, muscle and tendons. The knife just slid straight through with hardly any effort. He then placed a large screw driver into the joint and twisted and with surprisingly little force, the hand popped off.

Paul carried on up the arm to the elbow, employing the same method and again there was no great effort required. It was a bit more difficult at the shoulder with a bit more strength required, but Paul was on a roll and the adrenalin had taken over.

Mike had brought several boxes down and with squinted eyes so he couldn't watch what his big brother was doing and wearing his own heavy duty rubber gloves, he began to pack the boxes with body parts. They shared the parts out evenly as they'd decided earlier that two of Charlies thighs were not going to fit into a single box. They'd also decided that neither of the thighs would fit into a single trap either and the excess flesh would require filleting off the bone first.

There was a lot less blood than they'd anticipated. Charlie had mostly bled out in the house at the hands of Sally

41

his wife. They had everything all boxed up nice and neat and what remained was a torso with a semi severed head still attached.

Between the two of them they lifted and passed the boxed body parts up into the boat, then Paul went down and with a few deft strokes of the knife and a bit of a twist, he removed Charlie's head from his body.

The torso went into a large heavy duty polypropylene bag with the head in a black plastic bin liner. It was amazing how heavy a torso could be, even without head and limbs, in Charlie's case it came to just under nine stone or one hundred and thirty pounds.

Paul, with the help of Mike, then threw the bagged torso across his shoulders and climbed the ladder, dropping the remains of Charlie over the side into the bottom of the coble, his head following soon after.

They then wrapped the bloody rug back into the tarpaulin and that went into the back of the car again to be disposed of when they came back ashore.

Everything else went on board the Bonny Doris together with all the knives and other tools employed in the dismemberment.

'Right,' said Paul, 'that's him sorted, let's get this boat in the water and feed them fuckin' fishies.'

Mike took an old nylon broom from the boat and swept around the area used for the butchery. The soft sand that had blown up from the beach had absorbed all of the remaining spilt blood, but sweeping around had removed all other traces, leaving a relatively clean floor area.

Mike then took off his Nike trainers and threw them in the car, retrieving his waders out from the back. Fitting snuggly into the boots, he then pulled the big waterproof bib and braces over his shoulders. Once this was complete, he unlocked and opened the gates, driving the car out of the compound and parking it on the opposite side of the road.

Locked in the compound was a tractor used for towing the boats down to the slipway and onto the beach opposite the compound gates. This tractor was a cooperative motor, owned and paid for by the members of the local Fisherman's Society, each member of which had a key to the compound and the tractor. At the moment, there were around twenty boats in the compound. Some were away being rigged and refitted but there could be as many as thirty locked up at any one time when it was full.

Paul reversed the tractor back to the tow bar of the trailer and connected the lights and brakes, by this time Mike had returned and they pulled out of the gates, swung the trailer and tractor round and drove down the slipway onto the beach.

The dawn light was slowly coming up in the east now and the wind and swell had increased making the Bonny Doris roll and pitch a bit. They released the steel wire holding her on the trailer and Mike jumped on board, starting the 36 horse power Volvo Penta MD 17 engine. He turned the key, pulled the starter and the little beauty fired up first time.

Putting her in dead slow aft and with Paul pushing, Mike slid away from the trailer and the connections that Paul had unhitched.

'Back in a mo bro.'

Paul called to him and drove the tractor and trailer back up the slipway, across the Esplanade and into the compound, unhitching the trailer in their private allotted parking space.

Two other lads had just arrived by car to take their boat out, so he bid them a good morning and exchanged pleasantries, then parked the tractor in front of their boat for them to use. He then ran back over the road to where Mike was holding the Bonny Doris steady, waded out and without any effort, jumped on board.

They followed a north by north east heading off the beach and put the Bonny Doris into full throttle. She was able to keep up a steady five knots all day, even with a slight head wind.

Today they were lucky the wind was from the south west which was the direction of the normal prevailing winds in this area. The heading would take them off the shallows, past the steep slope into the twenty five metre deep water anchorage of the oil and chemical tankers dotted about, awaiting berths at the numerous terminals in the mouth of the river Tonnet, north of Seaborough city.

They anticipated around two hours to reach the lobster traps they'd checked on just a day earlier.

'You never know we may even have summit to bring back with us as well,' Paul thought out loud.

They steamed past the outer anchorage area until they saw the first of their marker buoys depicting the beginning of their submerged traps.

Upon arrival, Paul began heaving up the first trap by use of the eight inch Electroslaver hauler on the starboard side of the boat, while Mike put the engine into the stop position.

They remained drifting whilst the trap was brought on board. Inside they found a couple of small crabs, too small to be landed ashore, so Paul reached in and cautiously lifted them out dropping them promptly over the side.

The traps they used were metal welded, pvc coated and Japanese made. They were of a good strong construction and could be collapsed for storage and handling if required.

The brothers had been given a fair deal by a retiring lobsterman mate of their dads. The old lad had wanted fifteen pounds apiece for forty pieces, but canny old George Vickers had got him down to ten fifty each and a couple of pints in the Ship and Anchor after. These traps would last maintenance free for years.

'Okay, let's get this show on the road, pass me some of Charlie outta the cooler boxes Mike.'

Mike shook his head in exasperation but complied with a left forearm and a hand.

'Sick I'm tellin' yeh, you're fuckin' sick. How many bits do you think we should put in each one?' Mike asked.

'I don't think it matters too much mate, it'll either be eaten or it'll rot, but one way or t'other there should be only bones left at the end, hey what do I fuckin' know, I never done fuck all like this before 'ave I?'

They carried on from trap to trap placing pieces of dismembered Charlie into each one and removing a total of six decent size crabs and four good size lobsters all within the legal specification to be landed ashore.

Mike then washed out the cooler boxes over the side of the boat, removing any remaining blood that Charlie may have left behind and after putting elastic bands around the claws of the crustaceans, placed the crabs in one box and the lobsters in another, all they had left now was a head and torso.

'Right brain of Britain, what do we fuckin' do wi' this?'

Mike asked pointing with his rubber booted foot to the final remnants of a once upon a time, sort of human being.

Paul stood up stretching his arms above his head, opened his mouth and yawned.

'Right what we're gonna do is tie the fat boy to a weight and just drop him over the fuckin' side to the bottom. We can either hook him or just tie him with a bit of Kevlar line. Fasten it to a couple of those old knackered twenty mill' 'D' shackles and drop him, we can do the same wi' his fat ugly bald head as

45

well.'

Paul went into the standing shelter and brought out a reel of the braided 1000 pound Kevlar string line and cut off around two metres. He fastened a six inch shark hook to one end and two 'D' shackles to the other. With the shark hook he turned the torso remains of Charlie over and hooked from the right side of Charlies back just above what had once upon a time been his waist. Then around the spinal column and back through to the left side, securing the torso as if it were a side of beef in an abattoir.

The whole operation took a surprising amount of effort as Charlie was fast becoming very stiff and solid. Upon completion Paul needed to sit down to regain his strength.

They did the same with the head, but put the hook into Charlies mouth instead and through the bottom jaw bone, with only one shackle to weigh it down.

When they'd finished, they dropped the two shackles of the torso over the side. Paul then took the filleting knife and slit Charlies belly open from chest to groin. They had both taken an end each of the short remaining body letting it slide over the boats gunwale and gently into the water before the internal organs had a chance to drop out, there was hardly a splash. Paul lifted the remaining head and shackle over the side of the boat and let go.

'Cheers Charlie' he said, 'ave a good one.'

Mike then leaned over the side and finally dispelled the contents of his stomach.

By the time they'd finished and turned the boat around, the sea was dead calm and the sun was starting to set again. They could see the lights along the coastline flickering in the distance. They passed back in between the tankers at the anchorage area, all with their deck and accommodation lights on, looking like horizontal Christmas trees, it was a beautiful sunset and the end to a very long day.

'Hey, Mike me lad,' Paul was sat on the washboard at the aft end, letting the breeze blow over him, 'when we get ashore, I'll let you buy me a pint or three.'

Mike smiled at his big brother.

'Aye, why not mate?'

CHAPTER SEVEN

Sally opened her eyes slowly. She stretched and looked at the cheap digital alarm clock on the cabinet next to her side of the bed, it read ten minutes after seven. She was laid on her back in her comfy warm pyjamas with the now clean bed smelling of a spring garden scented washing powder.

The room was quiet and there was no one snoring, farting or shouting abuse. The world was at peace and she was about to roll over and doze back off to sleep again when it all came flooding back to her.

The shock of it kicked in the adrenalin and a chilling vision appeared in Sally's mind of what had actually taken place the day before. She threw herself out of bed, ran into the bathroom where she just managed to lift the toilet seat before the mad rush of acidic watery vomit erupted from her mouth.

How could she have slept after what had happened? What kind of an insensitive monster was she? She flushed the toilet and remained kneeling on the bathroom floor for a few minutes before leaning over the sink to rinse her face and clean her teeth. Standing upright she looked at herself in the small makeup mirror, examining her two black eyes which were now a blend of purple and shades of green. Her bottom lip had a scab the size of a five pence piece near the corner of her mouth and the left side of her face and cheek were still a bit swollen. Her sides still ached from a mixture of the kicking and the muscle straining work out she'd inflicted on herself during the clean up operations in the living room.

She pulled her pyjama pants down and sat on the toilet to have a pee, wondering why her brothers hadn't been in touch. What time did they leave and where did they take her dead husband.

She shivered involuntarily as she thought that maybe they'd been caught with Charlie in the back of the car and might have spent the night in a police cell. Would they have been able to get in touch with her, or would the police have prevented it with the intention of calling on her later in the day.

Too many questions started to form in her mind as she sat on the loo. Sally then went back into the bedroom to find her bathrobe and realised it still had spots of her own blood down the front. She put it on anyway and was about to go downstairs when her mobile phone rang in the bedroom. Sally froze, was it Paul, or maybe Mike, what had happened.

She grabbed the phone without looking at the display and half screamed into the mouth piece,

'Ya, who is it?'

'Hi Sally, it's only me Jenny. The kids are up and wanted to say good morning to you. Hope I never woke yeh pet. Is everything all right at your place?'

Sally relaxed and took a deep breath before answering.

'Yah everything's fine here, thanks Jen. Charlie's still sleeping, but I was up anyway, put the kids on and I'll call yeh later to give yeh an update.'

'Aye, alright pet, here's the bairns, speak to yeh later then.'

Sally spoke first to Georgia and heard all about how great it was staying at Jenny's house, then she tried to pry a conversation out of little Charlie but he was in the middle of a computer game and needed to get back before he lost all his lives.

She hung up with her heart still pounding. Sally then descended the stairs with trepidation and entered the living room.

She didn't know what to expect, but it was exactly as it had been the night before, minus Charlie wrapped up in the middle. It seemed so empty now though without the lads in there with her. There was a kind of silent echo as she walked across the floor in her bare feet to open the blinds.

After a quick look around and seeing no signs of blood or anything untoward, all the walls fresh and clean with the floor almost gleaming after the scrubbing it had been given, she re-entered the kitchen and saw the knife on the draining board.

It had been well wiped and washed, Paul had said to give it a good clean and keep it.

'You'll need that for peelin' tatties for the bairn's chips,' he'd said.

She filled the kettle with cold water from the tap and flicked on the switch for a cup of coffee.

Having made her coffee, Sally also made a slice of toast, she couldn't remember the last time she'd eaten anything. Sometime the day before yesterday she'd had egg and chips with the kids for tea. She covered the toast with some mixture of vegetable oil and butter substitute from a plastic tub and sat at the table eating whilst trying to gather her thoughts and decide what she was going to do next.

As she sat in total peace and quiet at the little pine table she could hear the sound of Ed Sheeran singing off in the distance. Sally stood and followed the sound upstairs reaching the halfway point before realising it was coming from the bedroom and sounded like Charlies ring tone on his mobile phone.

She found the phone tucked in the pocket of his knock off North Face fleece which was just to say hanging on the back of an old kitchen chair they kept behind the bedroom door.

She took the phone out of the pocket and noted there were several missed calls and text messages from various people, then the phone stopped ringing, it must have gone to voicemail she thought.

Sally sat on the end of the bed and looked around. Charlie's old Adidas trainers were under the chair where he'd kicked them off, his dirty socks with a big hole in the toe were lying next to them and his bright red and white striped football supporter's shirt was in a heap behind the chair where he'd thrown it.

Sally looked at all of Charlie's belongings laying around the room and decided she was going to have to get rid of them. What else could she do, if Charlie was not here, then he'd left and if he'd left, he would have taken or be wearing his clothes, so she had to make at least some of them disappear.

While she was thinking of what to get rid of and what to keep, Sally got dressed. She put on a clean pair of underwear and her skinny jeans, then pulled on the pale washed out pink sweatshirt that she'd been wearing the night before and retrieved her old worn and faithful pale blue denim flats from in the cupboard, putting them on again without socks. She combed her hair and quickly slapped on a few touches of make up around her eyes. She looked in the mirror and nodded with satisfaction at the results. She knew that everyone else knew she'd had a good hiding so there was hardly any point spending a lot of time and effort trying to conceal it.

Sally fluffed up the pillows and pulled the quilt straight on the bed, then went over to Charlie's clothes and started emptying the pockets, throwing the contents onto the bed and the clothes in a heap on the floor. She found his wallet in the inside pocket of his fleece and some small change in the outer pockets.

Sally was used to going through Charlies pockets after he'd had a good night out and fallen asleep unconscious, that was how she always managed to get her extra housekeeping. Charlie could never remember how much he'd spent, or what he'd spent it on. He was always trying to impress the big boys' by buying them drinks, trying his hardest to be a part of their inner clique. They used to take them laughing behind his back about what a total loser he was, they never ever bought him one back.

Sally picked up all the discarded clothing from the bedroom floor and started to fold and place it all in neat laundry piles. She then went to the cupboard, moved a canvas shoulder bag she didn't recognise, which was laid on the floor and continued by removing Charlie's hanging shirts and jeans, again going through the pockets and folding them neatly on top of the bed.

She picked up the discarded shoulder bag and after examining it from the outside, opened it.

Everything was contained in clear plastic resealable pouches and there were at least fifty little packets of white powder. She was shocked, but when she went deeper into the bags inside zipped pocket, Sally had to sit down to regain her composure.

She thought she knew what the white powder might

be, although at no time in her life had Sally ever had anything to do with drugs, she didn't agree with them and as a mam, wanted them as far away from her bairns as she could possibly get them.

To her knowledge, Charlie had never had anything to do with drugs either, but with the little white powder packets and the wads of money she'd just found in the strange little shoulder bag, she decided she knew very little about Charlie anymore.

Sally tidied and moved all Charlies clothes into neat piles on the floor and laid the white plastic envelopes just as neatly out on the bed. After counting she found there was a total of twenty four thousand nine hundred and sixty five pounds, she recounted and again came up with the same amount. She sat for a moment trying to take it all in, then conducted a few deep breathing exercises, her hands were shaking and she needed somewhere to stash her findings, somewhere the kids wouldn't find and no one else if they came snooping around.

In all her life she had never held such an amount of money. It wasn't quite a major lottery windfall, but Sally had never seen the likes of it before. The money she decided she would keep as things were probably going to be tight for a while, but as far as the white stuff was concerned, she didn't know what to do. Her heart was telling her to flush it all down the loo, her brain was saying, put it to one side and talk to Paul and Mike about it, they would have the answers. Where the bloody hell were they?

The knock at the door made her jump and startled her out of her contemplation. Who the hell was that, Should I answer or pretend I'm out, then she realised it was probably the lads back. She grabbed the money and the packages and quickly threw them back in the bag, then pushed the bag under her pillow with the quilt on top, smoothing it neatly over.

Sally ran down the stairs, taking them two at a time, unlocking the front door by the key that was still in the lock. When she opened it, a total stranger stood before her. Her heart beat faster and her stomach started doing summersaults again, Sally just stood and not a word came out.

The man in front of her was of slim build. He had a dark complexion, shoulder length, black wavy hair, and very deep dark coloured eyes. He was younger than Sally, maybe late teens, early twenties and was wearing a brown corduroy three quarter length jacket, old blue washed out denim jeans and a pair of cheap canvas trainers. The stranger was the first to talk.

'I like speaks at Charlie.'

Sally stood staring, her brain was numb, she was not sure of what to say but thankfully her mouth took over.

'He's not here at the moment and I don't know when he's gonna be back.'

'When he be back? We have meeting last night, and he no comes.'

Sally's mind was racing, at least this wasn't the police, or there again maybe it was, and he was undercover.

Sally neither knew what to do, nor what to say, so again her mouth took over before her brain went into gear.

'He didn't say where he was going, he just left early this mornin', when he comes back should I give him a message?'

The stranger nodded his head, looked up and down the road nervously then back at Sally.

'Okay, I been try' to calls 'im but he no answer. You say 'im Oggy come 'ere, an' you tells 'im I see 'im tonights same place, tells 'im not be lates though, 'cos I got explainin' to do to men's I don't even like talks to, okay?'

Sally nodded and Oggy walked down the path then turned left down the road towards the town.

Sally felt that at any moment her brain was going to explode, it was in turmoil, she was trying her hardest to understand what had happened to her life.

Was it only yesterday morning that she'd woken up, broken and bleeding from Charlie? Now he was dead by her own hands, she'd found drugs and money secreted away in her home, strange people of foreign extraction were looking for him and where the fuck were her brothers?

She looked at her phone and the time display showed half past ten. 'Is that all it is she thought? What a long day already.' After a quick tidy up, Sally washed and dried her cup and plate from breakfast, together with the ones from the night before that the lads had used, she then decided to walk around and see Mam and Dad.

The walk to her parent's house was a short one. They lived on the same estate just two roads away. As Sally got nearer, she could see her mam out on the front doorstep talking to a neighbour. Mam saw her coming and gave her a smile and a wave, said bye to the friend and walked up to meet her.

'Oh, our Sally,' Mam said, 'what's 'appened to your face my pet? Has that bloody Charlie been at it again? I don't care what you say, this time I'm getting' the lad's to 'ave a quiet word wi' 'im. I'm not 'avin this, you're our bonny little lass and it's not allowed. Your dad's gonna be so very upset when he sees yeh.'

Sally put her arms around her mams neck and the tears flowed.

'Oh Mam hug me, just hug me,' she sobbed.

'Oh my pet, away inside, I'll put the kettle on.'

Sally's dad was sat in his favourite armchair next to the fireplace, reading his morning paper. He had his mug of tea on the little table by the side of his chair, on the other side was his portable oxygen in case he became too short of breath.

There was a big smile on his face as he said,

'Here she is, here's our Sally, where yeh bin petal? We bin waitin' for yeh since yesterday.'

Then Dad saw her face and the smile disappeared.

'Well now I bloody know where yeh bloody bin and why we didn't see yeh yesterday, don't I? Wait 'til I get my bloody 'and's on 'im, I'll friggin' wring his bloody neck.'

Sally was not exactly sure what she was going to tell her parents. She knew it wasn't going to be everything. She also knew it wasn't going to be the truth, at least not all of it. Sally couldn't remember a time when she'd told so many lies to so many people she loved, but she had to say something. She started by telling them about Charlie coming home from the pub after watching the football match and the two of them fighting. Then she talked about the kids for a while, telling her parents that Jenny had kept the kids overnight because her and Charlie were going to try and make up and finally she told them that Charlie had got up this morning and gone out somewhere, but she didn't know where and that a man called Oggy had come to the house looking for him because Charlie wasn't answering his phone.

Sally failed to mention that she had stabbed Charlie numerous times in the neck with a very sharp kitchen knife and that her big brothers were at this very moment in time disposing of his body somewhere. At least that's what she hoped they were doing. She also omitted to mention the drugs and money she'd found in Charlie's shoulder bag, that had now been secreted under the quilt on her bed. No there was quite a bit that Sally hadn't actually mentioned.

'Oggy?' Said Dad, 'only bloody Oggy I know is a young dark lad with a bad reputation. He's supposed to be mixed up wi' a bad lot that one, what's he want wi' Charlie anyway? Charlie wants nowt to do wi' the likes of him, I'm warnin' yeh, bad news'll come of it, bloody bad news.'

They seemed to have believed what Sally had said, they always did. Sally could tell them just about anything she liked and 'if our Sally said it, then it must be true,' was the normal guarantee to whoever might be listening.

Mam and Sally talked on for a while, with Dad throwing his tuppence worth in every now and again. They verbally dissected the soaps on the television that Sally had missed over the past twenty four hours, had another cup of tea, dunked some more biscuits, then Sally prepared to leave.

'How yeh strapped lass?' Said Dad.

'You got enough to tide you over? I can give you a couple of bob if yeh need it.'

Sally smiled, bent over and kissed her beautiful Dad on the top of his balding pate,

'No our Dad, I'm alright for now thanks, may need a borra later though if that's okay?'

'Aye lass you know where we are and when that Charlie gets home, you tell him from me, I'm gonna be 'avin a word.'

Sally and Mam exchanged glances, they knew he wouldn't, then Sally bid them both, 'tarah for now,' and left.

Sally walked down the road outside Mam and Dads house feeling amazingly cheerful considering. The talk with her parents had somewhat restored her sanity and cleared her head a bit.

She was free of Charlie, she had money in her pocket, she was looking forward to seeing the kids after school, all she needed to do now was see her brothers and be reassured that she wasn't' going to be spending the rest of her days in a six by six cell in the woman's prison at Low Newton somewhere over in County Durham.

On the way home, Sally decided to call at Jenny's house. Jenny deserved an explanation or at least some sort of a reason for having to look after the kids the night before. Besides, Sally didn't want to go straight home, she felt strange about being in the house by herself right now. It would be better once she had the kids with her for company.

Jenny also lived on the same estate as Sally, but in the opposite direction to that of Mam and Dads house, so Sally had to walk past the end of Frazer Avenue to get there. As she was passing, she looked down the road to see if her brother's car was parked and was surprised to see the stranger Oggy standing a little way down from her own front path.

He definitely hadn't been there when she'd left to go to her parents' house, or at least she hadn't seen him, so he had either been hiding or he'd come back. Sally didn't want to talk to him again, not just yet, so she carried on walking, arriving at Jenny's' house a few minutes later.

Sally knocked on the front door and Jenny walked around from the side of the house with wet laundry in her hands.

'Hya pet,' she said 'just hangin out me smalls. Away round the back.'

Sally followed Jenny around to the rear of the house.

The small garden was very neat and contained a small tidy lawn with flowers in borders all the way around. There were also little terracotta plant pots dotted about, full of pretty flowers and small shrubs. Compared to Sally's garden, this was like the pictures she'd seen in magazines of Alnwick.

'What a pretty garden Jen,' Sally admired, 'I wish ours was even a little bit like this, it would be a pleasure to be sittin' out in this, rather than the jungle we 'ave.'

'This isn't me,' Jenny said shaking her head with clothes pegs in her mouth whilst continuing to hang washing on the line, 'this is our Geoff, he loves his garden, out in all weather pottering about. Yeh just missed him actually, he has an allotment as well, but that's only for his veggies, he's just gone to do some weeding, or at least that's what he says. I know one of those bloody mates of his has a home brewery up there and he'll come back tellin' me about how hard he's bin workin' and how he'll have to lie down for a while because of his bad back. Sleep it off more like it.'

Both lasses laughed, then Jenny invited Sally in for a cup of tea.

'So, Sally me love, what's bin 'appenin? I must say you look a lot bloody happier now than you did, 'ave you an' Charlie sorted everything out then?'

Jenny was a straight talking, no nonsense, short, buxom woman, that had a gentle spot for Sally.

'Sort of,' said Sally.

'He said he was dead sorry and promised he would never hurt me again. He said he was goin off for a while to stay at a mate's house to get his head together cos he were ashamed of hiself.'

'Well I'll believe that when I see it,' interrupted Jenny, 'we both know he's said that a dozen times before don't we? I hope for your bloody sake he bloody well means it this time pet, cos I hate seein' you get hurt so much. My Geoff has never laid a hand on me. He knows the first time he does will be the bloody last, he wouldn't wake up the next mornin' and my Geoff likes to wake up at some time after a good nap, so he does.'

Sally smiled, she only wished she'd been able to have

59

such a close relationship. In Sally's small restricted world, what Jenny and Geoff had, was idyllic.

The two women talked and drank tea for the remainder of the afternoon, or at least until it was time to pick the kids up from school. Then they both walked down to the Infants school together. The talk was light hearted enough with both of them adding their own sense of humour and nonsense to the conversation.

CHAPTER EIGHT

After leaving Charlie's house, Oggy had walked down the road towards the town centre but it came to him that he didn't believe everything that Charlie's pretty young wife was telling him. He mistrusted what she'd said, but didn't know why. Maybe it was her mannerisms, or maybe it was another of his inner senses telling him to beware.

Oggy didn't trust anyone, only his senses, they'd saved him far too many times before to be ignored. Instead of heading back into town he decided to hang around. Maybe, just maybe, the little bitch was lying and the fat bastard was still in the house hiding from him, 'I breaks his fuckin' neck when I gets hold of him,' he thought.

Oggy's full name was Oghuz Ahmet Galata and he was a Turk from a little coastal town in the southern part of the Turkish, Mediterranean coast, called Mersin.

He'd left the family home a few years before when his mother had died of cancer, leaving no one to protect him from his violent, ever dominant father and his bullying three older brothers.

He'd been the runt of the litter and at eighteen had

hitched, walked, begged, plenty of times stolen and would have done anything else that was required of him to get onto the shores of the United Kingdom, albeit illegally.

Once he'd arrived, he found and mixed with the villains of the London area who gave him an apprenticeship of sorts, inclusive of anything from picking pockets, extortion, keeping a stable of working girls and of course drug dealing.

He'd started at the bottom, but found he was a natural, quickly working his way into their trust. Drug dealing seemed to be his forte, making the most money for the least amount of effort. This was to become his trade of choice.

Oggy's biggest problem was that he stole, he just couldn't help himself. His fingers stuck to everything and anything if it wasn't nailed down and if he thought he could turn a quick profit. Unfortunately, his fingers stuck to objects that belonged to some of the very wrong people and those wrong people he stole from wanted their goods back. Then they wanted to find him and kill him, but not before they hurt him, lots and lots and really lots.

So Oggy had moved from London and headed north to Seaborough because at some point somewhere, he'd been told it was easy pickings up north and so one day it was decided that this is where he would settle and set up in business all over again.

He was extremely worried now though, not only did he have a bunch of London bad boys on his trail for pocketing a rather considerable amount of their illicit drugs without paying for it, but he also had a bunch of Albanians wanting their drugs and money which Charlie had been told to look after on his behalf and the fat fuck wasn't answering his calls, texts, or the fucking door. Where the hell was he?

He saw the pretty young wife walking back towards the house. He'd watched her leave earlier by herself, but now she was returning with two kids, a young boy and a little girl. He didn't know Charlie had kids, if these were his, it could be quite useful.

Sally and Jenny picked up their respective children and all walked home together, or at least part way together. Stopping outside Jenny's house to say their goodbye's and thank you's, they then carried on towards Sally's house.

The kids were full of it and never shut up all the way, talking of their sleep over, watching cartoons until late and drinking hot chocolate before they went to bed. Sally asked them what they wanted for their tea and it was unanimously egg and chips again, however when Sally mentioned the chippy it was a different story altogether and they all settled for a large battered sausage and chips each instead.

The chippy was next door to Mr Patel's, so Sally went in and bought a large bottle of Cola as a further treat.

When they all arrived outside the front path of their house, Sally looked around cautiously to see if there were any signs of Oggy, but he was nowhere to be seen.

They opened the front door and Sally went directly into the kitchen and started to serve out their tea's, when there was a loud shout from little Charlie.

'Mam quick!'

Sally's heart turned to stone as she ran into the living room with both kids glued to the spot.

'What's the marra?' She screamed.

It was little Charlie that answered.

'Mam we bin robbed! Dads chair and the rug 'ave gone, someone's nicked 'em.'

Sally gave a sigh of relief, 'if this is the worst then we should be alright,' she thought.

'No,' she said softy, 'your dad spilt,' what, she thought,

what did he spill? 'Your dad was opening the big jar of pickled beetroot and you know what he's like? Anyway it went everywhere, we had to get rid of everything in case we all got stains on our clothes.'

It worked, the kids looked at her then burst out laughing. To them, this was the biggest joke in the world, their dad had got knacked.

The kids finished eating, then watched some television whilst Sally washed the pots. After Sally took them up to get bathed and ready for bed. She read them both a bedtime story and tucked them in and was just saying night, night when there was a knock at the front door.

Again, that feeling of dread crept over her as she walked down the stairs.

'Please don't let it be the police, please don't let it be that Oggy, please, oh please, just let it just be the lads back.'

Sally unlocked the front door and opened it cautiously.

'Hya sis,' came the voice, 'put the kettle on.'

Sally smiled and flew into the arms of her big brother Paul, she then turned and hugged Mike.

'Where the hell have you two bin? I've bin bloody worried sick about yeh. I thought yeh'd been picked up by the bloody bobby's, you could at least 'ave called us.'

Once the kids heard the voices, they came running back downstairs to see who the visitors were. Both Paul and Mike fussed over them for a while, then Sally ushered them both back to bed. Whilst she was upstairs she grabbed the satchel with the money and the plastic envelopes and brought them down with her.

The lads had made themselves comfy around the kitchen table with cups of tea and biscuits. They would have enjoyed something stronger, but Sally didn't have anything,

Charlie had drunk it all.

'I guess you're not gonna tell me where you took 'im?' Sally asked.

'No!' Said Mike, 'the less you know, the better, it's enough to say he won't be found.'

Sally nodded her head in acknowledgement.

'I don't think I really wanted to know anyway, what do you think my chances of getting away with this are? I don't wanna go to prison or get me kids taken off us.'

'I would say pretty good,' replied Mike, 'first off, no one's gonna find the body. Second, no one actually knows or cares that he's missing and third, the police won't get involved unless they find summit, which they won't, or if someone files a missing person, which would probably have to be you sis, but yeh only have to say he's walked out on yeh, and yeh don't know where to.'

Sally brought them both up to date with what she'd told Jenny and their parents. They both agreed it was probably as good a story as anything they could have come up with under the circumstances, then she broached the subject of Oggy.

'Why the fuck would Oggy the Turk be coming around here to see the fat boy?' Asked Paul, 'he wouldn't give Charlie the time of day normally, he's only a small time drug dealer, but he mainly works for those nasty bad Albanian bastards. Now they are hard and fuckin' ruthless, best off steering well clear of them.'

When Paul had finished talking, Sally removed the packages and money from the shoulder bag, placing them all on the kitchen table saying to her brothers.

'Do yeh think maybe this has summit to do with it?'

'What the fuck! Where the hell did this lot come from?'

Mike had stood up and taken a quick step back away from the table as though the contents of Sally's bag were about to explode at any time very soon.

Sally explained she'd gone through Charlies clothes with the intention of getting rid of some of them when she came upon this cache in the bottom of the bedroom cupboard.

Both lads just stared at the piles of money and drugs on the table, looking from Sally to each other.

'Now what the fuck do we do?' Mike asked to no one in particular, 'this is really startin' to get a bit fuckin' daft man.'

'Right let's 'ave a think,' said Paul, 'it's pretty obvious that Charlie and Oggy had some sort of deal goin' on, but we don't know what that deal was. I think it's fair to assume that Oggy is lookin' for his stuff, but why Charlie would 'ave it, I don't fuckin' know. As far as Oggy's concerned, Charlie still has the goodies, but he don't know where Charlie is at the moment does he? Maybe he thinks Charlie's done a runner wi' it all. At least that's what I woulda bin thinkin'.'

While Paul was talking, Mike had opened one of the re-sealable plastic pouches, wet the tip of his little finger and dipped it into the white powder. He then rubbed the powder onto his top gum, with immediate results.

'I think this is pretty pure coke,' he said, 'I feel like I've just had a shot of Novocain at the dentist, except I feel a lot happier about it.'

Mike's brother and sister looked at him as much as to say, 'are yeh daft, why would you do that?'

'Oggy's not gonna go away, is he?' Said Sally, 'he's gonna keep comin' back 'ere lookin' for Charlie 'cos there's nowhere else for him to look is there?'

Paul shrugged, that seemed like a fair assumption, so he said.

'All you have to say is that Charlie hasn't come home

and you don't know where he's gone, or for how long. Sal you can even say you're worried sick about him 'cos he never stays away. No one can prove anything different. Maybe we need to get rid of some of his clothes and make it look as though he's gone off somewhere.'

'That's what I was doing earlier when that Oggy knocked on me door,' said Sally, 'I still have Charlie's mobile, there's loads of messages and missed calls on it, I guess some of them must be from that Oggy. We should check the messages and voice mail though, shouldn't we?'

So, for the next thirty minutes that's what they did, they checked Charlie's messages. There were a lot of missed calls, numerous voice mails and several texts, the three of them sat and went through them all one by one, omitting the inconsequential ones and recording the telephone numbers of the ones they believed may be of some importance.

All the important ones seemed to be from Oggy with voice mail messages ranging from.

'Call me soon you can mate,' to 'where da fuck are yeh, yeh fat twat?'

It seemed that Oggy was quite desperate to get in touch with Charlie, for whatever the reason might have been.

It was starting to get late now and there was nothing more to be done this night. Both brothers had now been on the go for over forty hours, so they all decided that it might be safer if the lads took the money, drugs and some of the clothes that Charlie would wear on a day to day basis.

Sally put the money and cocaine back into the shoulder bag and together with some of Charlie's clothes, put everything in a large Tesco shopping bag for Mike to carry. She gave the lads a kiss on the cheek, said, 'night, night,' and watched from the front door as they both got into the Mondeo and drove away.

Before they left, they'd made arrangements to be back the next morning bright and early to discuss plan 'B' whatever that was going to be.

Oggy was cold and hungry, he'd been stood outside Charlie's house for the best part of the afternoon and evening and he'd seen from a distance the dark blue Mondeo pull up outside the house and two big lads get out.

Both of them were fair sized, the bigger one had a full beard and a short cropped head of dark hair. He also looked as though he worked out a lot based on the size of his chest and arms under the sweat shirt. The smaller one had no facial hair and the hair on the sides of his head was cut very short, the top slightly longer and combed back. He was also quite muscular, although he was a bit leaner and looked faster than the big lad, he also looked as though he worked out, or at least had a very physical job.

Who were they? Had Charlie already made a deal with them using his stash, or were they just visiting? Up until now there was still no sign of Charlie and it was getting late, he still hadn't called him and Oggy didn't dare go back to his own place for fear of unwanted visitors. He was also not answering some of his latest calls, he needed Charlie, like it was yesterday.

There was no alternative, he walked the short distance back to the front door and knocked, it was answered soon after by Charlies wife who opened it by a small crack.

'What do yeh want at this time of night?' She asked, 'if it's Charlie you're after, then he still hasn't come home and I don't know where he is, or when he's gonna be back. I just told me brothers about yeh lookin' for 'im an' they won't be too pleased when I tell them yeh was round 'ere so late knockin' on me front door again.'

At least Oggy knew who the two lads were now, but

that didn't really help.

'Misses, I really needs to find him, is all.'

Funnily enough, he was starting to believe the very pretty young woman that was stood in the doorway. Even his instincts were telling him she could be telling the truth and that was even more worrying than when he thought Charlie might be hiding upstairs under the bed, trying to avoid him.

Then a thought struck him, what if the Albanians already had Charlie and that's why they were trying to call him. Maybe this was why Charlie seemed to have disappeared and nobody had any idea as to his whereabouts. But how would they even know about Charlie for that matter. Ya but, the Albanians were always one step ahead of everyone else, that's why they ran everything.

'Okay missus, you gets Charlie he must calls me, okay?'

With that Oggy turned and this time he headed into the town, where he kept a small one bedroom flat at the back of the railway station.

CHAPTER NINE

Donika Demaci was Albanian. He was a wiry, lean man of around five foot ten inches tall, with short black hair and a very neatly trimmed goatee beard. Not a huge man physically, but immense as far as his power and control were concerned.

He was the boss of the criminal underworld based around the Seaborough city limits. Demaci was a ruthless street lord and ruled by simple violence and terror, there was not one kind bone in his body.

There was however, little that perturbed Demaci and that included being on the wrong side of the law. He had no scruples and would have sold his mother, granny, sister or any other female member of his family to a Bedouin goat herder if he believed the price was right. In fact, he would sell all of them together, if he thought he could get a decent payback on a package deal.

He had no respect for women, he didn't hate or dislike them, on the contrary there was one or two that he was quite fond of, but they were there to be used and for a profit. Not by him of course, perish the thought, Donika Demaci loved boy's and the younger and prettier they were, the better.

The police, both locally and at a national level had tried unsuccessfully to apprehend Mr Demaci on various occasions in the past, but he was far too cunning to allow that to happen.

His underlings might be apprehended in the course of their everyday activities and some of those that had, ended up serving time in Her Majesties prisons as a result, but it was never going to be Demaci, he'd never been found anywhere near the scene of a crime yet.

Today Donika Demaci was slightly perturbed however. He generally knew what was going on, but today he didn't seem to understand where Oggy was. It wasn't like pretty young Oggy to ignore his mobile phone when summoned.

After waiting through the morning, a couple of the lads had been sent to Oggy's flat, but apparently after they'd knocked and got no reply, they knocked very hard and the door became open and so they walked on in as if invited. They couldn't find Oggy anywhere, nor any of the merchandise that was owed to Mr Demaci.

Even after they turned the chairs and television upside down in the living room, the bed in the single bedroom was also turned over to look underneath and the kitchen cupboard doors seemed to have fallen off when they swung on them, with all the crockery tumbling out onto the floor.

They didn't find any of the things that they'd come for and so they left, thinking that Oggy was one seriously untidy housekeeping Turkish individual.

This was all reported back to Mr Demaci who was starting to think that maybe he was being double crossed somewhere or even heaven forbid, disrespected. It wasn't so much the value of the items, although that was a fair amount, maybe a pittance to the likes of Demaci. It was more the principal.

71

He could ill afford to let anyone be seen to get the better of him, this would be an effrontery and a mark against his good name, it needed to be rectified immediately. They must find Oggy and quickly. There were other bigger fish waiting for his total concentration and this hiccough with Oggy was just something that was getting in the way.

Donika Demaci had just received the telephone call he'd been waiting for from the ships agent in the harbour area, notifying him that the vessel Rangoon Princess had finally arrived at the anchorage area and tendered her Notice of Readiness. The vessel had then been instructed to proceed directly to the first of the marker buoys at the entry channel, where the duty Pilot would board by launch on the port side and under pilotage, would manoeuvre the vessel to the Seaborough City Container Terminal, berth number two for the unloading and then backloading of three thousand containers of varying sizes and differing cargoes.

The vessel Rangoon Princess was a Panamax, fifth generation container vessel. Built at the Hankim Heavy Industries shipyard in Busan, South Korea in 2002 and had a maximum capacity to carry a total of 8,000 units.

The heroin being smuggled in, was coming from the port of Karachi and had been loaded on board the vessel at the Pakistan International Container Terminal.

The heroin had been packed inside a total of twenty bags of Portland cement which would be part of a larger consignment of one hundred tons of cheap dry cement powder being delivered by five, twenty foot containers to local construction sites within this part of the UK. Demaci had made contact via a network of international criminal type investors and brokers, devising what he considered to be a foolproof plan.

CHAPTER TEN

Oggy was knackered, he hadn't slept for days with worry, he hadn't eaten for hours, he'd been walking and waiting for what seemed like an eternity and he was no closer to finding Charlie than he had been the day before.

Charlie was definitely not at home, he felt sure of that now, so where had the fat bastard gone? And what for?

Oggy got his keys out of his pocket as he was approaching his front door on the ground level. The actual flat being up a narrow flight of stairs on the first floor. However, as he neared the door, he could see it was not closed properly and this concerned him.

He stepped closer and listened, there wasn't a sound coming from the inside. He looked around and couldn't notice anything untoward. Slowly he pushed the door open and stepped inside. Nothing, so he ventured up the stairs as cautiously and quietly as he possibly could.

When he reached the top and saw the immediate obliteration of his small flat, his first reaction was burglars. But he knew that all the bad lads in the area knew who he was and what his relationship was with Mr Demaci and based on that alone, he believed they wouldn't dare. Therefore he had to assume that it must be the second and much worse option, Mr Demaci was looking for him. Oh shit!

Oggy's choices of what he could do were starting to look abysmal. He could call Mr Demaci and explain why he didn't have the goods, which would probably result in some form of punishment, with hospitalization at the very least. He could run, but he didn't know where to run to, or he could find Charlie which he'd been trying to do and it was becoming more difficult by the hour.

All he wanted to do was sleep, wake up the next morning to find a happy smiling Charlie standing there in front of him with the shoulder bag, having cleaned and tidied his flat, made him a nice Turk kahvesi and a full menemen breakfast. Not too much to ask, is it? Not a cat in hells chance mate.

It had all started the night of the big football game, when all the lads had gone to the Ship and Anchor. Oggy wasn't too bothered about watching the game, he had a meeting with some out of town dealer who'd got in touch through Mr Demaci.

Oggy believed that this little venture might turn out to be quite lucrative, however he was very wrong and when the dealer walked into the pub with a couple of extremely large and very heavy associates that Oggy immediately recognised as being a particular dealer who had travelled up from London, and was wanting to step outside around the back to discuss business, then Oggy got what might be considered a senses overload. This just might turn out to be a rather huge mistake.

Especially considering what Oggy had already taken off him when he'd left London and further, considering what and who's goods Oggy had in the shoulder bag.

The match had long ago finished and Charlie was heading out to buy a six pack, then going home to sort his missus out, when Oggy turned to him and whispered urgently.

'Charlie, I needs favour now.'

Charlie thought he'd finally made it into the big boy's camp and was only too keen to help.

'Course Oggy, owt for a fuckin' mate, watcha fuckin' need?'

'Takes this to your home. Keeps it safe and brings it back 'ere tomorrow night, I see you is alright after, okay?'

Oggy handed Charlie the small canvas bag with the shoulder strap, which Charlie promptly placed over his head, putting his left arm through, then gave Oggy a very limp salute.

'No fuckin' probs mate, see yeh tomorra.'

He then staggered to the door and left.

Oggy on the other hand, made his way through the melee of football supporters into the back room and legged it out the back door into the yard and over the wall.

Oggy desperately wanted to sleep, but did he dare put his head down in his own flat or should he go off somewhere else out of the area. All his known associates were also known to Mr Demaci, so it would only take a phone call from any one of them to gain favour and for Mr Demaci to be advised of Oggy's whereabouts, in which case he was well screwed.

He may as well turn his bed the right way up and sleep on it and if the worst scenario took place then that's where he'd shuffle off this mortal coil, he could always beg. Begging sometimes worked.

Mr Demaci was not happy and if he was not happy he was going to make very certain that others were not happy. He was speaking to Bashkim Hamiti, his right hand man.

'So, you searched the flat and found nothing, right?'

'Yes Mr. Demaci, we searched it, but no, we found nothing. There was no sign of Oggy or any of the goods that you sent us to look for.'

Bashkim was also Albanian, a very precise and intelligent man. He'd once been a Kapter, or Staff Sergeant in the Albanian infantry, but the rank was well below that of his capabilities and intelligence and after leaving, he'd found there was only a limited calling for the skills with which he had been accredited to in the military.

That was until Mr Demaci took him under his wing and made him his own private lieutenant.

Bashkim was the most average looking man you would ever imagine and because of that, most people underestimated his skills and his gentle powers of persuasion. He was in fact deadly and as such, ideally suited to Mr Donika Demaci's special requirements.

He'd been married at one time, however whilst he was still serving, his now ex wife had taken their only daughter and fled back to her parent's home crying that Bashkim was mentally cruel, totally unfeeling and insensitive towards her and the child. Bashkim shrugged his shoulders, told her she was probably right, then wishing her good luck, he turned and walked out.

It was late evening and they were talking in the small study office of Donika Demaci' apartment in the Tower Flats, overlooking the busy river Tonnet in the centre of the city. Demaci was wearing his black, Japanese silk Kimono.

'Okay, before we are finished tonight, I want you to go back and see if he has returned. If he has, then take him to the lock up under the bridge and make sure he is made as uncomfortable for the night as you can and we will talk with him in the morning. If he is not there, then go home to bed and we will discuss what we will do in the morning, okay? All is understood?'

Demaci was still calm. Until now he hadn't lost his

temper, but he was starting to. He had the strongest feeling that someone somewhere was disrespecting him. Bashkim Hamiti nodded agreement as Demaci walked him to the front door, quietly locking it behind him.

Demaci then turned to face Simon. The young male model who was lounging on the black leather corner suite with a glass of chilled Moet and Chandon in his very soft looking, expensively manicured hands. The escort agency had sent him for Mr Demaci to assess and approve, it would therefore be Demaci's decision as to whether or not this tall, slim, dark haired and very pretty young man would be working full time for the agency or should we say, it really depended on Simon's powers of persuasion as to whether or not he got the job.

Oggy was out cold when the downstairs door burst off its hinges. The noise would have been deafening had he been awake, but as he was in a very deep and troubled sleep, it was just very bloody loud.

The sound of heavy footsteps thundering up the stairs did nothing to convince him that all was right with the world and in the few seconds it took for the uninvited intruders to find their way into Oggy's bedroom, he had in fact only just managed to pull his pants on and that was all he now wore, just his pants.

He was grabbed from both sides by very large hands and forced to his knees, whereby a not so gentle kick by Hamiti's heavy foot to the scrotum ensured he was fully awake.

'Mr Demaci would like to know where you have put both his money and his goods?' was the first thing Bashkim had to say.

The second was ever so slightly more of a threat.

'If you don't tell me now, then I have instructions to take you and make you feel very uncomfortable, what would you like to tell me?'

Oggy Galata thought about it, but only for a split millisecond.

'I don't know where stuff is,' was his un-rehearsed reply.

Hamiti readied himself for another of his now infamous bollock busting kicks when Oggy screamed.

'Wait! I have not got it, but I know who has, his name Charlie, he live at Westernside, I takes you now.'

Bashkim thought for a second before replying.

'No! We will now take you for a short ride to consider your answer and later in the morning at some time convenient, you will tell Mr Demaci all that you know, is that understood?'

With that, the large hands that had put him on his knees, now lifted him off his feet and dragged him down the stairs and out the front door to the white transit van parked on the opposite side of the road. Whereby young Oggy was thrown into the back onto the cold bare metal floor of the van, to be accompanied by a rather large Neanderthal type, whose sole purpose in life was to ensure Oggy Ahmet Galata did not leave without permission.

The drive from Oggy's flat to the unknown lockup under the bridge took around forty minutes. Oggy was confused, he didn't know if he was happier to stay in the van or to get out. In the van he was extremely cold and uncomfortable, whereas outside he was just as cold but as yet, not quite so sure how uncomfortable he was about to become.

He was manhandled again by the large hands that had bent and manipulated him in the flat. Shirtless and bare footed he was taken into a derelict looking brick workshop, with big wooden padlocked doors and most of the windows broken. The inside was no improvement on the outer shell of Oggy's new accommodation. It stunk of old oily rags, garbage and somewhere the toilets had overflowed, leaving raw sewage to leak across the old cracked concrete floor.

Oggy was placed against one of the supporting pillars with the end of a chain wrapped tightly around his waist and padlocked, the other end had previously been welded to a metal support.

Those now all familiar hands, held him tightly up against the support, whilst Bashkim Hamiti methodically punched the crap out of him. With his face a mass of lumps, bloody and bruised, he was asked if he felt uncomfortable and when he nodded to the affirmative, being unable to speak any more at this time, he was released and allowed to drop onto the cold, wet, sewage covered floor and await a time when Mr Demaci would see fit to pay him a visit, maybe sometime later in the day.

Bashkim Hamiti was not concerned about Oggy's chances of escape. The whole area was private property with chain linked fencing surrounding the total perimeter. It was all owned by one of Mr Demaci associates and therefore no one ventured to this part of town. Oggy could shout and scream to his heart's content and for as loud and long as he wanted, nobody was ever going to hear him.

CHAPTER ELEVEN

Sally awoke, looked at her alarm clock and smiled. The smile didn't hurt as much as it had the day before and she knew she was healing. To her left lay little Charlie stretched out with his arms and legs pointing to the four compass points and to her right a very tiny huddled bundle with a pink teddy that was Georgia. The two of them had climbed into her bed at different times through the night, Sally hadn't even been aware, she'd slept so soundly that she hadn't known a thing.

The clock said half past seven, but it didn't really matter because today was Saturday and that meant a no school day, so Sally turned onto her side and closed her eyes again. When she eventually woke later, the small alarm clock showed that she'd succeeded in having an extra half hour sleep. Sally then managed to get out of bed without waking the kids and slipped into the bathroom where she showered and dressed and was downstairs with her first cup of coffee, preparing breakfast for the bairns when the knock at the door came.

Answering cautiously and opening the door slowly, she was pleased to find big brother Paul stood there with a huge strong white teeth smile on his beautiful weather beaten face.

'Mornin' little sis, ave yeh got the kettle on then?'

'Where's our Mike then, didn't he come wi' yeh?' She asked.

The smile dropped and Paul shook his head sulkily

'No, he bloody didn't. We went for a pint at the Ship and Anchor after leaving yours last night and the jammy bastard only pulled didn't he, he always friggin' does man. Anyway we won't see him much this side of lunch time, I left 'im a note sayin' I was comin' 'ere tho'.'

Sally poured him a brew and they talked about the past couple of days and the dramatic changes that had taken place and were about to continue taking place. She also mentioned the late night visit from Oggy, but explained that he didn't seem to pose a threat.

Paul advised his sister that there was going to come a time in the not too distant future when she may have to report Charlie as a missing person, which she reluctantly acknowledged. He also explained about the fire they'd seen on the way to the pub the night before and that the clothes they had taken belonging to Charlie, together with his mobile phone and the blood stained rug, had all gone in to fuel the flames. Apparently, the car was stinking so badly of the dried and congealed blood in the rug they couldn't breathe anymore, they'd had no alternative but to get rid of it.

Paul also told her that he'd been up early and stowed the bag with the money and the drugs in a safe place in the engine compartment on board the Bonny Doris where nobody would find it. He'd removed a couple of hundred for Sally to get by with, but told her she was going to have to go to Social on Monday and ask for a hand out on the basis her husband had fucked off without leaving her with owt. This was more or less true in a roundabout sort of way that Paul had justified in his own mind.

At this the kids came down with all sorts to tell uncle Paul. Sally promptly ushered them into the living room out of the way, where they knelt on the floor at the coffee table to eat their breakfasts and drink their sweet weak tea, whilst watching Saturday morning television in their pyjamas.

Mike turned up half an hour later and went into quite graphic detail about the gorgeous young lass he'd spent the night with and how well him and her had got on. It was almost poetic until he found out from Sally that she'd been in her class at school and was well known for putting it about behind the bike shed with just about every lad in the school.

Sally and Paul brought Mike up to date with their earlier conversation over yet another pot of tea, re-iterating on what they'd already discussed concerning Sally's finances and the reporting of the missing Charlie. Mike confirmed he had nothing more to add to what had already been decided and so they all agreed, that it was, 'finita la musica, passata la fiesta,' so let's get on with the rest of our lives.

CHAPTER TWELVE

Mad Arrie was forty three years old. His full and proper title was Harold Arthur Stoke and he wasn't mad, that's just what the local kids called him.

Harry (to his friends), once had a very good job as an accountant at a law firm in the city, but his wife left him for a much younger toy boy and took the kids with her. The courts in their infinite wisdom gave her the house and everything in it, ordering Harry to pay full maintenance for the kids and the ex wife while they lived there. The courts believed he could afford it on the excellent salary he was being paid.

Joanne his ex, apparently couldn't take the boring humdrum life and was screaming out for some sort of excitement, which unfortunately was not a part of Harry's natural chemistry. Harry didn't like excitement, Harry enjoyed pondering.

After the divorce and after much pondering, Harry played his trump card. IIe walked into the offices of the law firm he'd worked in for nearly twenty years, handed them his resignation without working his one month's notice, then leaving instructions that all outstanding salary, holiday money, pension together with any investments and other moneys owing to him, were to be paid directly to the Battersea dogs and cats home. Not because he liked either dogs or cats, or Battersea for that matter, no, he just despised his ex wife.

After making the arrangements for his finances, Harry walked back to the bedsit he'd been renting, put on his comfy old Wrangler jeans and his even more comfy older sweatshirt that he used to wear whilst working in the garden back at the family home. He then slipped into his faithful Barbour waterproof jacket and favourite Timberland walking boots, locked the bedsit up and posted the key through the letterbox of the landlord's flat downstairs, then Harry went for a long walk.

Harry walked for five years, he never turned around and he never went back, but he did hear through the grapevine that his ex had lost the house. The boyfriend didn't last too long after, and the kids now all grown up, had left her. That was exciting, wasn't it? No, that was bloody justice.

Now days Mad Arrie was a dishevelled mess. His hair had grown way past his shoulders and was knotted and dirty, as was the impressive beard he sported. The clothes he'd left home in were long gone, but he was still able to attire himself with clothes left outside houses in various charity bags, taking anything that would fit him or could be of service, then retying the bags for the respective charities to collect when he'd finished.

Mad Arrie travelled light and rarely slept in the same place two nights in a row, moving about constantly. He would however, always go back again another time if it suited his purpose. He never strayed too far from town centres, there was always plenty of local eateries throwing good food out from the kitchens into the garbage in the back alleys. He did well from that and hadn't actually lost a great deal of weight over the past few years.

Last night Mad Arrie found the hole in the link fence of the boat storage yard he'd used many times in the past. Looking through the fence he could see there was nobody about, so he ventured in, sheltering under the boat nearest the wall, covered over in case it rained and out of the wind, protected by the wall itself.

It had been a good dry night and as he was gathering his bed roll, together with all his other worldly possessions ready to move on, he heard the big gate squeak open and a tall young man of around thirty years, with dark short cropped hair and a full beard, carrying a shoulder bag, walk over to a boat on the far side of the yard.

The young man climbed the ladder, lifted the lid of what looked like a big box on the front of the boats shelter and placed the bag inside, he then climbed back down and left, locking the compound gate behind him.

It can't have taken more than five minutes, but Mad Arrie's curiosity had got the better of him and although Harold Arthur Stokes was neither adventurous nor exciting, Mad Arrie had learnt over a very short period of time to be a scrounger and anything that might be of any use to him whatsoever was fair game and that nice little canvas shoulder bag looked extremely useful.

He made sure there was nobody about, swiftly climbed the ladder and opened the big box, surprised to find a huge engine inside, he hadn't expected that. The bag was just lying there so he scooped it up, throwing it over his shoulder and was back down the ladder from start to finish in less than a minute.

Arrie grabbed the rest of his belongings, then exited via the hole in the fence to his next destination, wherever that was going to be.

CHAPTER THIRTEEN

Donika Demaci woke early, which was his norm. A lot of his business was conducted whilst he was still in his Japanese silk kimono before he even dressed.

He'd slept naked as he always did, the big king size bed being empty when he woke, having ushered young Simon out much earlier when he'd finished with him, confirming of course that there was an excellent chance of him getting a full time position at the Escort agency. This of course was true from Demaci's point of view, he would advise the agency that Simon had been fun to be with and could be an asset to the agency that Demaci owned.

Demaci was drinking his second cup of espresso that morning and eating a fresh croissant when Bashkim Hamiti buzzed from downstairs. He was let in and when he arrived up to the apartment, explained about finding Oghuz Galata in bed back at the small flat and as per instructions from Mr Demaci, he'd transferred Galata to the lock up under the bridge and made him feel extremely uncomfortable for the night.

Hamiti then went on to further explain that the whereabouts of Mr Demaci's goods were still not entirely apparent, however young Oggy had mumbled something just prior to being placed unconscious, that maybe Mr Demaci might find somewhat beneficial and informative.

Donika Demaci listened tentatively to the Hamiti report of the night before and after checking his schedule for the day on his home computer, instructed Hamiti that there was no need for him to leave, they would complete business from the apartment first, then they could maybe pay a visit to young Oggy.

Demaci told Hamiti to help himself to fresh coffee and croissants, whilst he retired to the bedroom where he showered and shaved in the en suite bathroom. Dressing in a very relaxed Saturday morning attire of a dark blue, button down Hugo Boss, short sleeved shirt, with his tan heavy cotton Ralph Lauren chinos and his favourite comfortable, old brown leather boat shoes.

It took Demaci around two hours to complete negotiations between several clients on the telephone, after which he was ready to go out to interview young Oghuz Ahmet Galata as to the whereabouts of the misplaced goods. Both Demaci and Hamiti left the apartment together.

Whilst Hamiti went down to the underground carpark below to bring Mr Demaci's black Range Rover Vogue up, Demaci took the front door of the apartment block out on to the main road. Outside they found two of the big brawny minions waiting. Mouths wide open, snoring loudly, fast asleep in the front seats of the white transit van.

The drive from the centre of town to the lock up took an easy thirty minutes and gave Mr Demaci time to sit back and relax in the big comfortable car, listening to the Classic FM radio channel and watching the world go quietly by.

When they arrived at the lockup all was silent. There was no sound coming from the inside of the unused garage.

There was no one in the local vicinity to oversee what was happening or who was there. The weather was extremely mild for this time of year, although slightly overcast and Mr Demaci was in a relatively good mood, humming quietly along with Rimsky Korsakov's, Scheherazade.

CHAPTER FOURTEEN

Sally got the kids dressed and told them they were all going up to the local Tesco supermarket and they could each choose something nice, but they had to help carry the shopping back.

Little Charlie was wearing a worried expression on his little face and so Sally in the end had to ask him.

'What's the matter our Charlie? It's not like you to be so gloomy.'

Charlie stopped what he was doing and turned his serious little face up to look at his mother.

'Where's our Dad, Mam? We 'avn't seen 'im for ages now and you avn't even said owt about 'im', did you's two argue again and has he run away?'

Sally realised that with the exception of the very weak spilt beetroot story, she hadn't even mentioned a word to the kids about their father. It could only have been a matter of time before one or both questioned his disappearance.

'The fact is Charlie, after your dad hurt me really bad the last time, he was so mad wi' hiself that he's gone off to stay wi' a friend for a while to calm down. He said he'll maybe come back when he's sorted his head out, but I don't know how long that might take.'

It was gobby Georgia that chirped up.

'Well I hope he never comes back, he was always smelly and angry and kept on hurtin' you, our Mam.'

'Yeh,' said Little Charlie, 'he was always hurtin' you weren't he our Mam and I don't wan' 'im to come back either cos we're 'avin a good time wi' out 'im, aren't we? It's really nice, and quiet now.'

Sally smiled down at the two of them.

'We are happy just the three of us,' she said, 'we can manage and help each other can't we? We don't really need your dad to spoil all that right now, do we?'

Sally was talking openly to her own conscience rather than the kids. However, it was their heads that were nodding up and down in agreement with everything that was said.

CHAPTER FIFTEEN

'So, I understand you have some information that you would like to share with me young Oggy. I trust you had a quiet night. Maybe not quite the comfort you were expecting, but you must realise I cannot be seen to allow people the likes of you, to just wander about doing whatever they want. That would be detrimental to me as a business man and could be considered quite anarchistic. You have responsibilities to me and you now owe me a considerable amount of money and goods, so Oggy where is it?'

Mr Demaci was stood with his tanned, nicely manicured hands in his pocket. Although the weather was pleasant outside, within the confines of the dimly lit lockup it felt quite chilly.

Oggy was laid in the foetal position on the floor, his blackened, bruised and swollen eyes were only just able to open and focus on the speaker as long as he lifted his head at the correct angle. The skin on his cheek bones had split and had now scabbed over from the savage punches issued the night before. His lower jaw was set at totally the wrong angle, broken or dislocated would only be determined, if and when he was ever likely to see the inside of a hospital and to complete the scenario, there was massive bruising around his abdomen and rib cage, where he already knew he had at least two ribs that were fractured.

He was cold and totally exhausted from both pain and lack of sleep, but through inflamed broken lips and with tears running off his cheeks he tried to speak.

'I tells Mr Hamiti last night, before hims beat me up too much, I tell hims, I no haves you money, Charlie he have's it. Charlie, he live in Westernsides, I go many, many time to see hims, but hims lady say hims gone. What I can do?'

Demaci slowly walked around the recumbent body of Oggy, trying hard not to step in the excrement covering the floor.

'Well Oggy, I'm going to tell you what you should have done. You should have first answered my calls and let me know what the situation was, then I may have been in a position to have assisted you, now unfortunately I can't. Secondly this was all your responsibility, why this Charlie had anything to do with my business is beyond my understanding. I don't know him, I've never met him, he doesn't even work for me and yet, you say you've freely given him a considerable amount of my money and possessions, why would you do that?'

Oggy was shivering uncontrollably now, a mixture of cold, fear and shock, but he spent the next painful ten minutes trying to explain to Mr Donika Demaci the whole situation of how Charlie had ended up with the satchel of money and cocaine and how he'd visited and maintained surveillance on the house to no avail. He further explained about the comings and goings of Charlie's wife and her brothers. At the end Oggy was so exhausted he could only mumble incoherently to himself.

'I think we may be finished here Bashkim. Oggy seems to have served his purpose and is of no possible further use to either of us anymore. Do you happen to know this Charlie and where we might find him? If so, maybe you can speed young Oggy on to the remainder of his journey and after, please ensure word gets about that I'm not to be trifled with. You are fully aware of how I feel about respect and there seems to have been a complete lack of it lately. I shall wait for you in the car, please don't keep me waiting too long.'

Donika Demaci walked outside into the now brilliant sunlight and once inside the passenger side of the Range Rover, removed his aviator Ray Ban sunglasses from the glove compartment and put them on. He then switched on the radio and continued to listen to Classic FM whilst awaiting the return of Bashkim Hamiti.

Inside the lock up, Hamiti had gleaned as much information about Charlie as he could and knew there was no more to be had from Oggy.

He stepped behind the exhausted slumped body and told him to relax it was all over, he would now be looked after.

As Oggy relaxed, Hamiti placed a comforting arm around his shoulder and with a quick twist and jerk of Oggy's head, he broke his neck, cleanly, swiftly and very professionally.

The thin six inch, razor sharp flick knife that had been produced from Hamiti's back pocket, slid slowly across opening Oggy's throat from ear to ear, this was a symbol, a warning to others. Night, night, young Oghuz Ahmet Galata from Mersin, Turkey, sweet dreams.

CHAPTER SIXTEEN

'What about these our Mam? We love these,'
Little Charlie was up and down the Tesco aisles as though competing in the finals of the Supermarket Sweep, with Georgia's little legs running closely behind, trying her hardest to keep up.

'No Charlie, I know your tryin to help us pet, but we don't need all that, its only to tide us over the weekend and a few extra treats while we watch the telly.'

Sally was trying her hardest to curb the children's enthusiasm, but it seemed as though it may have been a lost cause. She also had to be very careful that she didn't give the impression of someone who had money. She was supposed to be going into Social on Monday, pleading poverty as a mother whose husband had walked out on her and two young children, without providing a penny for them before he left, the bastard.

Sally went to the checkout and started to place her shopping on the conveyor feed. As the checkout woman scanned the items, Sally realised how much it was going to cost and stopped her.

'I think maybe I gone a bit daft and put too much in the trolley. Can yeh tell us how much I've spent up to now, cos I may hafta put summit back.'

The checkout lady looked at her with a sympathetic knowing smile and nodded.

'Aye pet, at the moment it comes to fifteen pounds twenty five pence, is that okay or do yeh wanna change summit?'

Sally pursed her lips and blew.

'Okay, let's get rid of this, this and this, I only got a twenty on us and its gotta last us the weekend, what's that look like now?'

The checkout lady re-cashed the shopping and gave a final price of seventeen pounds and thirty pence which included the remainder of what had been left in the trolley.

Sally smiled, paid and left with three bags of groceries. We can live like kings on this she thought, must remember to be careful in future though.

The three of them walked home laughing and joking as they went and as they turned up the path to the front door they were totally oblivious of the white transit van parked at the end of the road, with two very large 'gentlemen' sat in the front seats, carefully monitoring and recording theirs and everyone else's movements on their Garmin dash cam.

Sally unpacked the shopping while the kids ran upstairs and put their pyjamas on for a night on the settee in front of the telly, watching cartoons and then later Britain's Got Talent until bedtime.

Sally made them all a little buffet and put it on a tray on the coffee table in the living room. Then whilst the kids were absorbed in watching Shrek for the umpteenth time on DVD, she went and gave her mam a quick phone call.

They both nattered for a good half hour with dad giving his considered opinion every now and then, after which they said their night, nights and hung up. Sally went upstairs stripped off and changed into her pyjamas and now clean bathrobe which she'd soaked in bleach, washed and scrubbed to remove all the remaining blood stains and was now looking as good as new. She then went down to join the kids for the rest of the evenings telly.

CHAPTER SEVENTEEN

'So, did he say anything?'

Demaci asked Hamiti as he was stepping back into the driver seat of the Range Rover for the ride back into the city,

'Yes, Mr Demaci, he gave me an address for this Charlie, but there seems to be confusion as to whether this individual is actually living there or has gone off somewhere.'

Donika Demaci was gazing out of the nearside passenger window at the old dilapidated ruins that had once been such magnificent buildings. Lived in by prosperous businessmen and their well to do families. Kept segregated from the slums of the workers who had toiled to make them rich in the first place. There seemed somehow to be a poetic justice that these once fine buildings would became the slums of the late twentieth century before they were demolished.

'Okay, after the boys get rid of the remains of Oggy, send them around to keep an eye on the house and see if this Charlie person returns. Do we know what he looks like? Have we got a description at all?'

Hamiti started the engine and gave the big car a few

rev's.

'Yes sir, I don't think it will be too difficult to recognise him,'

'Good, good, take me back to my apartment, I have work I can be getting on with. Keep your phone handy and call me if there are any developments, I shouldn't need you for the rest of the day, but make sure the boys keep you updated.'

Hamiti nodded acknowledgement and pulled away.

The drive back was without incident and neither of them spoke. Hamiti dropped his boss outside the front doors to the tower block, then drove off in the Range Rover to his own flat, farther outside of town.

Later in the afternoon Hamiti received a call from the two men watching Sally's house explaining that her and the kids had arrived back with their shopping and were in the house, but up until now there was no sign of the husband Charlie.

'Okay' said Hamiti, 'give it a couple of hours until everyone is settled for the evening then go in discreetly and look around. We need to somehow confirm that this Charlie person has not actually been hiding in the house all the time and before you leave, give the woman a word of advice. Tell her to get a message to her husband, we want our property back.'

After the skies had become dark, one of the large bulks of man mountain stepped out from the van and walked up and across to number 35 Frazer Avenue. He could hear the television on in the living room, so he tried the front door handle, it was unlocked and he quietly stepped inside shutting the door silently behind him. Sally was in the kitchen, he could hear her talking on her mobile. In the living room he could hear the kids laughing at Shrek the movie, so he warily climbed the stairs in the darkness to have a look around.

For a man of his bulk and size, it would have seemed impossible for him to move so quietly, but everyone else was preoccupied with whatever it was they were doing and no one gave a second thought to the oversized prowler walking around the house in the dark.

He checked the main bedroom first, making sure not to disturb anything, he looked under the bed, in the cupboard, nothing. The bathroom was small, too small for him to enter comfortably, so he just poked his head around the door, the last room was the kid's bedroom. Just as he entered, he heard Sally climb the stairs and enter her own bedroom next door, pulling the cord for the light switch by the side of the doorframe as she walked in. He waited a short while, then stepped out of the children's room to go quietly back down the stairs.

Sally's bedroom door was half open and as he walked past he could see her getting changed. She had her back to him and was totally naked, reaching for her pyjamas off the top of the bed. He watched silently for a few seconds, before walking back down the stairs to quickly look in the kitchen.

It was cluttered with the usual untidiness of a young family, but nothing of any interest to him, so he entered the living room.

Little Charlie and Georgia looked up at the huge bull of a man, who apart from the skin colour, could quite easily have passed as the green ogre himself.

'No be afraid, I no hurt you,' he whispered in a deep rumble to the now terrified children, 'Where you papa? Where Charlie? He is here?'

Just then Sally came bounding through the door, a second later she was swinging at him, she didn't even come up to the shoulder of his twenty five stone frame. The punches she was throwing were glancing off him and having absolutely no effect, he then held her firmly by the wrists, so he could pass on the message from his boss before he left.

Sally had heard a man's voice, but thought it must be the television. When she walked in through the living room door and nearly collided with the voice, it was with total shock and horror.

'Who're you? What you doin in my 'ouse? Gerrout now!'

Sally flung herself with arms flaying at the massive figure in front of her, but to no avail. Her wrists were grabbed solidly by two vice like hands.

'I no come hurt you okay lady, only speaks at you. Charlie he live here, you say him return things not belong him now and then no trouble, he no return, then big trouble. You tell him muss be quickly though.'

At that the massive humanoid turned and walked out of the door as silently as he had entered. Sally ran after him and double bolted the front door, she then turned back into the living room hugging both frightened kids to her on the settee.

Once Sally's heart had slowed to an almost steady rhythm again, she explained to the bairns that everything was okay and there was nothing for them to worry about. Then she phoned Paul.

This being Saturday night, Paul and Mike had walked up to the Ship and Anchor for a few bevvie's and a bit of banter with the local lads. They'd already consumed several pints each so were well on their way to being very relaxed when Paul's phone rang.

'Hya princess, whatcha after at this 'our?' Paul slurred down the phone.

'Are yeh drunk?' Sally questioned.

'Not yet our Sal, but well on me fuckin' way, why

whussup?'

Sally explained about the big man that had let himself in through the front door. The man who had terrified her and the kids and she asked Paul what she should do about it.

'Well, if yeh really wan' me 'onest fuckin' opinion, nowt,' Paul slurred, 'jus' fuckin' leave it for now and go on up to bed. I can't see anyone doin fuck all tonight, they're afta Chas an' he aint even there now is he? Tha's who they fuckin' lookin' for. I'll be round in the mornin and we'll talk proper then, you go off to bed an' don't you fuckin' worry sweetheart.' Paul then hung up.

Sally looked at her phone as though Paul's face was there looking back at her and mimicked her older brother.

'Just go up to bed he said, just go up to bed and don't worry he said, what's the point, how the fuck am I gonna sleep?'

'Away kids, give your mam a hand with this.'

There was only one thing for it, Sally needed to barricade herself into her own home and so she locked the front and back doors, removing the keys. She then had the kids help her carry the heavy wooden coffee table from the living room into the front passage and wedge it on its end under the front door handle. Now if anybody tried to enter, it might not stop them, but at least it would make one God awful noise when it was pushed over.

Sally then went into the kitchen and looked at what could be done to prevent the back door from being opened and with a lot of tugging and pulling, her and the kids managed to disconnect the plumbing at the back and push the heavy automatic washing machine in front of it.

All the downstairs windows had blinds on them. Vertical in the living room and venetian in the kitchen, which

Sally thought probably wouldn't stop anyone, but just might put them off trying to enter if they had to make too much noise getting in.

She didn't think the big man that she'd found in her house would be able to fit through a window anyway, not even if his life depended on it. He didn't need to, he could actually just walk through the bloody wall she thought with a shudder. But Oggy, now he would be able to climb through a window, he was young and looked nimble and agile enough.

'I guess Oggy must have got sick of looking for Charlie and sent his big mate around instead,' Sally thought, 'Jesus, I hope Charlie didn't take anything from that big lad or we're well knackered.'

She had no sooner completed her fortifications, when there was a loud banging at the front door. Sally froze, the kids ran to her with arms wrapped around her legs for protection. 'I don't even have a bloody weapon,' she thought. The knocking came a second time and with it a voice from the other side of the front door.

'Away our Sal love, lerrus in, I need a pee.'

Sally recognised the voice of her biggest brother and hurriedly removed the coffee table and after finding the front door key, unlocked and opened the door.

Paul ran quickly past her, legging it straight up the stairs. Mike followed, staggering slowly through the front door and standing in the small passage with a big stupid smile on his face.

'I went out in the front garden,' he grinned.

Paul completed his ablutions and came down the stairs, fastening his flies as he descended.

'Jesus man, I thought yeh wasn't gonna lerrus in there Sal, I was bustin'.' Paul said.

'What are you two doin here, I thought yeh weren't

comin' round 'til t'morrow,' said Sally.

'Aye, but I got to thinkin' while I was suppin. If it wasn't Oggy that came round, then it had to be one of them big bastard Albanian lads, sent by the boss man and if that's the case, then you shouldn't be here by yourself.'

Mike just stood swaying, nodding in agreement with everything his big brother said.

'So, our Mike and me, well we figured we may as well crash 'ere the night, cos you probably wouldn't a slept anyway, didn't we Mike?'

Mike was feeling no pain and his swaying was starting to make Sally feel seasick.

'Away in the kitchen, I'll put the kettle on.' Sally finally said.

CHAPTER EIGHTEN

Bashkim Hamiti woke early, showered and drank his coffee before phoning the two men who should be sat in the white transit watching 35 Frazer Avenue. It was six o clock and the telephone rang five times before it was answered.

'I hope you were not sleeping, because that would mean you were not doing your job and if you are unable to do your job, then I have no further use of you.'

Hamiti was speaking in the men's own local dialect of Gheg. They'd all lived close to the same area as each other in the northern part of their Albanian homeland.

'No sir everything is okay. Some men came late last night and nobody else. The men did not fit the description of this person we are looking for.'

'Okay,' said Hamiti, 'I'll get someone to relieve you. Please stay there until they arrive, and I think I may take a drive over myself in a little while to have a talk.'

Hamiti hung up and was about to leave when his phone rang, it was Mr Demaci.

'Good morning Bashkim, is there any news about this Charlie person yet?'

'No not yet sir, I have spoken with our people outside the house and they have advised me that he is not in the house and never turned up during the night. They did say however that two other men arrived. I'd intended to go over there later in the day to have a word if that's okay with you.'

There was a few seconds silence on the other end of the phone then Demaci replied,

'Yes, that might be a good idea. Find out from the woman where her husband is and put a little gentle persuasion her way. Call me later if you have something for me.'

At that the phone went dead, Demaci had hung up. Hamiti, went into the bedroom and dressed. Light blue jeans and a dark blue polo shirt were the order of the day. On his feet were his white Reebok trainers, very eighties looking, but we all know, some fashions never die.

He then went downstairs to where the Range Rover was parked and headed to the Westernside council estate to have a visit with Mrs Sally Oldham and her family.

Sally was the first to wake. For the second morning in a row, she'd woken to find that she'd shared the bed with little Charlie and Georgia. In fact, last night it had been her that had put them both into the big bed so that Paul and Mike could use the kids bunks to sleep on.

She put on her bathrobe and quietly crept barefoot downstairs to put the kettle on, surprised to find it had already boiled and Paul was sat there with a big mug of steaming tea and not the slightest sign of a hangover.

'What you doin up so early?' Sally asked the big lad.

'Hey, I'm always up early sis, you know that. Usually awake by half six at the latest. There's tea in the pot, ah, but your one of them posh mornin' coffee drinkers in't yeh? Anyway, water in the kettle should still be hot.'

Sally made herself a Nescafe in her 'MAM' mug and sat opposite her big brother.

'Who do you think it was came in the house last night then if it wasn't a mate of Oggy's?' she asked.

'I'm not a hundred percent Sal, but I got a really bad feelin' it could be someone that works for a man called Demaci and if that's the case, then Charlie's in the best bloody place. Oggy musta fucked up big time if Demaci the Albanian's become involved.'

Paul took the time to carefully explain to his little sister the pyramid of power that evolved around the underworld trade in the Seaborough area, with Demaci up at the pointy bit and Oggy way down at the bottom somewhere. He further explained how much more serious it had all become and why he believed Charlie might now have had the better option.

'It's all to do wi' them drugs and money int it?' Sally asked.

'It's the only thing I can think of, unless that useless fat twat of a husband of yours has been up to more naughty stuff that he shouldn't a been doin'. I'll be honest wi' yeh Sal, I never thought the fat fuck had that much energy in 'im, he's well fuckin' impressed me.'

Mike surfaced half an hour later, looking like death.

'I don't know why I try to keep up with 'im pint for pint, he's got hollow fuckin' legs, an' look at 'im, ready to start the fuckin' day an' here I am totally fuckin' knackered.'

Sally and Paul laughed, then Sally put a brew in front of Mike and not long after he started to come around.

'Right then folks, wha' we doin t'day then?' said Paul.

'Well I'm goin to go 'ome for a shower, shave an' a whatsit, then to our Mams for a nice Sunday roast. What yeh think? Are yeh comin?'

Sally and Mike thought it was just what the doctor ordered. Sally being the elected spokesperson phoned their Mam and told her to expect company. Mam was over the moon to have her family coming over for lunch and couldn't wait to see them all. Mike and Paul left to get ready and they all agreed to be there at Mam and Dads house for one in the afternoon.

CHAPTER NINETEEN

Mad Arrie woke with the sunrise. He'd spent last night in the old barn of a derelict farmhouse on the outskirts of town and a most peaceful and comfortable night it was.

Before settling down, he'd managed to rustle up some cooked chicken pieces and fried vegetables with noodles found in a used food bin outside the back of a Chinese restaurant. He'd crammed it all into his new bag, which, since obtaining it the morning before had not been taken off his shoulder or even used.

'I knew this would be useful,' he said out loud to nobody in particular.

As it was breakfast time and he should be on his way soon, he opened the bag and removed the food morsels. Licking his fingers clean of any remaining grease or food particles. Then he happened upon the original contents of the bag.

Oh, my goodness. Having been an accountant, he couldn't help himself and he counted the money with no interest at all in the little white plastic parcels which were left remaining in the bottom of the bag. No, it was only the money that interested Mad Arrie this sunny Sunday morning, all twenty four thousand seven hundred and sixty five pounds of it.

Then Mad Arrie had a ponder.

'I've got no possible use for the drugs and as for the money, I left all that behind me five years ago and I've been so much happier since. I have no real use for the money either to be fair.'

And so Mad Arrie decided that he should get rid of it all. He could either give it away, bury it, or even put it all back where he got it from, minus the bag of course, but he definitely didn't want it.

After much thought and consideration, Mad Arrie was of the opinion he was not a thief as such. Yes, to take the bag might be considered stealing, but if he was to give the contents back, then surely that would be an honourable thing to do. Based on that early morning ponder and supplied with an alternative to being classified a thief, Mad Arrie collected his items and packed up, preparing to return the borrowed goods back to the rightful owner.

CHAPTER TWENTY

After lunch, Sally helped Mam clear the table and wash the dishes, while all the men folk sat in the front room finishing their cans of lager, watching rugby league highlights on the television. The kids had gone outside to play in the back garden, Sally felt as though it was safe enough to let them out at her mam's house.

Mam asked if everything was going alright and had Charlie been in touch, but Sally wasn't sure what to say. She wanted more than anything to tell her mam the whole truth but knew at this stage it wasn't possible. Mam and Dad would want to wrap them all up to protect her and the kids, but big brothers Paul and Mike were already doing that, so she just said.

'I don't think Charlie's gonna be coming back Mam. I think he's maybe got hiself into big trouble with some really bad lads and gone on the run somewhere. I've had that Oggy round lookin' for him a few times and he's not answering his phone or owt, but I think he may 'ave done a runner wi' whatever he took from him.'

'Well that's the best news I've heard all day our Sally

and good riddance I say. I expect your dad will agree wi' me as well.'

'I know Mam, but what about the kids, it is their dad at the end of the day.'

'The kids'll be fine, you'll see pet. Believe me they're resilient and a lot better off wi' out a father the likes of 'im and you're much better off by a thousand percent wi' out 'im as an 'usband. He were a fat useless bag of tripe that lad and I'll be glad to see the back of 'im, good riddance I say.'

Sally felt much better having sort of told Mam what had gone on. The whole story would have been far too disturbing for both her parents to comprehend and she didn't feel at this time there was any need for the whole truth, hopefully there never would be.

Sally and her mam had a pot of tea in the kitchen while the lads were watching the end of the game, then she gathered the kids up and said it was time to be going home.

There were big hugs and kisses all round and Sally said she would call in the next day once she got the bairns to school. She told Paul and Mike to call in when they were passing and headed out the door to go home two roads away.

The kids were in a great mood and when Sally thought about it, they had been since their dad had left. Maybe Mam was right, they were better off without him.

As she came into Frazer Avenue Sally noticed the white van that had been parked there for some time now. She knew it didn't belong to any of the neighbours, everyone knew everybody else's business in Westernside. As she turned to walk up the path, she noticed the big man in the passenger seat was the same one that had been found in her house and she shuddered, hurrying the kids straight in the front door, slamming it hard behind her.

She then immediately called Paul on her mobile,

'Hya pet, yeh can't be missing us already, you've only been gone ten minutes, what's up?'

'Paul, we just come up our path and that big man we found in the house last night, is parked in a white van with another man over the road watchin' us.'

'Right Sal, Mike and me'll be straight round, pet.'

Within two minutes the brothers arrived running and out of breath with the exertion of a big roast dinner, two cans of lager each and a jog. They didn't knock but came straight in the door and looked secretly like nosey neighbours through the front blinds.

As they were looking a black Range Rover pulled up behind the white van and a very nondescript man wearing pale blue jeans and white trainers got out and spoke to the driver. After several minutes of conversation, the man in the jeans pointed to Sally's house and then approached the front door.

Sally and her brothers heard the knock and after Paul nodded for her to answer, Sally cautiously pulled the door open.

'Yes, can I help you?' Sally said formally,

'Good afternoon, Mrs Oldham, yes?'

'That's right, what can I do for yeh.'

'Good, good, yes you can please tell me your husband Charlie Oldham's whereabouts?'

'I'm sorry but who are yeh?'

'It's not really important who I am, suffice to say I wish to speak to your husband.'

'Well he's not here and I don't know when he'll be back, are you a friend of that Oggy? Cos, I already told him all of this.'

'No, I am no friend of Oggy's, in fact you could say the opposite and I can assure you, he will not be bothering you at all in the future. The problem I have is that Oggy entrusted your husband Charlie Oldham with something that belongs to my employer and my employer is keen to have his property returned immediately. So as you might understand, I'm rather keen to speak with your husband.'

'Well then, I really can't help yeh 'cause like I keep telling everyone that asks, I don't fuckin' know where he is. So now do you understand me?'

The back hander came out of nowhere and landed right in the middle of Sally's face knocking her back into the kitchen. Paul was the first to react with Mike right behind him.

Hamiti wasn't expecting Paul to be as big and sturdy as he was, but it really didn't pose such a great threat. Paul came rushing out of the front door totally unprepared. Hamiti on the other hand was well prepared and relaxed, breaking Paul's nose first, then landing several rabbit punches to the kidneys dropping him on his knees like a sack of potatoes. Mike flew out the door and after several taps, punches and kicks was laid alongside his big brother.

Hamiti then walked to the front door and called back in to Sally,

'Please Mrs Oldham, consider this the one and only warning I will ever give to you and your family. Get a message to your husband, we want our property back immediately. He has twenty four hours and please, have a very pleasant day.'

Hamiti then turned and walked away, without a hair out of place.

Sally ran outside to try and help her brothers to their feet whilst holding her own nose from bleeding. They all managed to get inside and shut the door going straight into the kitchen where Sally handed out tea towels to staunch the bleeding from Paul's nose. Mike didn't appear to be bleeding, but seemed to be in a lot of pain.

'What the fuck happened there? I dunno who the fuck that was but he broke at least two of my fuckin' ribs, I can 'ardly breath.'

'Fuckin' Albanians, well I'm gonna be breathing out me fuckin' mouth for a while, God that fuckin' hurts,' said Paul straightening his nose.

Sally who was sat with her head tipped back to stop the bleeding from her own nose just muttered, 'I'm used to it, just like bein' back wi' Charlie.' They all looked at each other and laughed.

CHAPTER TWENTY-ONE

'So, Bashkim, have you found our lost friend Charlie Oldham or is he still missing?'

'No Mr Demaci, he was not at the address of his wife and family. To be honest sir, I don't believe he's been there for some time and according to his wife, he went off somewhere, to stay with a friend. Personally, I would bet good money that he may have left the area.'

'Well this is most unfortunate and upsetting, I'd hoped this episode would have been completed by now. What are we to do?'

'I explained to his wife that I would allow her twenty four hours. Then I expected his whereabouts to be confirmed.'

'Yes, yes, Bashkim, but what are we to do if he has done a runner and his good wife has no idea where he is?'

'Then sir, I suggest we leave him a message. One that might guarantee his attention.'

'Okay, what is it you suggest then?'

'It would have to be something that affects his wife, because if anyone would know how to get in touch with him, it will probably be her. I would rather not touch the children yet as that would only ensure police involvement, but it must be someone close to her to make her understand we are not playing some trifling game.'

'Okay, Bashkim, I'll leave this to you, please get it resolved as soon as possible, we've already spent far too much time and effort on it.'

'Yes sir, I understand.'

Mr Demaci hung up the telephone and turned to his new toy boy Simon, lying naked across the king size bed in Donika Demaci's apartment, his hand gently stroking his full erection.

'So, Simon, I understand you managed to get your name on our list of escorts. Congratulations, now let's see if we can work on your promotion and maybe get you a bigger rise, here let me do that, you must be exhausted by now.'

CHAPTER TWENTY-TWO

The bleeding from Sally's nose had stopped. It wasn't broken, just very sore. Her eyes had also stopped watering, so she went over to make sure Paul was okay. He'd reset his nose as best he could, it wasn't the first time he'd had to do it and it probably wasn't going to be the last. Mike was in pain but could breathe much easier now he'd relaxed.

'So, who was that then? Funny way of introducing yourself if yeh ask me,' Sally said whilst filling the kettle.

'I think I know who it was, but I wish I didn't cos he's a tough little fucker. Apparently, the big boss Donika Demaci uses him. He's ex military and you really don't wanna fuck with 'im cos he looks like fuck all, but he's hard as nails and doesn't take prisoners. If he's involved then this has just jumped up an almighty bunch of notches and we really need to consider what we're gonna fuckin' do.'

Paul was trying to talk whilst holding his nose together and the speech coming out of his mouth was like that of a geriatric BBC radio announcer.

'Well one things for fuckin' certain, we can't get Charlie

to bail us out, can we? That fat fucks never there when yeh fuckin' need 'im is he?'

Mike laughed at his own stupid joke, then coughed and had to hold his arms around his chest to try and stifle the pain.

'Right so we know, or at least we think we know who that was, but what do we do now? I think I could've handled Oggy, but it would seem it's in the hands of a totally different foreign gentleman who isn't as easily handled.'

Sally had finished making the tea and was getting the mugs out of the cupboard as she spoke.

'Nay lass, this has just gone from an amateur bottom of the league five a side, into the Premier division. We gotta get that fuckin' stuff back and pay those bastards off or there's gonna be a fuckin' blood bath and rock all left of us after, I can promise yeh that.'

'Ya, but are you and Mike in any fit state to go and get it?'

'Mikey can stay 'ere with you Sal. I can go by me self, won't take but 'alf an 'our. The way he looks right now, I'll be faster on me own anyway.'

They all finished their tea's and while Mike went into the living room and laid on the settee to watch cartoons with the kids, Paul went out to get the bag back from the boatyard.

His nose had stopped bleeding but the start of two beautiful black eyes were well on their way and his head was resonating like a blacksmiths anvil, what a mess.

He had to walk back around to Mam and Dads house to collect the Mondeo from where he'd parked it before lunch, keeping an eye out to see if he was being followed, but there was no sign of anyone.

Paul parked the Mondeo outside the boatyard and unlocked the gate. The Bonny Doris was laid by over on the far side of the yard, but he was up the ladder with the engine cover open within a few short minutes. Then he just stared into the open hatch not comprehending the message his eyes were trying to convey back to his brain.

'Oh fuckin' no!'

He looked inside the engine box, poking his hand around the sides and any other orifice that he could get his great paws into. He searched the whole boat but could find nothing.

'We are in so much shit,' he said out loud, 'what the fuck do I tell our Sal and Mike, they're relyin' on me, we're all gonna fuckin die, and that's only if we're fuckin' lucky.'

'Everything all right up there, mate?'

Paul looked down and there stood the same policeman that was talking to Mike the night they'd butchered Charlie beside the boat.

'No, it bloody isn't. Some bastards nicked me tool bag off the boat,' replied Paul in his most perturbed manner.

'Was it all locked up? Anything been broken into?'

'No, you know what mate, some bastards probably borrowed it and just not returned it yet, 'ang on a mo' I'm coming down.'

'Ooh! That looks sore, how'd you manage to do that then.'

'Me nose yeh mean? Bloody Sunday league, got bloody nutted didn't I. That was another bastard, yeh know what? The worlds fuckin' full of 'em officer, I blame the parents.'

Dave Riley laughed.

'So, you must be Mike Vickers brother then, Paul, is it?'

'Aye mate, how'd you know that then?

'I was passin' the other night and Mike was all locked up in the yard gettin' ready to take the boat out.'

'Right yeh, he had a head start on me. I caught up a bit

later though. Not safe keepin' those gates open of a night 'round 'ere, you don't know who's passin' by.'

'That's what Mike was sayin'. Listen Paul, that sister of yours, Sally? Is she seein anyone? Or what's the score? Real bonny lass if I recall.'

Paul looked at young officer Riley in disbelief. 'You must be fuckin' joking,' he thought, 'I've got the headache from hell, my nose is throbbin' like fuck. I've lost nearly twenty five thousand fuckin' pounds give or take, plus a major stash of dope and your trying to get fixed up with me fuckin' little sister, who's only just finished butchering her fat fuck of a husband that me and our Mike were trying desperately to fuckin' chop up, while you was busy reminiscing at the fuckin' gate and now I've got the whole fuckin Albanian mafia chasin' after us,' but instead he said.

'Yeh, a bonny lass our Sal, married though. But the fat twats fucked off and left her wi' the two bairns and no money. Personally, I think he's done a bunk cos some bad lads might be chasin' 'im.'

'Oh, so who was she married to then?'

'You'll probably know 'im, Charlie Oldham, he'll 'ave bin around yours and Mikes year in school.'

'You're jokin'! Shit, what did she see in him? Your Sally could have had anyone, and I mean anyone. Every lad at school used to watch the girl's netball just to ogle her in tight shorts. We all worshiped her, Sally was what fantasies were made of.'

'Well mate I'm her big brother and I have no idea of what you're fuckin' talkin' about. Never saw it personally, know what I mean? All I saw was me pretty, skinny little sister married to a fat ugly bald twat. I really wanted to wring his fuckin neck, but the law say's no, no, no, don't be a naughty boy, you're not allowed to do that.'

'So, Paul, if there's nobody else around, is there any

objection if I give her a call sometime, do you mind or owt?'

'I'll tell you what, Dave is it? I have no objection at all personally mate, that's our Sal's business, but she's had a real shitty time of it wi' the fat twat and I really don't want her bein' messed about, okay?'

'Oh, hey Paul, no way. Wow! Sally Vickers, right, I best be goin', but put in a good word for us will yeh? And take care mate, thanks.'

With that, police constable David Riley ran across the boatyard compound, jumped into his police car and drove away at high speed, sirens blaring. Maybe on his way to a serious crime scene, or maybe just very happy, who knows?

Back in the yard Paul felt sick to his stomach. He now had to go and explain the loss of all the stash. But hey, at least Sally had gained an admirer.

Paul pulled up outside 35 Frazer Avenue, walked up the broken path, knocked and walked straight in. Mike was fast asleep on the settee having taken four paracetamol for his pain.

Sally was busy in the kitchen, making a peanut butter and honey sandwich together with fairy cakes for each of the kids to eat at the coffee table in the living room while they watched the telly.

Paul walked over and not too gently shook his little brother awake.

'Away mate, in the kitchen, I think the proverbial's just hit the fan.'

'Oh, what the fucks 'appened now?' Said Mike, pain written all over his handsome face.

'Away in the kitchen man, too many little ears in 'ere.'

Paul sat them all down around the kitchen table. Sally had just made a fresh pot of tea and poured it first.

'Right gang, there's no easy fuckin' way to say this, but

it's all fuckin' gone.'

Paul spent the next fifteen minutes explaining about what he hadn't found on board the boat and about the police officer Dave Riley's conversation. Answering all the questions fired at him as best he could from both Sally and Mike.

Mike's questions mainly applied to who could have taken it and how would they have even known it existed in the first place.

Sally questions on the other hand appertained to, how tall officer Riley was? Was he good looking? Was he fit? What did he say about me? Did you tell him me husband's run off and I'm more or less single now?

Both brothers just looked at their youngest sibling in astonishment. They were about to die at the hands of Albanian gangsters, probably by means of a most horrendous nature and she was looking in a mirror straightening her fuckin' hair.

CHAPTER TWENTY-THREE

Mad Arrie had watched from behind the broken chain link fence. First the quite irate bearded young man on the boat looking for his stashed bag and not finding it, getting more irritated by the second as he searched.

Then the bearded young man was talking to the fresh faced police officer. 'Don't the police look younger and younger?' He thought. 'Is it possible that the man with the beard may have reported the loss of his bag to the police, probably not, considering what it had contained.'

Oh dear, something else to ponder. Everyone had left and the main gate at the entrance to the compound had been relocked by the big man, so Arrie squeezed through the hole in the fence and cautiously crept across the compound, crouching low under the hull of the Bonny Doris. There was still nobody about, so Arrie quickly climbed the ladder he'd found laid alongside the coble and taking the stash out of his newly acquired shoulder bag, placed it back where he'd found it within the engine box. This time however, it was all contained in an old plastic supermarket carrier bag, of which Arrie had many, collected over a very long period of time. That's better, he sighed with relief, he would have hated to have been considered a common thief.

The next question was whether he would stay the night here or move on. There was still plenty of daylight and it would probably be better if he was not found nearby in case the big man with the beard came back. Arrie pondered for a few minutes then decided to pick up his belongings and move on. He knew a nice place not too far away, with some derelict buildings that he could shelter for the night.

Sally asked the lads if they would be staying over, but they graciously declined saying they would be going home and calling for a pint later. They would both be back in the morning so Sally didn't have to face Demaci's man Bashkim Hamiti by herself.

Sally kissed the two of them on their cheeks and set them to the door. She scanned the road, but there was no sign of the white van or the two large men. She waved bye to her older siblings, then went inside and locked the door before running a bath for the kids. Tomorrow was a school day, so up and out early.

Sally wondered about barricading the front door again but decided against it. A barricade wasn't going to stop anyone if they really wanted to be in.

She was upstairs tucking the kids into bed, when there was a knock at the door. Sally's stomach did a flip and with total trepidation she walked back downstairs and opened it.

Stood in the doorway was a tall man in his mid twenties, he had short blond hair, sparkling blue eyes, looking muscular and fit. He was wearing blue washed out jeans and a navy t-shirt and an open Superdry hoody with a pair of well worn Adidas trainers on his feet.

Sally stared for a few seconds before asking,

'Hello, can I help yeh?'

'Hya Sally. You probably don't remember me, but I was talking to your brother Paul today. He said it's probably alright for me to call around. Dave Riley, I was in the same year as your Mike back at Thornton secondary.'

'Right, ya, he did mention it and of course I remember yeh, I just wasn't expectin' to see you so soon that's all. Em, away in Dave, I'm just putting me bairns to bed, if yeh can give us a few minutes, just go in the living room and I'll be down soon as I can.'

Sally showed Dave into the clean but sparsely furnished room and after he'd made himself comfy on the settee, she legged it up the stairs, pulling off her old sweatshirt as she went.

She ran into the kid's bedroom, kissed them both a quick goodnight, then ran into her own room, slipping into a clean ironed shirt and hurriedly brushing through her short brown hair whilst applying a few splashes of makeup and a smear of lipstick. All done in less than five minutes, she was back downstairs and ready.

'Can I get yeh a coffee or tea or summit Dave? Sorry I don't have anything stronger.'

'Coffee would be great please. That's if it's no trouble.'

Sally returned to the kitchen and put the kettle on. She quickly scanned the room and it looked reasonably clean and tidy, lived in, but clean. When she turned around Dave was stood in the doorway.

'Thought you might need a hand,' he said.

'No, I'm good thanks,' she smiled, 'I've made coffee before once or twice, it's only Nescafe though, nowt posh. Milk? Sugar?'

'Yes, to both please, just half a spoon of sugar though.'

Dave sat on one of the kitchen benches while Sally

fussed with the coffee. After placing it in front of him, Sally took hers and sat on the bench opposite, a look of total curiosity on her pretty face.

'Well, this is one for the books David Riley. What made yeh wanna see me?'

Dave smiled, then went a deep shade of red.

'The fact is Sally, I've always wanted to see yeh. Right back when we were at school together. But yeh just suddenly seemed to disappear and I lost touch with just about everybody that knew yeh. After a while I ended up getting married meself. It only lasted a year, no kids or owt, then she was off. I joined the force and that seemed to fill a lot of me time, but then the other night I saw your Mike and it all came flooding back. To be honest, I haven't been able to get yeh out of me head since. Look I'm not normally as forward as all this okay? But what I've found, especially through my job, life's too short and yeh gotta grab your chance when it comes along, otherwise, it'll just pass yeh right by again. Anyway, I really liked yeh back at school and I know there's gallons gone under the bridge by now, but considering your husbands buggered off, is there any chance we could maybe start seeing each other?'

Sally's heart was fluttering. Nobody had ever spoken to her like this before. He was gently spoken, looked gorgeous, she fancied him like mad and he seemed to fancy her and that's while she looked a mess. Today was not one of her, I really look good today, days. It didn't stop Sally from smiling whilst holding the cup in front of her mouth though.

'Look Dave, I think you're really lovely and I'm totally flattered, but what are yeh gonna do if Charlie walks through that door?'

'What do you wanna do Sally? Would yeh want him back?'

'Not a chance, thank you very much,'

'Right then, we'll deal with that if and when the time comes. All yeh gotta say for now is you'll give us a chance and we'll take it slow and see how things turn out. We can take our time, there's no hurry.'

'You know what David Riley, why not?'

With that Sally put her slim, long fingered hand out for Dave to shake. He took gentle hold of it with his own and they both stood up. Then Dave stepped around the table, bent over and gently kissed Sally on her lips. This was the first kiss by a man since meeting Charlie and she thought her legs would buckle beneath her. She stepped back with a slight gasp and sighed, 'Well, I wasn't expecting that.'

'Right,' said Dave, 'I'm gonna go for now. Give yeh some time to mull over what I said. I gotta say, I'm well chuffed yeh willing to give us a try though. I know It's what I want, but more than anything I really want you to be happy about it too.'

With that Dave stepped towards the front door with Sally close behind. He opened the door then turned, bent and kissed her again on the lips before smiling and saying, 'tarah, see yeh soon eh.'

Sally stood watching as Dave got into his yellow Volkswagen Golf. They waved to each other as he drove off.

Sally came in and shut the front door leaning against it from the inside thinking, what the fuck just happened there?

CHAPTER TWENTY-FOUR

Paul and Mike had left Sally's house and gone back to their own place for a shower and a change of clothes. For the time being, the two brothers were sharing a terraced street house in the centre of town.

Paul had put down a deposit after leaving Mam and Dads house to join the Royal Marines Commando unit. Initially as a rifleman and after completing a five year stint leaving as a Corporal. He'd joined at nineteen to see the world and returned home at twenty four to help his little brother with the fishing boat after Dad had taken ill. If truth be known, Paul really hadn't enjoyed the regimentation and had been somewhat disillusioned with the whole job. He'd been totally okay with the friendship of his fellow squaddies though and made loads of good mates.

Mike moved in with Paul just after his final return from Afghanistan. It just wasn't possible to bring lasses home to Mam and Dads house. Neither of the lads had ever had any long term relationships with any of the local girls, much preferring the one night stands. No complications and free spirits as they say.

The girls on the other hand would have loved to have got their claws into either one of the Vickers boys. Both were good looking, both strong and both more than capable of looking after themselves. At least under normal circumstances and what's more, they always had readies in their pockets. Neither of the Vickers lads were ever known for being skint or short of a bob or two. To complete the picture, each one of them were totally sexually ruthless givers and takers with the lasses in the bedroom department and neither had ever had any complaints. The Vickers boys were well known and loved by just about everybody.

While Mike was in the bathroom getting ready, Paul had a quick wipe around the kitchen and living room area.

The wall between the kitchen and front room had been knocked down after Paul bought the house and a large downstairs open plan living space made. All modern and functional with low maintenance being the operative words.

Upstairs, they both had their own decent size bedrooms and were each responsible for their own space. Neither of them encroaching on the others privacy. The bathroom had been modernised when the downstairs had been done and the old cast bath removed to make way for a big walk in shower unit instead.

Essentially, the house was a very masculine lads pad, with no frills and no female influence. However, it had never put any of the young ladies off and when invited they were all too keen to come back for more.

Paul was watching the telly, halfway through a can of lager when his younger sibling finally came down in clean jeans and a long sleeve designer shirt with the tails hanging out over the waistband of his denims. He also had on a pair of

Adidas Gazelles and was smelling of some very expensive aftershave.

'Right finish this off while I get ready, be down in half an hour,' Paul said handing Mike the remainder of the can.

They were only going down to the local Ship and Anchor. Knock back a few beers, have a bit of banter with the lads, then back home for an early night, unless of course they fell lucky with the local lasses, then hopefully, not such an early night.

They decided to walk rather than take a taxi, it was only twenty minutes and the exercise and fresh air would do them both good. As they were walking and chewing the fat, Paul was aware that someone seemed to be following them.

He'd first noticed him sat in a black Audi across the road from the house as they came out the front door earlier and after he'd exited the car, shutting it behind him. He'd then walked in the same direction as the brothers, but a few paces behind on the opposite side of the road.

As they stepped into the front door of the pub, Paul turned quickly to look over his shoulder, but there was no sign of the stranger. Just nerves he figured, too much going on in his head, too tired maybe.

As the brothers walked in, there was a big cheer went up with numerous well directed, derogatory remarks aimed at Paul.

'What's the other guy look like Paul,' and 'Give us his fuckin' name and we'll go round and sort 'im out for yeh mate.'

All the usual banter that goes with the territory of a broken nose and now two beautiful black eyes in an area such as this one. Everyone was leaving Mike alone, hard to see cracked ribs under a shirt. He was very aware of them though. It seemed that everyone in the busy pub wanted to brush past, making him wince with each slight contact.

The pub was full by the time they got there, all seats were taken and it was three deep standing at the bar.

The back room with the wide screen was also full and noisy. It sounded as though there might have been a boxing match being watched on the wide screen the way everyone was shouting. That together with the many obscenities being bantered about.

A couple of the local lasses made a beeline for the boys. They'd all spent time together in the past, both day and night times and feelings between them all were very relaxed and cordial. The girls brought drinks over for both themselves and the two Vickers brothers. The girls had seen them walk in and as they were already being served, thought they'd save the lads the trouble of having to fight at the bar.

There was plenty of flirting being done tonight by the ladies. Both of whom were tall and leggy, wearing the shortest of skirts and the highest heels imaginable. Makeup and hair seemed to have come straight out of a top shelf glamour magazine and their bodies were simply to die for, all the curves being in exactly the right places. Even Mike was feeling no pain when blonde Chrissy was rubbing herself all over him in time to the background music. It seemed to be out of simple unpretentious horny lust, while Paul was fairing equally well with Julie, the simmering hot brunette.

They all stood around and the laughter and banter was good, however Paul couldn't get the mysterious follower out of his mind and seemed to be slightly preoccupied throughout the evening.

They left the pub before closing time, missing the mass of drunks and revellers and arriving back at the house in record time. Paul was the first through the door and turned the lights on with the girls and Mike following very close behind, laughing and joking in a real Mardi Gras atmosphere.

The girls had removed their shoes along the way and were now at least four inches shorter than when they'd left the pub. Of course, the first thing on the agenda when they walked through the door was a need to pee, so the two of them ran straight up the stairs leaving the lads behind.

Paul turned to Mike and said.

'It's all wrong Mikey.'

'Okay, then I'll take Julie and you can have Chrissy, I don't mind.'

'No kid, everything in here's wrong, we've been turned over.'

'How do you figure that out then? Everything looks the same.'

'It's not. I tidied up while you were in the bathroom earlier and it's not the way I left it. It's fuckin' subtle and professional but someone's been in.'

'But there's nowt of any real value to take.'

'They didn't necessarily come to take anything mate, they came to fuckin' look for something, or maybe even someone.'

Both girls came slowly and seductively down the stairs giggling. Neither of them were wearing a stitch of clothes. They both just stood at the bottom posing coyly in just their very high heeled shoes. These girls had been created simply for men's desires and were both fully aware of the power they possessed.

Paul looked at the girls, then his younger brother and shrugged.

'Fuck it, we'll sort it all out in the morning mate.'

CHAPTER TWENTY-FIVE

Sally woke before the alarm. Both kids had joined her again at some time through the night and managed to climb into the big bed without her knowledge.

She woke feeling on top of the world. Leaping over little Charlie who was laid sprawled out as normal. Considering how last week had started and developed, this week was looking quite positive.

Sally hadn't been able to get Dave out of her mind and it had taken quite a while before she'd been able to drift off to sleep. She was unsure how the kids were going to react to him, but that was a worry for another day.

She went into the shower and had a long hot all over wash. Then just stood under the spray, letting the hot water rinse over her long lean body taking all her troubles and reservations with it.

After, she went into her bedroom, dried her hair and put on her makeup. All the swelling and previous damage done to her face by Charlie had all but gone, there was still a slight bruising to her nose from yesterday. Good old Max Factor was the answer to that little problem.

Sally looked at her hands and even thought of doing her nails later. They weren't very long, but they were a nice shape and could be made pretty and feminine. Then she noticed the rings and dragged them off her fingers, went into the bathroom and tried to flush them down the toilet, but they wouldn't go. She dipped her hand back into the bowl to retrieve them, dried them on the bath towel, then put them to one side to be thrown in the garbage on her way out. Good riddance she thought.

Clothes were next on the agenda, but unfortunately Sally didn't have too many nice ones to choose from. She'd always looked good in her pale blue skinny jeans though. She had the long legs and pert bum for them and maybe a nice summery looking shirt to go with it. The white long sleeved one to hang out over the top. She dragged out her old pair of black stiletto heels from the bottom of the cupboard that had been hidden away for such a long time, but still looked in pretty good nick. Stiletto heeled shoes were always hot and never went out of fashion she thought and to finish off, she put in her big gold loopy earrings.

Sally stood up and inspected herself in the mirror and the person looking back at her was not the Sally who had spent the past seven bleak years being dominated, tormented and abused. No, the person looking back was stunning. Standing tall, slim, sexy and full of the youthful vibrancy that had once been there so many wasted years before.

When she turned around, both Little Charlie and Georgia were wide awake, sat up in the bed staring at her. Both kids had smiles as big as the Cheshire cats and when she did a twirl and asked what they thought, she was given a rapturous round of applause and a cheer with little Charlie saying.

'You're the most beautiful mam in the whole wide world and yeh look just like a real life movie star princess.'

Sally thought she was going to cry, it had been such a long, long time since anyone had thought about her in that way.

'Right you two, up and washed and don't forget to clean your teeth. I'm goin' down to make your breckies, then dressed and school, come on, chop, chop.'

Sally clapped her hands to hasten them quickly along.

The kids jumped out of bed laughing, hurrying into the bathroom to get ready, whilst trying to keep the joyful atmosphere going for as long as they possibly could.

CHAPTER TWENTY-SIX

Donika Demaci was up and dressed when Hamiti rang the downstairs door bell. Demaci released the door lock allowing him to enter the building and he rode up in the lift to the eleventh floor of the Tower Flats.

The door to Demaci's apartment was open when he got there, so he let himself in. Mr Demaci was sat behind his antique mahogany green leather topped desk talking on the phone, but was able to signal to Hamiti to pour two cups of coffee from the filter coffee maker in the kitchen.

Hamiti did as instructed and returned a few minutes later, placing Demaci's cup and saucer on a place mat on the desk and taking his own to sit at the big black leather corner sofa. Hamiti sat quietly relaxed, gazing out of the large picture window watching the boat traffic on the busy river Tonnet, awaiting Demaci to finish his phone call.

Eventually Demaci turned his attention to Hamiti.

'Okay, my friend, what news do you have that will make me very happy this morning?'

'Sorry Mr Demaci. Nothing that might make you very happy, but I've had one of our people search the brothers house last night and there was nothing to be found. This means that both the wife and the wife's brothers houses have been searched with no sign of the missing goods or this Charlie person.'

Donika Demaci walked over and sat on the sofa with Hamiti.

'Do you know what Bashkim? If this wife and her brothers were to have denied in the beginning that there had ever been such a person as this Charlie, I think I would have been very inclined to have believed them and would have just thought that maybe young Oggy had made up this name to cover his own loss. We must try one last time and failing that, I think we have spent enough time and effort on the subject and we might just have to assume that this Charlie has gone 'walk about' as our Australian friends say.'

'Yes Sir, I was going to visit the house again later today and see if there were any further developments. Do you still want me to go, or do you have something else planned for me?'

'No, go, and give it one last try. There is nothing for you here today, so concentrate on this small issue. Then we must move on. Anyway, I'll be working from home today, we have that rather large shipment arrived and once it's been customs cleared, it must be delivered later in the week, so we will be very busy soon.'

At that, Hamiti finished his coffee and took both his and Demaci's cups and saucers to the kitchen, washed them, dried them and put them neatly away, before bidding his employer a good morning and leaving.

CHAPTER TWENTY-SEVEN

'Away Julie pet, get up, Mike and me we gotta get goin'.'

'Just another ten minutes Paulie, yeh fuckin' wore us out man. I'm knackered and probably gonna be walkin' like fuckin' John Wayne for a week.'

'No love, come on, we have somewhere we need to be and we can't be fuckin' late, it's dead important.'

With that Paul jumped out of bed, slipped into his boxers and ran into the bathroom to empty his over stretched bladder. He could hear little brother singing downstairs and the smell of sausages frying was drifting up to the bedrooms at the top of the stairs.

He finished in the bathroom and went down and sure enough, there was Mike in his navy blue briefs and white sport socks, dancing a rumba and twerking to his own singing while frying sausages in the big pan.

'How many yeh makin' our kid?'

'Enough for all of us. Did we 'ave a fuckin' good night? Was we a good boy? Or maybe we was a very, very, dirty fuckin' bad boy then?'

Paul grinned, he could never keep a serious face when

his kid brother was in this mood and he was always in this mood when he'd just got laid, which was pretty regular.

'So, where's Chrissy then?'

'Probably the same place as Julie, tucked up in bed. I couldn't get her to wake up man, she said she was fucked and I know that's true cos I fuckin' did it and may I add, I did a very fine job of doin' it, even if I do say so meself.'

'Ya I know. Yeh kept putting me off me fuckin' stroke yeh noisy little bastard and might I just add as your older brother, our mam woulda' bin fuckin' disgusted if she coulda heard some of the stuff you was shoutin' out. You really need to wash your dirty fuckin' mouth out before yeh kiss our mam again.'

'Darlin' bro, I shall never wash this mouth, nor this tongue, they have travelled to places that beautiful memories are made of.'

'Oh, fuck off yeh dirty little twat, there are some things big brother's don't need to know.'

'What don't yeh need to know then Paul?'

Chrissy and Julie had finally surfaced and come downstairs with Chrissy wearing Mikes shirt from last night and Julie wearing Paul's. It should be noted at this point however, that both girls looked far better in them than the lads ever did and the lads had always looked pretty good.

Food was eaten around the breakfast bar sat on tall stools with lots of tea for the boys and coffee for the girls. Again, the banter was good natured with a lot of embarrassing comments directed to all sides. Nobody was free to take verbal prisoners this morning.

They all took it in turns to use the bathroom and shower, but when Paul entered for his turn, Julie joined him and after going down on her knees and making such a good job

139

of getting him big and hard again, Paul helped her to her feet, gently pushing her against the wall, Julie turned offering her pert round butt to him. Paul being the total gentleman, accepted the offer and slipped into her from behind, a gentle back scuttle in the shower was exactly what the doctor would have ordered, had there been a passing doctor to consult with that is.

The lads dropped the girls off at Chrissy's place with kisses all round, promising to meet up again soon, then they turned the Mondeo around and headed for Sally's house.

CHAPTER TWENTY-EIGHT

That morning, Sally walked the kids to school with both bairns laughing and telling her their stories. As they approached Jenny's house the two of them ran off ahead and caught up with Jenny's two. The four of them then went on talking away like a congregation of washerwoman. Jenny stood by the front gate waiting for Sally to catch up.

'What the bloody hell happened to you?' She said eyeing Sally from top to bottom then back to the top again, a look of utter shock and surprise on her face.

'I always knew, given half a chance yeh might brush up a bit tidy like, but lordy me, yeh look absolutely bloody gorgeous our Sally. Charlie had nowt to do with this, did he? Please say he didn't'

'He did in a roundabout sort of way Jen. He hasn't come home or owt, but I think I've met someone else and we've decided that if Charlie does come back, we're just gonna run 'im off.'

'Well, whoever he is you've met Sally me darlin', I take my hat off to him and me, well I personally already like him and yeh can tell 'im that an all. Do I know him? Right, listen, tell Aunty Jen all the gossip there is to know about this mysterious man and what you've bin up to and Sally it's okay, yeh can exaggerate as much as yeh like please.'

Jenny linked her arm through the crook of Sally's and they both walked to the school laughing and talking, revelling in their own conspiracy like a couple of teenage school girls. Totally ignoring the conversation of the four kids walking along in front of them.

When they arrived at the school yard there was total silence as they both walked past all the other mothers. The look of total amazement in the faces of some of the bedraggled women was more than obvious and so was the jealousy of many others. The false sympathies and knowing nods were there when the beatings and bruising had been apparent, but once the beauty of the inner person had manifest itself, then it was the turn of the green eyed monster to be released from its nasty little cage and the vicious tongues would start wagging overtime.

The school bell went and with all the kids locked away inside for the day Jenny and Sally walked out of the yard.

'Are yeh coming round for a brew then Sal? Do yeh have time pet?'

'Not right now Jen, I need to get home, I got our lads coming 'round to sort some stuff out for us.'

'Okay pet, the doors always open. Yeh know that don't yeh? Just call us if yeh need owt and if you and that new fella of yours need a babysitter, yeh know to just drop the bairns off anytime, they're never a bother.'

Sally thanked Jenny for the offer and with that, walked up to Mr Patel's convenience store for milk, bread and biscuits.

Mr Patel was behind the counter sat on his high stool serving with one of his granddaughters stacking shelves when

Sally walked in.

'What is this? Who is this? It must be a vision from the Gods. This can't be the Sally we all know and love, this must be someone else, but who?'

'Good morning Mr Patel, how are you and Mrs Patel today?'

'I know that voice, it is the voice of young Sally Vickers, metamorphosed from that of a duckling into that of a beautiful being. We are both well my dear child, but thank you for your kind consideration, may I just say however, so much, much, better for having seen you this morning.'

By this time, Sally was blushing bright red. She had never in all her life had so much positive attention thrown her way and she would be quite happy for it never to stop.

'Mr Patel, just milk, bread and chocolate chip cookies if you please.'

'Of course, of course, please excuse the ramblings of an old Indian who has just been given a glimpse of nibbana. Here you are Sally my dear and may I say whatever has happened, I hope and pray it lasts forever.'

Sally paid for the goods and gave a flirty little wave to Mr Patel as she walked out of the shop, whispering a quiet bye to Mr Patel's giggling granddaughter as she left.

Sally walked the remainder of the way home by herself, but whilst strolling along she was made aware of being followed by a car keeping pace with her at a slow walking speed. She was too frightened to turn in case it was Hamiti come early, or even one of his monstrous goons about to throw her into the back of the van and drive away to some horribly secluded spot in the middle of nowhere.

She most certainly couldn't out run anyone in the stiletto heeled shoes she was wearing, so she stopped and as

143

she stopped so did the car. Slowly she turned and the first thing she noticed was the luminous yellow and blue checks down the side and the blue light on top of the police car.

A young, very handsome uniformed officer opened the door, stepped out and walked towards her. The smile that crept across Sally's face was a picture in itself, but when the officer approached and said.

'That must be the most perfectly beautiful arse in the whole world Miss. I would follow that arse anywhere.'

'Aye, and a good morning to you too officer. Taking a wee bit of a liberty though, aren't we?'

'That's nothing compared to what I would like to Miss. You should be arrested for looking this good. Where yeh off to then? What yeh doin'?'

'Firstly officer, I'm minding my own bloody business and what makes yeh think it's any of yours? Or have I broken the law in some way?'

'I wish you had Miss because it would fulfil nearly every one of my personal fantasies to be able to handcuff you in the back of this car and interrogate you down some quiet country lane for an hour or three.'

'Well make an appointment and just maybe we can fulfil some of those dirty, disgusting, little fantasies of yours, but for now officer, I have urgent business to attend, so if there's nowt else, I bid you, have a good day.'

'Are yeh busy after lunch then, can I call on yeh later Sal,'

'You bloody better David Riley, I didn't go to all this bloody trouble for nothing yeh know.'

Dave ran over, looked quickly around and then gave Sally a quick kiss on the lips, she on the other hand didn't reciprocate, she was smiling too much and missed a great opportunity for a snog with a man in uniform.

They both waved to each other as Dave drove away, but Hamiti sat watching in the Range Rover down the road was very intrigued. What kind of arrangement could there possibly be between this Charlie Oldham's wife and a police officer? How could it be? If this Charlie is her husband, would she blatantly act in this way in a public place. Charlie couldn't be anywhere near, could he?

Paul and Mike pulled up outside Sally's house, just as she turned the corner at the top of the road. Both brothers were sat watching and were busy daydreaming about the very pretty young woman in high heels walking towards them, when the harsh realisation struck them that this was in fact their own little sister. They looked at each other in the knowledge that they'd both been thinking the same disgustingly perverted thoughts.

Both brothers got out to stand somewhat self-consciously by the side of the car as Sally approached, smiling, walking tall and confident, hips swaying sexily with each step she took.

'What the fuck do yeh think you're doin man?' asked Paul angrily.

'I just took the bairns to school and picked up some groceries at Mr Patel's why?'

'I don't fuckin' mean that, I mean the way yeh look an' that.'

'Why, what's wrong with the way I look? You're the only one complaining up to now our Paul.'

'Well I mean, it's not right is it? You look, you look too grown up that's all.'

'I'm probably older than some of the lasses you's two take to bed on a weekend. I have two children and I'm twenty four years old. How old do I have to be to wear nice things?'

'Well I know that Sal, it's just, we never ever saw you lookin' this way before, that's all.'

'Okay, well get used to it then lad's cos this is who I am, not who I'm allowed to be, okay?'

Sally walked up the path and unlocked the front door letting the brothers follow her in. She walked straight to the kitchen, filled the kettle and switched it on.

'Right who wants what? Have you two eaten this morning or do yeh need me to make yeh summit?'

'We already ate thanks Sal, tea for me, that's all please.'

It was the first time Mike had spoken, having taken a step back to watch his older brother dig a bigger and bigger verbal hole to bury himself in with his little sister.

Paul was sat quietly sulking, trying his hardest to get his head around the fact that baby sister was actually a beautiful grown woman.

'Tea for me too, please Sal.'

Sally turned and realised the inner turmoil her older brother was having with his emotions and her heart melted. She walked up behind him wrapping her arms around his massive neck and kissed him on his cheek.

'I love you our Paul and you Mikey. There's no way I could 'ave got through any of this without the pair of yeh by me side. Trouble is, now I gotta learn how to grow up and stand on me own two feet. I got two bairns to raise and I think I might go and try lookin' for a job soon. Oh! and bye the bye, I think I might 'ave got meself a new fella too.'

The brothers looked at each other and smiled, it was Paul that said.

'We aren't gonna end up with a fuckin' bobby in the family are we? Talk about bringin' the tone of the fuckin' neighbourhood down Sal.'

'You just behave yourself our Paul, he's lovely. We

haven't had much chance to talk properly yet, but he came round last night, and we spoke for a little while and funnily enough I saw him round the corner just now when I was comin' home.'

'Well you take it slow our kid. He seems like a decent lad and I've already had a quiet word wi' him about treatin' you right. I think he's probably good for you after that fat, useless, idle twat you was married to.'

'Well if you want my opinion,' said Mike, 'I think you both'll make a great looking couple. Yeh both look well suited, hey what the fuck do I know. I remember he was a good footballer at school though.'

'There's just one word of advice Sal and you probably know, but I'm gonna have to say it anyway. Be careful what you say to Dave about Charlie leaving. Just remember he is still a cop okay?'

'I know our Paul, I already thought of that and if he asks, I'm only gonna say I think he got into trouble with some bad lads and has dumped us and disappeared somewhere.'

'Ya sweetheart, that sounds about right, just be careful.'

As they all sat around the kitchen table, drinking tea, talking and making fun of Sally's new look and her new found relationship with Her Majesty's Constabulary there was a knock at the door. They all looked at each other but it was Sally who rose to answer.

CHAPTER TWENTY-NINE

Bashkim Hamiti had sat watching patiently as Sally first talked, then waved goodbye to the young police officer as he drove away. There was no point in phoning Mr Demaci, there was nothing to report. Nothing that he had seen or heard, that would suggest that Charlie Oldham was at this address or that his wife had any idea as to his whereabouts. Based on the performance that had just unfold this morning, it seemed to somewhat suggest the pretty young wife didn't really give a damn where he'd gone anyway.

Hamiti sat in the car listening to the radio, contemplating what to do next. The reports from his man who'd been watching the brothers also suggested there was no evidence of any involvement on their behalf. Two brothers shared a house, went out for a drink with friends and brought two beautiful young women home, who then spent the night. What could possibly be wrong with that?

After a while, Hamiti exited the Range Rover. Leaving it parked where it was and walked the short distance around the corner to the Oldham house, knocking hard several times.

It was the young wife who answered the door and the transformation from the dowdy woman of the day before was immense.

'Good morning Mrs Oldham. I mentioned to you yesterday that I would return to ask if there had been any developments and if your husband Charlie Oldham had been in touch.'

Sally was being cautious and keeping well back from the door. Both Paul and Mike had walked up behind her and were stood either side, still protective of their sister, irrespective of the damage incurred to the three of them from Hamiti the previous day.

'Mr Hamiti, as I said to you yesterday, I really have had no contact with me husband since Thursday last week and I'm so sorry if you and Mr Oggy have suffered as a result of his actions, but you gotta understand this has nowt whatsoever to do with either me or me bairns.'

The young woman was being respectful and appeared to be telling the truth. There was nothing more to be said or done, but leave and report the loss to Mr Demaci.

Hamiti nodded in acknowledgement of the statement Sally had just given and turned to walk back down the broken path to his car parked around the corner.

There are times when there is no possible explanation for the actions of a person and if asked 'why on earth did you do that,' they would quite often shrug their shoulders and say, 'I don't know.'

The following was one of those occasions and must be attributed to, youthful exuberance, stupidity, bravado, whatever the reason. Michael Vickers came flying out of the house grabbing Bashkim Hamiti by the shirt collar, spinning him around and landed a resoundingly headbutt to his nose, breaking cartilage and laying the nose at a very odd angle in the middle of Hamiti's face.

By the time Paul had reacted to go after his younger sibling, several more two handed punches had been landed to the face and Hamiti was on his knees. This didn't stop Mike and several kicks were also issued to leave imprints on Hamiti's appearance. It had all taken less than fifteen seconds for Paul to wrap his massive arms around his baby brother and pull him away.

'That's for yesterday yeh Albanian twat, now fuck off back to where yeh came from and tell yer faggot Albanian friends they're not fuckin' welcome around here either.'

Paul in the end pushed his impulsive younger brother back inside the house. He then helped Hamiti back to his feet apologising in no uncertain terms for the actions of his younger sibling.

It did no good. Bashkim Hamiti walked away holding his broken face, shaking his head to control his blurred vision, with blood pouring between his fingers from his somewhat lopsided nose.

'This will not be forgotten, there will be a heavy penalty to pay for this, you stupid, stupid, people,'

'What the fuck 'ave you just gone and done yeh stupid little twat? He was fuckin' walkin' away man. Sally had cracked it, he believed her and he was fuckin' leavin', this is really gonna end in fuckin' tears now.'

'I don't know do I, I just saw 'im walkin' away after what he did to us yesterday and I saw red. Who the fuck does that Albanian nowt think he is comin' 'round 'ere like he fuckin' owns the place and treatin' us the way he did?'

'Well my little bro', I 'ave an 'orrible feeling we're about to find out exactly who he thinks he is and what he's fuckin' capable of.'

Sally was shocked, she didn't know what to say, she knew Paul was right, Hamiti had been going to walk away and it felt as though he was finished with them. He seemed to have accepted what she'd said to him. Oh Mike, she thought, what the fuck have you just gone and done.

They all sat around the little kitchen table talking and trying to decide the best course of action.

'I don't think anyone's gonna do owt tonight do you?' Paul was talking while trying to get into the mind of an assassin.

'Hamiti's gonna go home and clean himself off. He's not gonna do owt while he's fuckin angry, I think he's too professional for that. In fact he's probably gonna go and ask Demaci's permission to do summit or at least check on whatever he's gonna be allowed to do, cos this is now very personal and nowt to do with his boss's business anymore. There's no way Demaci is gonna wanna draw any unwelcome attention to his business, is there?'

'Do yeh think he's gonna come after us then our lad?'

'I don't know. He's gonna wanna fuckin' hurt you really bad though and I mean really, really bad.'

CHAPTER THIRTY

'So Bashkim, you are saying that it looks as though this Charlie character has left the area with no sign of our goods, there is definitely no sign of him anywhere?'

'That's correct Mr Demaci, we've checked all his usual haunts and the people he knows and nobody has a clue where he might be. He has, to all intents and purposes dropped off the face of the earth.'

'Okay, we have already spent far too much time and effort on this, we must put it aside and prepare for the big shipment delivery at the end of the week.'

'There is just one small thing sir, I feel I should bring to your attention.'

'Of course, Bashkim, what is it?'

'Well when I was at the house, the younger brother brought, let's say embarrassment and disrespect to me and I feel punishment is due.'

'Okay, but the problem I have with that Bashkim, is that these people are civilians and have no loyalty to our organization. Civilians have a totally different set of rules, so punishing them if they have done something, is rather a very private and personal matter and may bring the wrath of the law down upon us. I will leave this up to you to do as you see fit. But Bashkim, keep me and my business out of it, is that understood?'

'Yes, I understand Mr Demaci, thank you and I will speak to you tomorrow.'

With that Bashkim Hamiti hung up and went into the bathroom of his small flat to straighten his nose and release the swelling around his eyes which had already discoloured into black.

Hamiti had already decided upon retribution. It would be swift and it would be extremely violent. The young upstart will forever regret the day he laid a finger on Bashkim Hamiti, the Albanian twat.

CHAPTER THIRTY-ONE

The lads finished their last cup of tea and decided there was nothing to be gained in hanging around at Sally's house. There was a bit more painting to be done on the Bonny Doris to bring her up to pristine condition, so they both kissed their sister goodbye and told her they would be in touch later in the day sometime.

Sally had just finished washing the remaining dishes from the kid's breakfast and the numerous cups from the tea and coffee they'd consumed when there was a light knock at the front door.

Sally wondered if there would ever be a time in the future that her stomach didn't do somersaults when someone came to her house. She worried needlessly on this occasion, stood at the doorstep in his off duty clothes was her favourite policeman, with a big bunch of flowers.

'Away in Dave, I didn't expect yeh so early.'

As the young officer stepped into the small passage Sally came closer, put her arms around his neck and snogged him. It wasn't a fast lip crushing passionate snog. It was more of a soft welcome to my life type of kiss that was really meant to show him that this is what she wanted as well. When they drew apart for air it was Dave's turn to be surprised.

'That was nice, what did I do to deserve that then?'

'You knocked on me front door, what am I supposed to do?'

'What? Do you kiss every man that comes to your front door like that?'

'Only the one's I really like. You just happen to be the first one up 'til now.'

'Aye and I better be the last as well, I'm not sharing you with anybody.'

'Treat me nicely mister and you'll never need to.'

'Well, I brought you these, so is that a good start?'

'It could very well be. But now I'm embarrassed cos I don't have a vase. No one's ever bought me flowers before.'

'Oh! I never thought of that, sorry.'

'No need, it's not your fault you're the first one to ever buy me flowers. Come on let's get this over with, we're goin for a walk.'

'Where to?'

'Me Mam'll have one. Let's go meet me Mam and Dad. Think of it as a baptism by fire.'

With that Sally gave Dave another kiss and they both stepped outside hand in hand. It was Dave's turn to have butterflies in his stomach as they walked together the short distance to Mam and Dads house.

Sally gave a quick knock on the door and walked in. Mam was in the kitchen making a brew and Dad in his armchair watching the horse racing.

'Away in pet, hey George it's our Sally. Oh! She seems to have a strange young man holding her hand.'

'Hya Mam,' Sally walked over and gave her mam a kiss

155

on the cheek, 'this is Dave and we're seein' each other, so be nice.'

Mam wiped her hands on a tea towel and shook Dave's, he in turn kissed her on the cheek bringing an immediate blush and smile to Mams face. They both then did a U-turn and walked into the living room to meet Dad. Dave walked over and shook Dads hand.

'Dad this is Dave, Dave this is me dad and I love him to big bits.'

'Hello sir, pleased to meet you.'

'Whoa there son! They aven't knighted me yet, so Im either Dad, or George, you decide. I don't mind one way or the other, but before we go any farther, can you both sit yourselves down and explain to your mam and me what the bloody hell's goin on and who this young Dave person here is?'

Mam walked in with a tray full of mugs and a big pot of fresh tea with biscuits. Placing it all on the small coffee table in the middle of the neat little room, while between Sally and Dave they brought her parents up to date with everything.

'Well you two, I'm bowled over. I have to say though, I can't remember ever seeing my little lass looking so beautiful and if I must thank you for that young Dave lad, then I do from the bottom of me heart.'

Dad had gone all misty eyed, but everyone could see how happy and proud he was of his beautiful daughter.

Mam was equally as pleased and even more surprised that Dave had met both Sally's brothers and not only managed to survive the ordeal, but had got on well with them. Nobody mentioned at this point that Dave was a policeman. One serious shock per day to the system was a reasonable tolerance.

CHAPTER THIRTY-TWO

'I'll go get the paint out the back of the car and you get the brushes out of the turps in the standing shelter our kid.'

Paul had calmed down during the drive to the boatyard, but Mike could see he was far from happy and his mind was ticking over like a time bomb ready to explode.

Very few people ever see Paul when he's angry, mainly because they don't know. It's not a loud aggressive thing, on the contrary it's a very quiet, calm determination to seek vengeance for whatever the hurt might be. Mike had figured it must stem from his military training.

Paul very rarely, if ever, spoke about his time in the Marines, always saying there was nothing to talk about, but you don't live your life as a kid brother and then as a best mate without knowing when things aren't right, and Mike had always known, the Paul that came home was not the same Paul that went out there.

'Do you want me to start up at the bow, starboard side and work me way back?'

'Aye go on then young'un, I'll start portside aft and meet

yeh somewhere in the middle for a cup of tea.'

Mike could hear Paul was trying his hardest to control the fear of the unknown. Mike had put himself into massive danger with the Albanians and Paul was worrying about the consequences and the possibility of his kid brother getting seriously hurt.

Paul had already been on his mobile half a dozen times since leaving Sally's house, but Mike had no idea who he'd been talking to, or what he'd been talking about. It had seemed to be light hearted enough though, with a lot of laughing and joking so Mike was not too perturbed. Paul would tell him when he was good and ready but not before. Big brother could be a stubborn ox about sharing information, best to just wait.

'Bro where have yeh put the scrapers?'

'No idea mate, have you checked in the cover?'

'Yep, not there.'

'Check under the washboard, or failing that the engine box.'

Mike searched everywhere for the scrapers, then opened the lid of the engine box cover finding a Marks and Spencer's carrier bag. He lifted it out with the expectancy of finding the long lost scrapers in the bottom and allowing him to get some work on the boat started.

'Big bro, I need you to look at summit rather important.'

'Away man I'm tryin' to get summit done 'ere.'

'That's nice, but yeh really need to see this our kid. I shit you not, when I say this might be summit really important.'

'Okay, what the fuck is it?'

Of all the things that were on the important shelf in Paul's overworked and tired brain, the contents of an M and S carrier bag were not included and the shock of those contents made big Paul speechless.

'Where the fuck was that?'

'Right there on the top.'

'So, who could 'ave put it there?'

'Maybe you just missed it bro.'

'Not a fuckin' chance. I turned that engine compartment inside out and found nothing, besides it was in that shoulder bag when I put it in there. Who do you know that can afford to shop at M and fuckin' S, cos it's nobody I fuckin' know, that's for sure?'

CHAPTER THIRTY-THREE

'Right my love, that's the easy part, now it starts to get a bit more difficult.'

Sally had left her mam and dads house with both Dave and a vase in tow. Both Mam and Dad giving her the secret thumbs up, with a wink and a smile as she exited the front door.

They were both now heading towards the school where the sure test of Dave's diplomacy skills would be established.

'That went well don't you think?' Sally was looking at Dave for his reaction to meeting her parents.

'They're really lovely people Sal, how longs your dad been ill?'

'It's been a few years now, that's why the lads run the boat. They coulda got rid of it but it woulda broke me dads heart. Paul came back from Afghanistan to help Mike when Dad took his bad turn. None of us thought he was gonna make it through he was that bad, but he did.'

'So, Paul was in the forces then? What section?'

'Ya, he was a Corporal in the Royal Marine Commando's, he's a big roughy toughy, pussy cat.'

'If he was in the Green Beret's he's definitely a bit on the roughy toughy side. Pussy cat, I'm not so sure about, maybe mountain lion.'

The two of them laughed as they came to Jenny's house. Sally went straight around to the back door and there was Jenny with her husband Geoff, both pottering in the garden.

'Hya folks, I brought someone to meet yeh.'

Jenny and Geoff both turned to see who the new stranger was holding on to Sally hand. It was Geoff that came straight over dusting the soil off on the side of his overalls and shaking Dave's proffered hand, followed closely behind by Jenny, who had scrutinized him within seconds of their arrival and had already made up her mind as to whether she liked him a millisecond later.

'I'll put the kettle on, away in Sally.'

Sally let go of her new beau, leaving him behind to discuss the garden and weather with Geoff while she went indoors to get a first hand assessment from Jenny.

'Ooh, he seems a bit of alright, I do like the looks of him our Sally. When you've finished with 'im, pass over what's left for me to play with will yeh?

'Sod off, he's mine, I think I might just be keepin' 'im forever.'

'Well my girl, I don't think I would be blamin' yeh for that. So, are you taking him to the school to pick up the bairns?'

'Ya, figured I'm gonna have to get it over and done with and the sooner the better. I don't know what's gonna be worse, the kids or those nasty cows waiting for their kids.'

'Oh, believe me our Sal, it's not gonna be your bairns, there adaptable. He's young, friendly, nice looking, your bairns are gonna take to him. Does he like kids? Has he got any?'

'I know he hasn't got any, but I didn't think to ask if he

likes 'em or not.'

'Well I wouldn't worry too much pet. Lookin' at him he likes you a ton load, so he's probably prepared to like what comes with yeh as well.'

The tea was made, and the lasses took it out to the lads in the garden where they all sat on the picnic bench in the warm spring sunshine. Everyone got to know one another before it was time to get ready and go for the bairns.

It was Jenny who spoke to Dave in her best imitation of a deep manly voice.

'Right Dave lad, you 'ave succeeded in completing yer first two challenges. The parents and the mates, now the final two are the most difficult. The kids and the other mothers, how do yeh feel? Ready to back out yet?'

'No, not yet, I think I should be able to handle the kids, but I gotta admit the other mothers are makin' me feel a bit queasy.'

They all laughed and agreed, then Sally said.

'Well come on then, let's go and get this over with.'

CHAPTER THIRTY-FOUR

Everything was set. Hamiti had spoken to his man and explained what he wanted and how he wanted it doing. It was all a matter of playing the waiting game now.

There was no need to speak to Mr Demaci. The boss had already expressed a wish to keep out of this affair. He had far more important dealings requiring his organizational skills and had left this personal hiccough to Hamiti to sort out. Demaci didn't want to get involved.

This jumped up English nobody, could not speak and act the way he did to Bashkim Hamiti, not without reprisals being forthcoming. He was going to wonder what had hit him and when he did, he would carry the scars very deeply and the pain would last for the rest of his days.

Hamiti had spent the earlier part of the afternoon resetting his nose and bathing his face to allow the swelling to recede. This being completed, it was now time to consider something to eat, which he hadn't really thought about all day. All this retributional organizing had made him lose his appetite for a while, but now it was back with a vengeance. Besides he had a few hours to kill before his plan would be put into action.

163

CHAPTER THIRTY-FIVE

'So, our Paulie, what we gonna do with this fuckin' lot? Are we just gonna hide it all again, or give it back to its rightful fuckin' owners? Or maybe give it to our Sal even, she could probably do with it about now.'

Mike couldn't believe what he was holding and after counting it again, found it all to be there, not a penny or a packet missing.

'I really don't think there's any point givin' it back to those fuckin' Albanian's now, do you? I mean, they already think Charlie has it and after what you did earlier to Hamiti, it's not likely they're gonna let bygones be fuckin' bygones are they? They're just gonna think we fuckin' lied in the first place and we just want them to leave us alone now, aren't they?'

'I guess, so do we give it to our Sal then?'

'No, I don't think so. Well at least not yet anyway. Sal's seein' Dave now and she doesn't really need something like this getting' in her fuckin' way, does she? Him bein' a bobby an' all. No, I think we should either take it home, which I don't wanna do cos we already been searched once, and they may just come back again, or we hide it in some better fuckin' place.'

'We don't need to keep the drugs though, do we? I mean, it's one thing bein' caught with big pennies, it's summit else bein' caught with coke and a smile.'

'You're right Mikey, we get rid of the fuckin' smack and hide the pennies, okay?'

With a plan of action, the lads took the little parcels out of the bag, wrapping the rolls of notes back up in the greasy M and S bag. Mike then pushed the bag into the toes of his big steel tipped waders, tucking a pair of heavy woollen socks in after them and throwing the whole lot into the back of the car with the fishing gear on top.

There were a few of the other lads working on their boats at the other end of the compound and it wasn't unusual to see some of them lighting small stoves to heat soup or water for a brew while they worked. So that's what the brothers did. They poured water into the small pan they carried on board and lit the Calor Gaz primer stove dissolving the small packets of cocaine into the boiling water. Mike then lobbed the whole liquid cocaine soup from the top of the boat over the chain link fence into the waste ground next to the compound. The little plastic envelopes were also put into the small pan and melted down into a single plastic mass. Once the little blob had cooled, that too was Frisbeed onto the waste ground over the chain link fence. The lads figured there were all sorts of drug related paraphernalia over in that area, a bit more wouldn't be noticed. No one was going to be able use it at least.

'Right mate, another good job done. Shall we give this paint work a bit more attention before we fuck off. Then at least it won't be a total waste of a fuckin' day.'

'Aye okay, do you know where the scrapers are then?'

'Fuck off.'

CHAPTER THIRTY-SIX

Sally and Dave walked hand in hand to the school with Jenny walking alongside.

The two of them made a very impressive young couple, tall, slim, fresh faced. This was going to give the women of the school yard something to talk about for a very long time.

As they stood outside the gates, they were amazed how many smiled and some actually came over to talk to Sally waiting to be introduced to the new man in her life. Was it just a short while ago these same vulturous women condescendingly smiled at her from a distance for wearing two black eyes, a bust lip and being married to a fat waste of space. Smile they might, friends, they never were.

They'd been stood outside the gates for less than ten minutes when the big doors opened and that mass of infantile humanity spewed out. All shouting and calling to each other, dragging jackets and coats on the ground with oversized school bags thrown over their tiny little shoulders.

They saw the two kids in the yard talking to their friends and not paying the slightest attention to Sally and Dave. Little Georgia was the first to walk over and hold her mams hand, still talking to her small friend, totally unaware that her mam's other hand was holding that of a complete strangers. It was in fact little Charlie who walked out of the big school gates observing his mam was with someone new.

Sheepishly he came closer and Sally smiled saying to the two of them.

'Charlie, Georgia, I want you to meet a really good friend of mine. His name's Dave and I think you're really gonna like him and get on well with him.'

'Hello,' said Charlie in a shy quiet whisper.

'Are you gonna be our new Dad now cos the old one's left us,' asked gobby little Georgia in a far from subtle, much louder and more forceful voice.

It was Dave who took the initiative saying.

'I'm not too sure about bein' your Dad or anything, but how about we start by getting' to know each other for a while and maybe we can become really good friends to start with?'

Both kids thought that being really good friends was a great idea and nodded in agreement.

Sally then asked the kids if they thought that maybe Dave might like to stay for his tea at their house, with a resounding 'yes' coming from them both.

Then Dave asked Sally if she would mind him treating them all to pizza from the local takeaway, which won him some serious brownie points all round.

While they stood waiting for the pizza order to be completed, Sally walked around to Mr Patel's and bought a large Pepsi. When she stepped back outside, there was Dave with one hand holding a pepperoni, a margarita and a mushroom pizza and it looked like Georgia had made claim to the other hand. They shared the pizzas out with Sally, Dave and little Charlie carrying one each and Georgia carrying the Pepsi, heading home for their afternoon feast.

The four of them walked back with both kids telling Dave all he would ever need to know and some things he really didn't need to hear, about their young lives.

Their likes, dislikes, favourite games and movies, in the space of the few minutes it took to arrive outside Sally's front door, Dave was fully conversant with the total history of both Sally's children.

Plates and glasses were set out in the kitchen at the little bench table by little Charlie trying his hardest to impress their new guest on how grown up he was. While Georgia tore lengths of kitchen towel for everyone to wipe their fingers and mouths on. Sally put her flowers into the vase she'd been carrying and had managed to get home in one piece.

Everyone was having a good time and they were sharing the last of the Pepsi out when there was a knock at the door and Paul and Mike walked in.

'Now then, what's goin on 'ere? Are yeh 'avin a party and yeh didn't bother to invite us?'

'This is Dave, uncle Paul and uncle Mikey. He had tea at our 'ouse and he's our Mam's very goodest best friend.' announced Georgia.

'Well, in that case, we're very happy to meet yeh Dave and we're really pleased that you're our Sally's goodest best friend.'

Both kids laughed at uncle Paul as he picked little Charlie up by the waist of his pants and sat down in his place at the table. There was plenty of left over pizza for the two brothers and it didn't take them too long to devour the remainder.

The brothers went through the game with the two little ones, showing that everyone was happy, then the kids left to watch their telly before bed time.

The grownups chatted in general and Dave announced

he was going to have to leave because he'd been called for a midnight shift and wanted to grab a couple of hour's kip first.

Sally walked him to the front door, closing the kitchen door over as she went through.

She put her arms around Dave's neck and kissed him. This was a long lingering kiss with a lot of feeling and Dave reciprocated in the same manner. They'd moved on in such a short time and were starting to enjoy each other both mentally and physically.

'That wasn't so bad then, was it,' said Sally pulling her mouth away.

'No, it wasn't, you can do that any time yeh like Sal.'

'I didn't mean that,' she said chuckling quietly, 'I meant, meeting me family and kids and stuff.'

'Oh, no it wasn't sweetheart, but I can't say I'm not glad that bits finished. I guess that's the hardest part over with then eh? But listen me bonny lass, I really gotta go and I'll see yeh tomorrow okay.'

'Aye, okay, see yeh tomorrow then, bye for now Dave, an' take care.'

They both kissed again and Sally stood on the step waving as Dave started the Golfs engine and drove off. Sally let go a big sigh, I'm really starting to enjoy this, she thought.

Back in the kitchen, Sally had to take a ribbing from her big brothers, then Paul said.

'Right Sal, now that your goodest best friend has left, we got stuff to discuss.'

Paul explained about finding the cash and smack and how they'd stashed the money again and got rid of the drugs. Sally was gob smacked to think someone could have taken it and then brought it back again. Who would do that? Now what do we do?

'The thing is Sal, you should start and make that claim with social, cos nobody's gonna believe Charlie left you with owt before he fucked off.'

'Right, I shall do that first thing after I drop the kids off at school in the morning. What else?'

'Be careful, I know yeh really like Dave an' all, and he seems quite taken by you as well. God only knows why mind, but just remember, he is and always will be a cop.'

With that the brothers said their farewell's and told Sally they would see her sometime later tomorrow.

CHAPTER THIRTY-SEVEN

Bashkim Hamiti had showered and put on fresh clean clothes. Tonight, he was treating himself to a nice meal in a good Greek restaurant in town. He might even partake of a few drinks and a bottle of red wine he thought.

Hamiti was not celebrating anything special, well at least not yet, the young pup was going to get his comeuppance but that would be cause for celebration at a later date. No, Bashkim Hamiti was working on his alibi and he figured the best one to have would be whilst sat in a nice restaurant surrounded by other diners all able to vouch that he was there when young Mr Vickers was punished.

He had a reservation for nine at the Athena, a Greek restaurant in the middle of the city. His taxi was booked for eight thirty and so that was another witness to add to the list should he be asked. A bit of a shame there wasn't a young lady to take with him. It seemed like it had been quite a while since he'd had any female company and a much longer time since he'd had any sex. Maybe that was why he was so angry with the young Englishman, Bashkim Hamiti probably needed to get laid.

The car was on time. Hamiti ordered an Ouzo at the bar while he looked over the menu, ordering the grilled saganaki and a squeeze of lemon as his starter, followed by the Greek salad and fried calamari for his main course with dolmathakia, green olives and several other side dishes as was the Greek tradition.

The waiter sat him at a decent table with his back to the wall, a personal preference of his to be able to watch who entered and who left, with little chance of someone coming up behind him unexpectedly.

Hamiti also ordered a nice bottle of the Xinomavro red to drink with his altogether very pleasant meal.

Halfway through eating, his mobile rang. He answered before the third ring and listened without saying a word. At the end of the very one sided conversation, Hamiti replied.

'Yes, go ahead and let me know in the morning how you got on.'

Hamiti then continued with his nice Greek dinner.

CHAPTER THIRTY-EIGHT

The lads had left and Sally bathed the kids ready for bed. She then read them a short story, whilst watching them fall asleep half way through. It had been a long day for all of them, but Sally couldn't remember one quite as happy as this.

She tried watching a bit of telly but there was nothing on to take her interest, so she figured she may as well have an early night herself. She got into her pyjamas and was just getting comfy when her mobile on the bedside cabinet rang.

'Hello?'

'Hya sweetheart, it's just me.'

'What you doin phonin' single women at this time of the night? Anyway, I thought you was goin' to get some sleep?'

'I was, but I couldn't, I just can't get you out of my mind Sal.'

'Good, isn't that how it's supposed to be like, or are yeh just supposed to drive away and just forget about us.'

'I don't think there's any chance of that happenin'.'

'Well good again. I was havin' the same problem actually. I came up to bed early meself. It's all quiet here, the lads 'ave gone home and the bairns are in bed fast asleep, so I figured I might as well have an early night as well.'

'Well I'll let you go then, just thought I'd call.'

'It's always nice to know the local constabulary is takin' such a keen interest in the safety of us single mams and checkin' in on us before we go nighty, nights.'

Both Sally and Dave were flirting and smiling on their respective ends of the phone.

'Hey Sal?'

'Yes David.'

I think I'm fallin' in love with yeh.'

'Oh fuck Dave! Now what do I do?'

'Go with the flow I guess.'

'Aye, okay then cos I think I'm fallin' in love with you too. Night, night.'

With that Sally hung up quickly. No one had ever told her they loved her except Mam and Dad and she most certainly had never said that to anyone herself, other than her two bairns that is.

This was a whole new ball game and Sally was feeling a bit out of her depth, but that didn't stop the huge smile from creeping across her face and as she snuggled down sleepily into the nice comfy bed. She dreamt of a tall handsome police officer coming to her rescue.

CHAPTER THIRTY-NINE

The silver grey Toyota pulled up quietly along the road, a bit closer to the house he'd been watching for the past few hours.

The street lights and surveillance cameras in this area hadn't worked for years. To be honest, no one really gave a rat's ass about crime around here and the actual statistics were quite low anyway. Whether that was a product of there being no crime at all, or the result of the local inhabitants of the area dealing with criminals in their own special way. Whatever it was, there was very little need to report anything to the authorities.

The lights of the house had been off for quite some time now, so he could only assume everyone had been asleep for a good while. Quickly and quietly he donned his woollen ski mask, picking up his shoulder bag, he ran around the back of the house. He then took the glass cutter with the suction cup fitted out of the bag and made a large circle in the back window, pulling and removing a large round of glass. As he had expected, the window was double glazed, so he cut a smaller circle in the second inner glazing, removing the centre.

Taking the large plastic bottle of ethanol from his bag, he squeezed several forceful sprays all over the inside of the house, saturating furniture and carpets throughout the whole of the living room area.

His next job was to light a cheap book of matches and throw that through the hole in the window. The living room erupted in a blue flame. Now all being well he would have enough time to go around to the front, which he did. Spraying the remainder of the bottle through the letter box onto the staircase and as before lighting a book of matches and throwing it in. Watching as the blue flames rose higher and higher. Job done, the quiet assassin then went back to the Toyota he'd stolen earlier and watched.

Within minutes, the whole of the downstairs was engulfed in a furnace of heat, smoke and fire. There was absolutely no chance of anyone escaping, he'd done this too many times before and was an expert. He also knew from past experience, there was positively no chance of survival.

Within minutes there was a massive explosion from the downstairs living room, the upstairs was now engulfed and in his expert opinion the survival rate was well below nil. Time to leave, this assignment was complete.

CHAPTER FORTY

Sally's beautiful dreams were disturbed by flashing lights and sirens passing the end of her road. She tried to pull the bedclothes over her head, but in the end both little Charlie and Georgia had climbed into her bed awakened by the noise and outside commotion.

Next, there was the banging on her front door. Both the kids were terrified and begged her not to go down, but the banging continued with excited shouting as well. Sally grabbed her bathrobe and slipped into her denim flats and descended the stairs cautiously. She unlocked the front door, opening it carefully and as she did, it was helped by Dave with Jenny standing behind him.

Dave grabbed Sally in a hug and buried his face in her neck.

'Oh Sally sweetheart, I'm so sorry my love.'

'Why? What's 'appened? What's the matter?'

Jenny walked past and took hold of her friend.

'Sally love, something terrible has 'appened and I need you to be brave pet.'

'Ya but what is it? Has there been an accident or summit? Is it the lads? Are they okay?'

'It's not the lads Sally, it's yer mam and dad, they've gone my love.'

'Gone? Gone where? It's late, they wouldn't be out at this time of night, where 'ave they gone to?'

'Sally love, there's been a terrible accident, a fire at yer mam and dads house.'

Behind Jenny stood Dave in full uniform, he was as white as a sheet and behind Dave stood two female uniformed officers. They pushed past and took Sally into the living room. Quietly they explained what had been found at her mam and dads house and that the tenders were still putting the remaining flames out. Two bodies, that of a man and a woman had been recovered from the upstairs bedroom.

Sally screamed and a low animal moan escaped from deep within her as she fell to her knees. Dave followed her down and knelt with her, his big strong arms around her and his tears of sorrow mixing with Sally's tears of anguish and pain.

'I'm so sorry my love, so very, very, sorry.'

'But how? Why? What happened?'

'Nobody knows anything yet sweetheart, it's far too soon. They'll need to investigate first. Nobody will make any assumptions at this stage.'

Sally's grief stricken face was looking up at officer Dave Riley's for answers he didn't have. The tears were flowing out of her beautiful hazel eyes and Dave's heart was breaking because he was unable to do a thing to protect her from the hurt.

'Has anyone told me brothers yet?'

'Not yet sweetheart. We've sent a car around to their place,'

'Shouldn't I phone them? Let them know?'

'No Sal, let the officers deal with it, they know how, it's

their job.'

CHAPTER FORTY-ONE

'Who the fucks that knockin' on the door at this time of the fuckin' night, man?'

Paul grabbed his jeans off the bedroom floor and slipped them on. The heavy knocking on the front door continued as bleary eyed, he descended the narrow stairs and cautiously opened the front door.

Stood at the door were both a young male and an older female uniformed Police officers. It was the male that spoke.

'Mr Vickers?'

'Yes.'

'Sorry sir, may we come inside please?'

'Aye of course, away in, what's up mate is it our Sally? what's happened?'

By this time, Mike had also come downstairs woken by the noise, wearing his big blue terry towel bath robe.

'Im sorry to have to tell you this sir, but there's been a fire. The whole house has been gutted at 26 Gallowgate Avenue on the Westernside council estate.'

'But that's our mam and dads house, what's happened?'

'Yes sir, Mr George Vickers and Mrs Doris Vickers we

understand. Two bodies were brought out from the upstairs bedroom and have been certified, deceased at the scene. We have no further details at this time however, there will obviously be a full enquiry to follow.'

'Has me sister been told, she lives just round the corner?'

'To the best of our knowledge, yes sir. We understand a friend of hers, Constable David Riley went 'round with a neighbour and two female officers to advise her of the tragedy.'

'Okay, thanks mate, we best get around to her house then. She's gonna need us.'

'We're so sorry for having to bring such sad news, but is there anyone else you'd like us to notify?'

'No, cheers mate, we'll sort it out from here. Thanks very much though.'

The officers let themselves out the front door as Paul looked at Mike and quietly spoke.

'So, this was the payback, was it? Those stupid fuckin' Albanian bastards have no fuckin' idea what they've just brought down on themselves and their fuckin' organization. I promise you this our Mike, the person responsible for this will be severely fuckin' punished.'

Paul had gone very quiet as both he and Mike climbed back up the stairs to get dressed and go to comfort their baby sister. Mike couldn't say anything he was too heart broken. Had he been the cause of all this? Was this all his stupid fault?

CHAPTER FORTY-TWO

Sally was sat in the kitchen with Dave and Jenny. The police women had left, and Dave had told them to take his patrol car with them, he'd get a lift back to the station later. He wouldn't be finishing his shift, he was staying at Sally's.

Jenny went over and put the kettle on and made coffee for everyone. As she was handing the mugs out, Paul and Mike walked in through the front door. Sally jumped up and ran crying into their arms and the three stood in the little passage way, arms around each other, locked together in their grief.

After a few minutes, they all came back into the tiny kitchen. It was cramped even under normal circumstances, now it had become almost claustrophobic and Jenny whispered to Sally that she was going to go home. There was no reason for her to stay any longer, not now Sally's brothers had arrived.

Sally hugged and thanked her friend and all the lads in turn showed their appreciation for her looking after Sally. Jenny left shutting the front door silently behind her.

Dave was the next to get up.

'Listen sweetheart, I'm gonna walk around to your

parent's house and report to my boss. Then I'll get a lift back to the station and sign off. You guys are gonna need to talk in private, so I'll leave you for now and call back a bit later, if that's okay?'

Sally got up and hugged her new man, then she held his face in her two hands and kissed him on the lips. The two brothers thanked him and stood to shake his hand, a bond had now been made between them and he'd been accepted into their family.

Dave left as quietly as Jenny had, closing the front door softly behind him.

'We drove past on our way round here Sal, the house or what remains of it is a fuckin' mess. They wouldn't let us anywhere near, but one of the firemen said he didn't think it was an accident. Dad's oxy canister hadn't helped mind, apparently that had blown up as well.'

Paul was talking and trying his hardest to hold it all together in front of his kid brother and little sister. His hands were shaking with anger, grief and frustration. Sally reached over and took hold of them in her own and through the sobs and tears she said.

'We don't know for sure if this was an accident or not just yet, so we're all gonna wait and not do anything stupid until we have confirmation one way or the other, okay? There's nobody in this room to blame for what's happened, so if either of you's two are thinkin' it's your fault in any way, now's the time to stop it. Mam and Dad are gone and that's tragic. It's just us three now and we stick together like we always did as a family. Whatever happens next, we all have to agree to do it together, okay?'

The lads nodded their heads in acknowledgement as Sally got up and put the kettle on. It was going to be a very long

183

day, with lots of decisions to be made. They were going to be needing lots of tea.

CHAPTER FORTY-THREE

Bashkim Hamiti woke early as was his norm. So many years in the military, rising early was a habit not easily broken. He was just about to step into the shower when his phone began to ring.

'Hello, yes, okay, it is completed? Yes, yes, okay I will call you later about the balance of payment. Thank you, yes, goodbye.'

There seemed to be an apprehension with Hamiti this morning. In the cold dawn of day, there was a side of him that had begun to think he may have over reacted and allowed his anger and pride to displace common sense. But no, they had to be taught a lesson. Mr Demaci would have done the same, or maybe not. He'd been told not to go too far and have any police involvement and that's exactly what he'd gone and done. It wouldn't take the brain of Britain to realise who was responsible and even if they couldn't pin it on him lawfully, the brothers would know who to go looking for. They were not fools, English maybe, but not total idiots.

Hamiti was sat at his kitchen table drinking his second cup of coffee when his phone rang again, this time he recognised immediately who was calling.

'Good morning Mr Demaci, how are you today sir?'

'Yes, good morning Bashkim, I'm fine thank you, or should I say I was fine. That was until I received a phone call a few minutes ago. Apparently there's been a fire during the night, a substantial house fire in the local council estate and two elderly people have died as a result. Now that in itself doesn't concern me, but when I was told who those people were, I became extremely perplexed and thought of the conversation you and I had yesterday afternoon. Now I know you're not a fool Bashkim, so please, just confirm to me that you had absolutely nothing to do with those people dying.'

'I'm sorry Mr Demaci, but I felt they had disrespected us and believed the punishment justified.'

'You felt justified in having an elderly couple killed in their sleep, to punish a young man that you had already beaten the day before for no reason at all and who you found by your own admission, probably had nothing whatsoever to do with the missing goods. Is that what you're saying?'

'It wasn't exactly like that sir, he was very disrespectful.'

'Bashkim, I don't give a flying fuck if he'd tied your sweet old grandmother to the back of a running camel and watched as the whole Albanian army fucked her in the arse. What you did was beyond stupidity, you have brought more pairs of eyes from the outside world into our world, can't you understand that? Please just get over here, we need to get this fucking mess resolved before it bites us.'

'Yes, Mr Demaci, I'm on my way.'

CHAPTER FORTY-FOUR

Dave Riley had gone back to the station where his desk sergeant had told him to file his report. Then he was told to take off home and look after his girlfriend. He was also told to take forty eight hours leave of absence and if he needed longer, he only had to ask. Dave thanked the desk Sergeant, went out into the car park, retrieved his yellow Golf and drove around to Sally's house.

When he got there, the blue Mondeo was still parked out front. Dave walked up the path and knocked. It was Mike who answered the door.

'Away in mate, Sal's just upstairs for a shower and getting' dressed, she won't be long, away in the kitchen.'

'Cheers Mike, how you guys coping? How's Sally?'

'She's sad, confused, angry and all the other things that go with losing your parents in a fuckin' fire I guess.'

'That was a stupid question, wasn't it?'

'Ya, but that's okay mate. You're a cop and cops always ask lots of stupid fuckin' question's, don't they?'

Dave realised the lads were taking the piss, he shook his head in disbelief and smiled.

Sally came down a few minutes later. She had on an oversized sweatshirt, with high cut denim shorts showing off her very long legs with pink sponge flip flops on her feet. Her hair was still damp from the shower but she'd bothered to put on some make up and looked and smelled great. Dave felt a real pang of guilt for even contemplating what he was thinking about her at a time such as this.

She came over, kissed him and promptly sat on his lap with her arms around his neck.

'Hya sweetheart, how yeh feelin'?' she said to her new man.

'Shouldn't I be askin' you that?'

'Ya, well yeh can if yeh like, but yeh know I already feel real shitty, so I wouldn't even bother askin'.'

At least they had all retained that dark sense of humour associated with the area. It all went hand in hand with the people of the estate, no matter how bad it was, you just had to laugh it off.

It was Dave who started the conversation.

'Where's the kids? Are they still up in bed?'

'No love, Jenny came round for them and took them to her place. She's gonna let her bairns stay off school with them so they've got someone to play with.'

'Okay, so there's only us four in the house then?'

'Well ya, why?'

'Cos I managed to get some info, but you all have to understand it's off the record. Yeh can't go quoting me on anything I'm about to say, okay?'

They all agreed and the two brothers sat forward to listen while Sally got up and put the kettle on.

'Right, first off, I'm sorry to have to say this, but it seems as though it wasn't an accident. The back downstairs window had been blown clean out with what they believe was your dads oxygen tank exploding. Anyway, they found most of the window still intact in the back garden. It had two circular pieces neatly cut out of the double glazed unit. They believe that's how the arsonist sprayed some kind of alcohol into the living room, then lit it.'

'Why are they saying alcohol and not petrol or kero or summit?' Mike asked.

'Petroleum based products leave a distinct after smell when they've burned. Apparently, there was none of that aroma, but there was an odour of sweet burnt alcohol. Yeh know like on a Christmas pudding. It was very faint but a couple of the brigade lads noticed it when they first went into the house.

Secondly, this has the same M.O. as some other arson attacks that've been carried out as assassination's around Europe. Whoever did this, has been setting fires in the homes of the rich and famously wanted by the criminal fraternity. This arson attack didn't come cheap, the guy who did this is a professional and is wanted in several European countries, so we have to ask ourselves, who would want to place a hit on your mam and dad and why?'

The three siblings looked at each other. Dave had confirmed what they already believed to be true, but it was Paul who took it upon himself to enquire.

'Dave, I got a question to ask you mate and I need a straight answer. First off, whatever gets said in this room now, fuckin' stays in this room okay? It's real important to all of us as a family and obviously, that now affects you and our Sal as a couple as well, so here goes. How much can we trust you? Not Dave the policeman, but Dave the lad?'

'That sounds ominous. Truthfully that would depend. I'm still an officer of the law and as such I have a certain duty, but I'm also human being and for that I have a separate set of loyalties. Same as everyone else I guess, why?'

The three siblings looked at each other and Sally gave a slight nod, giving Paul the go ahead.

'Right here's the deal mate and to us, it's a fuckin' big deal. We don't need any police involvement. It appears that Sal's husband Charlie, was in cahoots with a low life dealer called Oggy, who in turn was in with the Albanian mob. Now Charlie seems to have fucked off somewhere with whatever these people are looking for and they obviously want it back. They came 'round here questioning our Sal about Charlie's whereabouts, but she told them she had no idea, he's just fucked off. Anyway, this guy, Bashkim Hamiti they call 'im, originally didn't believe her, and belted her one in the face. Me and our kid went out to sort him and to be honest he gave us a fuckin' good hidin', thus me wi' two black eyes and a broken nose and Mike 'ere with a couple of cracked ribs. Anyway, he fuckin' comes back the next day and we think he believes what Sal's told 'im, but Mike here gives him a few slaps and sends him fuckin' packin' with a flea in 'is Albanian ear. Consequently this has happened to Mam and Dad and we think it's either Bashkim Hamiti or his boss Donika Demaci who are responsible.'

'So why no police involvement? You must realise these people are already wanted, we just can't pin anything on them for the moment.'

'But that's exactly it, and you fuckin' won't ever be able to pin this on 'em either. They're not daft Dave man, you said it yourself. They've used someone from outside to do this job. He's probably on the fuckin' ferry over to mainland Europe by now and yeh might have his fuckin' M.O. but you don't have a fuckin' clue who he is or what the fuck he looks like do yeh?'

Paul was right, at least Dave believed he was right, but was unsure what they wanted from him.

'Okay, I take on board what you're saying, but what

exactly is it you want from me?'

'Okay mate, now for the nitty gritty stuff. Really, we don't want owt from you, other than a bit of a blind eye that is. I know some people who are very professional at what they do and I've been in touch with them and they're prepared to come up and help out. Let's face it Dave, we can go places and ask questions that cops can't and we can get the fuckin' answers a lot fuckin' quicker, especially 'round here mate.'

Dave nodded, what Paul was saying had the basis of truth, the law was so tied up with red tape that it was common knowledge the judicial system appeared to be more on the side of the criminal than the public.

The police themselves were fed up with making the arrests to have criminals back on the street before the paperwork was complete. Or some wide boy solicitor had them released on a technicality and even if it finally got to trial and they were convicted, some geriatric judge or magistrate would slap them on the wrist, tell them to behave and release them because there weren't enough prison cells available. Or failing that, give them a fine that they had no intention of ever paying anyway.

Dave's mind was working overtime, he was duty bound to uphold the law, but around this area, there was no law. He knew they were never going to catch the arsonist and it didn't matter who'd paid him. They would never be able to prove it without reasonable doubt, at least not in a court of law.

'So, is that all you want from me? Just turn a blind eye?'

'More or less mate. But if yeh happen to be able to get us any tasty morsels of intel, that wouldn't go amiss either, yeh know.'

'Listen lads, I'm not against yeh sortin' this mess out on your own. The local cops are stretched to the limit in any case,

191

so there's no way they could give it their full attention and do justice to your poor Mam and Dad. I'll help as much as I can, but if my bosses find out I've assisted yeh, or passed info onto yeh, I'm gonna go down big time. The only thing I'm gonna dig me heels in over is there must be no harm to any civilians okay? I really don't care and neither does anyone else, what happens to the Albanians and their crew, but no innocents are to be caught in any collateral damage, understand?'

'That sounds good to me, bro' couldn't 'ave put it better meself.'

Sally walked over to Dave, sat back on his knee with her arms around his neck and said.

'Thanks gorgeous and welcome to the family.'

CHAPTER FORTY-FIVE

'I'm sorry Bashkim, I just can't seem to get my head around what you've done and how your trying to justify your stupidity. You've jeopardised not only the deal I've been working on for months, but the whole of what I've spent my life trying to build and for what? For the sake of your fucking pride. Yes, you could have had him beaten, or even put away never to be seen again, but no, what you did is so fucking stupid to be beyond ridiculous.'

'But sir, you are always talking about respect.'

'Yes, you're right Bashkim I am. But you may have noticed I mean respect for me, not for you. Who the fuck do you think you are? I brought you here to ensure my problems were resolved, not fucking created. To put my business in such a precarious position for the sake of your pride? Let this be an end to it, just make damn sure this cannot come back to me, do I make myself absolutely clear? Or do I personally have to ensure that you join young Oggy? Now, can we get onto the business of the goods awaiting customs clearance and hopefully delivered before the weekend and how they are to be shipped out?'

'Yes sir.'

Bashkim Hamiti, stood in front of his employer like a

school boy attending the Headmaster's office, reciting from memory the full details of the delivery plan appertaining to the drug deal that had been months in preparation.

'I understand all the goods are in polypropylene bags marked forty three grade, ordinary Portland cement, and there will be a total of twenty bags on the pallets, with red sealant across the top.'

It was intended that Demaci's men would follow their marked container to the building site and after watching the unloading of the pallets, would leave with the white van laden with their twenty bags of Portland cement and the site foreman a thousand pounds better off.

'That is correct, inside each of those fifty kilo bags is a one kilo polypropylene bag of pure heroin. If our maths are correct, that means twenty kilos of uncut heroin at two, two, five thousand a kilo, that should equate to a street value of around four million five hundred thousand, give or take. Not bad for a lay out of a hundred thousand Bashkim. Please do not fuck this up. I must check with the shipping agents later in the week to see if there is any update for the customs clearance and delivery, until then Bashkim, I suggest you go home and rest. Your face is a fucking mess and for the moment I really don't wish to look upon it. I'll call you if I need you. Please just go and let yourself out, goodbye.'

CHAPTER FORTY-SIX

Paul sat at the little kitchen table with his mobile phone and a small kiddies exercise book to make notes in. Mike was sat opposite watching and listening, with Sally having taken Dave into the living room out of the way so they could talk. Dave felt it better this way, then he wouldn't know or be witness to anything that Paul might be planning.

Paul made the calls and wrote names and times down in his note book, then he looked towards his kid brother.

'That's the two I wanted, Timothy Harrison, we call him the Timber. Big fuckin' black lad and I mean big. We may need his weight and strength. He'll be coming in from Liverpool and Jimmy Calbert, a wee Scotsman. Hard as fuck and can be as nasty as they come. Must be his ginger fuckin' hair, or maybe his lack of it. Jockie they call him, he'll be alright with us though. But once I point 'im in the right direction, he's like a fuckin' terrier and I don't mean the cute fuckin' cuddly type either.'

'When they gonna get here bro.'

'They reckon, they can be here by later this afternoon. We'll put them up at our place, then we can come and go as we please without disturbing Sally and the kids.'

'So, we need to do a shop then?'

'Ya, we do amigo. Food, rations and equipment, Jockie

and Timber are bringing their own personal gear and I've got mine in a kit bag upstairs in the loft. We only need a few bits and pieces that can be picked up at the local boat chandlers. You and me can do that later. We're gonna need some food as well, especially Timber, he can eat a scabby horse between two pissy mattresses for a fuckin' snack. There's no fillin' him sometimes.'

'When we goin' then big bro?'

'We'll say bye to Sal and Dave, leave them to spend some time together, then we'll call back after we've got the stuff.'

'We could do with talking to some of the lads at the Ship and Anchor, find out what the news is on the streets, then at least we'll have a heads up for when your mates arrive.'

'Ya, maybe we'll call in for a pint and find out. Best doin' it before the lads get here though cos no one's gonna wanna talk in front of strangers, are they?'

CHAPTER FORTY-SEVEN

Dave was sat back on the big sofa in Sally's living room with Sally laid full length, her head resting on his lap.

There hadn't been much talking between them. Both were tired having been up all the day before, and most of the night. Every now and again Dave would hear Sally give a big sob and a sigh and he would gently comb his fingers through her hair.

Paul poked his head around the living room door and said that he and Mike were going out for a few hours but would be back later. He asked if there was anything anyone needed picking up, but nobody could think of anything and so they just left.

Sally sat up, swinging her bare feet onto the cold floor. She took Dave by the hand, walked out of the living room pulling him gently behind her as she climbed the stairs to her bedroom.

Dave was a bit taken aback and not quite sure where this was leading. That was until Sally put her arms around his neck and up on tip toe kissed him a long lingering kiss. She then started to remove her big sweatshirt and shorts standing in front of him in just her underwear.

'I really need to be close to someone right about now Dave. Me, myself and I had a vote, we elected you as the one I want, whatcha reckon?'

'I reckon you all made a very good decision. I woulda picked me for you as well.'

Sally lay herself on the bed, looking long legged and beautiful. Dave kicked off his old trainers and threw his shirt in a heap on the floor, showing his lean muscular frame before climbing alongside to face this vision of sensuality on the bed. They lay looking into each other's eyes for a few seconds before Dave took the initiative, stroking Sally's back gently before kissing her.

This kiss was unlike all the others. There was a physical electric charge between the two of them this time and within seconds of their lips meeting, their mouths opened, and their tongues introduced themselves to each other. Their hands began the first of many explorations, touching, stroking. This was like a no holds barred confrontation and they both went to the secret places of each other's bodies that only couples prepared to be extremely intimate would readily allow.

Sally reached down and unfastened Dave's belt, unzipping his jeans and while he managed to kick them off with just his feet, he undid Sally's bra clasp one handedly and as she lay on her back he took one of her aroused pink nipples into his mouth and began to suckle it softly. Sally in turn reached inside his boxers to find him already hard and as she slowly stroked his hardness she slipped her last vestiges of modesty off, throwing her panties across to the other side of the bedroom.

In all this time, not a word had been spoken. Their mouths never leaving each other's bodies for more than a few seconds at a time. Dave slowly climbed between Sally's parted legs and as she raised her knees higher, he entered her slowly, gently sliding himself inside her already moist cavity with the minimum amount of effort, allowing the rhythm of desire to take over and they both writhed to the silent music of lovemaking. Both their mouths and groins firmly locked together on the bed.

Throughout the heavy breathing and the deep groans of desire that Sally had for so long never known, the crescendo built to its finale and as Sally gasped her orgasm, Dave released his own, deep inside her beautiful body.

Afterword's they both lay naked, breathing heavily, their arms and legs still entwined, gently kissing each other's faces and sweat soaked bodies. Touching and holding each other's intimate places as they slowly started their second arousal. Sally then looked at her new lover and said questioningly,

'Dave?'

'Yes sweetheart,'

'Can you do summit for us,'

'Of course, I'll do anything for you Sal,'

'Well, next time, will yeh take your socks off an' look as though yeh might be stayin?'

CHAPTER FORTY-EIGHT

Paul and Mike went first to the boat chandlers picking up a five kilo bale of nylon line, shackles, duct tape and a multitude of bits and pieces, probably never to be used but purchased just in case. Everything was paid for in cash from the money in Mikes waders so no trace could be made. Not that the owner of the shop would say anything detrimental to anyone about the boys, he'd known them since they'd come in with their dad as young lads.

The next stop was the big supermarket near the high street where they bought enough provisions to outfit a full battalion.

The last stop was the Ship and Anchor, it was a bit early but there were always a few of the local lads in there who worked the night shifts or never worked at all. It was a good place to pick up local gossip and someone always knew what was going on in and around the city limits.

The lads walked into the bar and Dougie, the owner walked over placing two pints in front of them.

'These are on the house lads, it's not much, but we all

heard about your mam and dad and if there's owt any of us can do, you just gotta say the word and I mean anything.'

'There is summit Dougie, if yeh got the time that is?'

'You go ahead Paul son, the place is quiet for now, what's on yer mind?'

'The fire wasn't an accident Dougie. It looks like it was set on fuckin' purpose by a pro from outta the area. We don't know who he is yet, but we do know who sent 'im and we intend really hurtin' those Albanian bastards.'

'You are jokin'. Why on earth would they or anyone else wanna harm your sweet mam and dad? They were both well respected and highly thought of around these parts lads.'

'We can't go into the details mate, but we do know for certain it was them. Who around 'ere would have any intel about them?'

'Well the only one I would know would be Jacko. He spends most of his time wi' low lives, him bein' one hiself. Ya, if anyone would know owt it's gotta be Jacko.'

'Where can we find this Jacko then Dougie?'

'Oh, he's out the back making phone calls and playin' pool wi' 'imself. No one else'll go fuckin' near 'im. Ugly little twat wi' greasy hair, black teeth and yellow headed spots. Never gets fuckin' washed, mucky, dirty little bastard. I keep barrin' 'im, but the sneaky little fuck keeps getting' back in somehow when I'm not lookin'. Probably has the cheek to use the fuckin' front door.'

'Thanks Dougie, we'll go an 'ave a word if yeh don't mind?'

'Yeh go right ahead lads, feel free. Yeh can drag 'is skinny arse outside if yeh like, an' give 'im a good fuckin' hidin' too. No great loss to me or the rest of the world.'

The lads picked up their pints and walked through to

201

the pool room out the back of the pub. It was almost empty except for one skinny, scrawny, ugly individual practicing his shots.

'Ow mate! Are you Jacko?'

'Why? Who the fuck wants to know?'

Jacko didn't see the slap coming, but he saw the stars and felt the tears as Paul laid one on his nose.

'I fuckin' wanna know, that's who. Now let's start again, are you fuckin' Jacko?'

'Ya, ya, what I fuckin' do to deserve that?'

'Nowt Jacko. When yeh do summit I'll give yeh a good fuckin' hidin' okay? Now listen and listen very carefully cos it might be well worth your while. I want to know everything there is to know about the Albanians mobs business in this area. Where their dealin', how and to who, do yeh fuckin' understand?'

'You're fuckin' jokin' man. I won't survive ten fuckin' minutes out there if I spill on them. 'Ave yeh seen the size of some of 'em bastards? And didn't yeh hear what they did to fuckin' Oggy? Poor little Turk fucker.'

'No Jacko, this solemn face of mine doesn't fuckin' joke and you won't survive one minute out there if yeh don't tell me what I want to know. Besides we never heard fuck all about what 'appened to Oggy, so please enlighten us.'

'His body was found on the waste ground by the railway lines. He'd been well battered. Broken jaw, broken ribs, broken neck and his throat cut from fuckin' ear to fuckin' ear. He was left as a fuckin' warnin' mate.'

'Right now Jacko, we're gonna buy you a pint of whatever it is you want and while you're drinkin' that delicious pint of whatever it is you want, we're gonna listen to everything you've gotta fuckin' say about those Albanian twats. Afterwards, I'm gonna give you a hundred fuckin' quid and my telephone number and you're gonna phone me with anything you might hear. If you don't phone me, I'm gonna tell those fuckin' Albanians bastards a whole bunch of fuckin' lies and give them your name as the person who told them to me. Do you understand?'

'Ya, ya, ya, I understand, I need to make a phone call first though and you can go get me that fuckin' pint?'

CHAPTER FORTY-NINE

Sally and Dave lay naked on the bed holding hands and feeling the warm glow of after sex. They were both physically drained after their lovemaking, but neither wanted to be the first to break the magic and get out of bed. Although Sally was desperately busting for a pee, it was Dave who spoke.

'I suppose we should get up then.'

'Why? Don't yeh like layin' here all naked next to us then?'

'I absolutely love it Sal, but Paul and Mike will be back soon.'

'Well that's alright, they know where the kettle is don't they?'

'I'm sure they do, but I don't know how they'll react when they know what I did to their little sister.'

'What you did! Hey listen mate, who dragged who up those stairs?'

'Oh ya, it was all your fault, I forgot. I somehow don't think Paul's gonna believe that though.'

'Well then that's his problem not ours. We haven't done owt wrong. We're two consenting adults that decided to go to bed and shag each other's brains out. What's the problem with that?'

'Well I'm on your side Sal.'

With that Dave put his arm around Sally and she snuggled in closer, spooning him.

'Did yeh really mean what yeh said to us on the phone then Dave?'

'What was that sweetheart?'

'Oh, forgotten already ave we? Yeh said yeh thought yeh loved me, did yeh mean it?'

'I thought I did at the time, but now I know I do.'

Sally sat up, threw her long legs over his waist and straddled him, bending over to kiss his now quite sore lips.

'I know I love you David Riley.'

'Well I know someone else that loves you Sal and if you insist on sitting there much longer he's gonna wanna jump up and prove it all over again.'

Sally giggled like a school girl, jumped off the bed and ran naked into the bathroom for a pee.

When she came back, Dave was sat on the end of the bed still in his birthday suit. Sally jumped on his lap facing towards him with her arms around his neck, her knees on either side of his slim hips and her feet tucked between his knees.

Her small breasts were at mouth height so Dave gently went from nipple to nipple, sucking and kissing each one in turn. Within a very short time, he was hard all over again and entered her in that position, laying back and letting Sally do all the work. Surprisingly it didn't take too long for either of them to reach their final destination, arriving at the same time.

'Right woman, you win, I'm empty and I'm knackered. You've had your evil way with me.'

Dave lay back on the bed with Sally still straddling him.

'Oh, no you don't mister. I've only just started. It was you that released the beast in me, now it's gonna take a lifetime for you to tame it.'

'Ya, I can do that,' he said and kissed her.

The two burly brothers knocked on the downstairs front door and burst in.

'Sal, Dave, where the fuck are yeh? Away man put the kettle on we're parched.'

'Hang on, we'll be down in a minute.'

'Down in a minute, what yeh fuckin' doin up there in the first place man?'

'Don't be so bloody daft our Paul. Mike try and explain to your older brother the facts of life will yeh, while I put some clothes on.'

'So, what you two been up to while we been out busy graftin' then?'

Mike was sat at the kitchen table with a stupid knowing smirk on his face. Struggling hard not to burst out laughing, at the same time trying his hardest to stir it up between his little sister and big brother.

It was Sally who answered, while Dave sat back quietly, an extremely satisfied glow covering his face.

'Do yeh really need me to answer that question Mikey? cos I will if yeh really want us to and I'll go into lotsa detail and exaggerate as well if yeh like.'

'That's enough, shut up you's two. I don't wanna fuckin' know. We 'ave other more important things we need to be considerin' here, other than your fuckin' love lives. So can we just get on with it please?'

The four of them having now all settled down, were sat around the small kitchen table. Mike had brought in some bread and cooked meats and Sally had made sandwiches for them all to share. This was the first food any of them had eaten that day and they'd only just realised how hungry they all were.

'The other two are on their way and should be 'ere sometime soon. I told them to come to your place Sal, then Mike and I can give them a quick look 'round and they can get a feel for the place. We'll all be sleepin' at our house though, so we shouldn't disturb you's two love birds and the bairns, if that's all right?'

'Ya, no problem Paul, whatever you feel's right is okay wi' us.'

'How much do you wanna know Dave? I don't wanna put you in an awkward situation mate.'

'Thanks Paul, I'll just sit in if that's okay. If I feel my position's being compromised, then I might have to go up to the bathroom for a while.'

'Okay mate, well understood. I'm not gonna start 'til the others get 'ere otherwise we're doin' it all fuckin' twice. Let's just sit back and relax, cos I gotta feelin' we won't be able to once this gets fuckin' started.'

The four of them didn't get much time to relax, a short while after they'd eaten there was a loud knock at the door. It was Paul who answered it and stepped outside, picking up in a bear hug a relatively small balding Scotsman with a very big attitude.

'Put me doon yeh wee fucker, 'ave a bit o' respect will yeh.'

'Jockie me old mate, it's so good to see yeh.'

'Aye a ken, it's bin too long laddie. I'm so sorry for yeh loss though mate. It's a very sorry affair to be losin' yeh mammy and da like that.'

'Cheers pal, away inside and I'll introduce you to

everyone.'

Introductions were being made, when there was another gentle tapping on the front door. This time Sally went to answer it thinking it might be a neighbour.

What she saw was not any neighbour from around this area. He might have been described more as an eclipse of the sun. His massive black frame covered the whole of the doorway, blocking any outside light from entering the tiny passageway.

'I guess you must be the Timber then?' Said Sally, tipping her head back to try and make eye contact.

'Yes miss, that would be me. I'm looking for the Vicker,' the big man replied in the softest, deepest educated baritone of voices.

'Away inside then Timber love, they're all waitin' for yeh.'

Once the huge frame entered the house, there was no possible way out for anybody else. Hugs and handshakes were made and Paul's big frame was dwarfed by that of the Timber standing next to him.

As there was no room in the little kitchen, the table and benches were carried through to the living room and everyone made themselves comfortable there instead. Sally had already gone around and taken orders for tea and coffee. It was agreed by all that no alcohol would be allowed until all operations were completed and then they would either celebrate or commiserate.

Paul took over, explaining what his proposals were, with everyone free to question or add any ideas after he'd finished.

'What I wanna do, is bring the lot of them Albanian bastards to a grindin' halt. I wanna close their drugs on the streets and I really want the two at the top to feel pain. This town will be a much better place without them. I'm not naïve, I know that once they're gone someone else will fill their place, but what I don't wanna do is the bobby's job. We let them do that cos they can do it far better than we can. We'll be goin' covert and we'll start by hittin' the pushers on the streets. Once we've done that, the big boys will stick their heads out of their shells to find out what's appenin', then hopefully we can make our move on them. Any questions?'

It was the Timber who spoke first in his deep rumbling voice.

'What sort of measures do you want us to use on the pushers Vicker? How much force and to what outcome?'

'Okay, from my point of view yeh can be as hard and ruthless as yeh fuckin' like. They're fuckin' scum so take the drugs and money off them. We'll store it somewhere out of the way an' give it to a charity or summit after. The money I mean, not the drugs. No killing though. A good hiding and a warning not to come back, but I don't want the police lookin' into our affairs for leavin' dead fuckin' bodies in the high street. Anyone else?'

'What we gonna do wi' the drugs laddie? None of us have any use for 'em, do we destroy 'em or what?'

'Im not too sure Jockie. We can either get rid of it all later or hand it anonymously to the police and let them deal wi' it.'

It was Dave who asked the final question of the day and probably the one on everybody's mind. The one that no-one wanted to ask.

'Paul, what's gonna happen to the two at the top when and if yeh get to them?'

'Fair question mate and I really wanna give yeh a straight honest answer, the truth is I don't think I can right

209

now. All I will say to you is they won't be allowed to walk away from what they did to Mam and Dad. I just can't allow that to happen, so if there's no other questions I call this meeting officially adjourned.'

'Wait! does anyone want owt from the kitchen, before I close it?'

There were smiles all round and the shaking of heads at Sally's only input of the whole afternoon.

'No thanks little sis. Mike and me are gonna take these two for a ride 'round our fair city and show them the sordid sights, then back to our place. I think if we start to hit them later tonight they won't be expecting it, at least they won't think it's us involved. I did manage to get a list of names and addresses to start us off with though. If yeh got a mo' Dave can yeh step outside mate.'

'Ya, of course.'

Dave followed Paul out into what was loosely termed the back garden of the house and they turned to face each other.

'Listen kidda, our Sal thinks the world of you. Yeh can see that a fuckin' mile off and I got a hunch your quite smitten wi' her too, but I need a big favour from yeh?'

'Just ask mate, if I can I will.'

'Good lad. I don't know how this is all gonna pan out and I need to know my little sister's gonna be okay. For the next while I'm gonna be busy, so I need you keepin' an eye out in case any bad lads turn up. Yeh know what I mean?'

'Paul, are you askin' me if I wanna have a sleep over with your sister?'

'Uh ya! I guess that's exactly what I'm fuckin' askin'.'

'Have no fear mate. I can't get too involved with what you're doin', but there's no one gonna get near Sal and the bairns, I'll make sure of that.'

'I kinda thought you'd say that our lad, welcome aboard.'

The lads all said their goodbyes to Sally and Dave, leaving them on the doorstep while Mike got in the Timbers white Ford transit van and Jockie got into the Mondeo with Paul, leaving his red Mini Cooper parked outside Sally's house. They all waved and followed Paul out of the estate.

Dave had his arm around Sally's shoulder holding her close to him, then he turned to her and asked.

'Hey Sal, I don't suppose there's any chance I could sleep over at your place tonight is there?'

'Did our Paul put you up to this?'

'He may 'ave hinted it would be a good idea, but I was gonna ask yeh anyhow.'

'Well only cos you was gonna ask us anyhow, then ya. But we gotta get the kids yeh know that don't yeh?'

'Ya, I figured.'

'Good, cos yeh can come with us now and fetch them from Jenny's place.'

CHAPTER FIFTY

Paul had Jockie in his car, followed by the Timber and Mike behind, driving around showing them the abysmal sights of the local slum districts.

They all managed to pass several of the dealers standing cold and damp in the abandoned streets of the city, while driving around the derelict areas where nobody in their right mind would want to wander at night unless they were desperate.

They drove, watching the young girls on the street corners, some no more than children. Trying their hardest to trade their wares, with no buyers currently interested. All the punters knowing that the longer the girls waited the more desperate they would become to make money for their pimps and then the prices would begin to plummet.

They drove past at least half a dozen of the drops on Paul's list and knowing there were at least another twelve left that could be sabotaged in the early hours when honest working people were fast asleep in their beds and not so honest people were out trying to make a score of one description or another.

The two vehicles circled around for another hour and nobody seemed to be taking any notice of them. Why would they, no one had ever posed a threat in the past, so why would they start now.

They did one last quick tour of the immediate area, then headed back to Paul and Mikes place for a few hour's respite and food before they made the first of several midnight sorties into the world of drugs, prostitution and unequivocal violence.

CHAPTER FIFTY-ONE

Sally and Dave walked hand in hand out of the little council house towards Jenny's place to pick up the kids. As they came to the end of Frazer Avenue a fire tender went past in the opposite direction making Sally catch her breath.

No more would she be able to walk the other way to visit her sweet Mam and Dad. No more cups of tea in the afternoon while gossiping about the evening soaps on the telly the night before, with dad giving his opinions. Or surprise Sunday lunches with all the family together. The tears started to flow all over again and she buried her face in Dave's chest sobbing uncontrollably.

They both stood on the corner with Dave's arms wrapped tightly around her, eventually the sobbing subsided.

'Do yeh want to go back home sweetheart?'

'No, I think I'll be alright now, it just came over us when I saw that fire engine go past and I realised I'm never gonna see me mam and dad again.'

'Up to you Sal, we can go to Jenny's or home. Whatever you want. In fact, I could go and get the kids by meself and you could have a lie down.'

'No, babe. Life goes on as me Mam would 'ave said and life is in them two bairns. Besides they make me laugh and I could do wi' a good one of them about now.'

At that, hand in hand they continued with a more determined step up to Jenny's house and knocked.

Jenny answered almost immediately and stood aside to let them both in. Once inside Jenny took Sally in her strong arms and held her. The tears flowed all over again and Sally's shoulders wracked with the sobbing. After a few minutes Sally regained her composure and wiped her nose on the back of her hand.

'Yeh 'aven't got any tissues 'ave you Jen. I've got snot everywhere.'

'Aye lass, here's some kitchen roll, use as much as you like.'

'The way I'm feelin' I may use it all Jen. Oh what a baby I've turned out to be.'

'Nay lass, your no bloody baby. Your just a sweet young thing whose hearts been broken and yeh need time for it to repair itself. Away, I'll put the kettle on, the kids are watchin' telly, they've had their tea's so just leave them be for a while.'

Sally and Dave sat at the kitchen table with Jenny making coffee for everyone. They talked about what the kids had been doing and saying and it seemed they were unaware of what had happened to their nan and grandad. That was something Sally was going to have to rectify when they got home later.

'Do they know how the fire started then Sal, has anyone said owt yet?'

Sally looked over at Dave before answering

'All we know is what our lads found out from one of the

fire bobby's earlier this mornin' and that it appeared to have been started on purpose. But we don't know who or why, that will be investigated by the police later. There's nowt official been said yet.'

'But who would wanna hurt your mam and dad, they were a lovely couple.'

'I know that Jenny, but there's some really sick people out there yeh know.'

There was nothing mentioned to Jenny about Albanians or what Paul and Mike were up to. That was on a strict, need to know basis.

They both drank their coffee, then collected the kids from the living room. Thanking Jenny for having them.

All four walked the short distance home, listening to the little one's telling them what they'd been up to all day and what their plans were going to be at school the next day and who they were going to be playing with.

Sally ran their baths and got the two kids ready for bed. But tonight, instead of telling them a bedtime story, she and Dave sat together on the edge of the bottom bunk to talk to them and between the tears and the hundreds of questions, they managed to let the bairns know that nana and grandad had passed away and they wouldn't be seeing them anymore.

Sally kissed them both before shutting the door over. Then her and Dave went downstairs into the living room and cuddled up on the sofa.

'Shall we 'ave an early night then Dave? Cos you were up all last night.'

'You must be knackered as well sweetheart, yeh didn't get much sleep yourself.'

The two of them went upstairs and got into bed. Holding each other close and with one thing leading to another, they made gentle, slow love, falling into a deep sleep in each other's arms after.

CHAPTER FIFTY-TWO

'Okay lads, we all ready to go? Have you all got everything yeh might need? If we can use your van Timber it's a bit less conspicuous than my car. A couple of us can get in the back with the gear and if we alternate, hopefully no one will be able to give a clear description of anyone in particular.'

Paul had taken charge. The two ex green berets were used to this. Paul had got them out of many a nasty scrape when they'd served in Afghanistan so the two of them were more than comfortable with this arrangement.

They drove into the city and found their first victim in a darkened doorway, handing out a small package to a dishevelled punter using only one hand, the other never leaving his jacket pocket.

'I'll take this first one wi' you Jockie. You walk straight past, then when I start talkin to 'im you can double back behind and keep an eye out. You two stay in the van out of the way, but if yeh see or hear owt let us know.'

The two lads stepped quietly from the back of the van. Paul gave Jockie a head start allowing him to walk past, then stepped forward himself and approached the skinny youth in the doorway.

'Watcha got?' Said Paul,

'Nowt why?'

'Empty yer fuckin' pockets into this bag then.'

'Fuck off, who'd yeh think you fuckin' are like?'

Paul broke the youths nose, tugging his hidden hand out of the jacket pocket to find he'd been holding a long razor sharp hacksaw blade with electrician's tape wrapped around, making a handle.

He emptied the pockets ripping the linings out of the clothing so they couldn't be used again, finding loose notes and change together with a mixture of tablets, powders and small wrapped parcels in tin foil. Everything went into a clear plastic bag. Paul then took the youths mobile off him, bringing his heavy booted heel down on it, rendering it totally useless.

'Right lad, this is the only fuckin' warnin' yer ever likely to get from me, so fuck off and don't ever let me see yeh back here again, cos next time, I'm really gonna fuckin' mess with yeh.'

With that Paul walked back to the van, waited for Jockie to come along from the opposite side of the road where he'd been watching and they all drove off to the next drop.

'Well that was relatively simple. I don't expect them all to be quite so easy though, keep yer eyes open lads and watch each other's fuckin' backs.'

Mike and Jockie were the next up. Same arrangement, they parked the van along the road away from the drop. Mike walked past as the spotter, while Jockie approached the dealer.

'Now then sunshine, what yeh fuckin' sellin'?'

'I don't fuckin' know you do I?'

'Och aye, a'course yeh fuckin' do mate. I'm yer worse fuckin' nightmare. We musta met sometime afore laddie.'

With that Jockie lifted his leg and stamped his heavy military boot into the side of the seller's knee, snapping the leg joint and dropping the drug pusher onto the floor whereby Jockie then brought the heel of the same boot down on his nose, splitting the skin and snapping the cartilage to one side.

'See, now do yeh fuckin' remember me? I bet yeh dinna want me to fuckin' come back though. So why don't yeh be a good laddie and pull all yeh fuckin' pockets inside out afore I get really pissed off wi' yeh. Cos next off, me boots gonna' make fuckin' contact wi' yer wee fuckin' knackers and when I kick yeh balls up inta yeh fuckin' throat, yeh gonna end up looking like yeh got a wee case of the fuckin' mumps.'

The pusher did as he was told, emptying his pockets into another plastic bag. Jockie then got down on his knees and cut the pocket linings out from the jeans and jacket of the piece of scum.

'Now then laddie, it may not feel like it right at this moment in time, but tonight's yer lucky fuckin' night, cos I'm no gonna kill yeh. However, if I should ever catch yeh out here again, then your gonna wake up in an intensive fuckin' care unit. Now then my little ray of fuckin' sun light, where's your mobile?'

The pusher put out his hand holding his phone while Jockie stamped hard on both hand and phone smashing them to pieces.

'Och sorry yeh wee daft twat. Yeh shoulda left fuckin' go first shouldn't yeh?'

As Jockie turned to go back to the van, one of the pusher's partners came running across to aid his mate, passing close to Mike who turned on him swiftly throwing him off balance over his shoulder and laying him flat on his back with a resounding crunch as his head made contact with the concrete pavement. Mike followed him down with a sharp fist in his teeth loosening the top front ones.

'Okay mate, now empty yeh fuckin' pockets.'

'Do you 'ave any fuckin' idea who owns this shit fuck face?'

'Yes, as a matter of fact. I do mate,' said Mike emptying the downed teens pockets and cutting away the linings before dismantling the mobile phone with his boot.

The two of them walked casually back to the van, climbing in the back, closing the doors behind them.

'Okay,' said Paul, 'well done lads, next on the agenda is a flat and I've been told these lads are the ones supplyin' all the streets in this area, so we can expect it to be well guarded and secured. There should also be a lot of cash and dope kicking around, so we all go in together for this one. Jockie your gonna be lead man so tatty yeh self up a bit. Timber you'll probably need to take down the door so bring that fourteen pound sledgie with yeh and don't let them see yeh through any spy holes. You're our secret weapon.'

The drive to the flat took nearly fifteen minutes. It was situated above a shop with the entrance around the back up a flight of concrete stairs.

From below, the door looked to be a simple double glazed unit. There were no cameras that could be seen anywhere nearby, so they weren't being watched by anyone. The whole system was so complacent and laid back, it really deserved to be raided.

Jockie went up the stairs loud and singing, acting the drunk in need of making a hit. He banged hard on the door, shouting abuse at whoever might be inside and eventually it was opened by a huge man in jeans and what may have been, once upon a time, a white vest.

'What fuck you want,'

'I need to fuckin' score mate. I'm fuckin' desperate.'

'Who say for you to come here?'

'Fuck off laddie, every fucker in town knows to come 'ere.'

'I got notting for you, now fuck off.'

'Away man, summit just to tide me over.'

With that Jockie pulled out a twenty pound note. The big man looked at it, then took it off him, shut the door and returned inside to get Jockie's fix.

While the door was shut the other three came silently at full speed up the stairs pulling ski masks down over their faces. As the door was unlocked and started to open Timber hit it with all his strength at the handle. The door buckled, the big man inside went down on his knees having taken the full slam to the face and Paul followed by Mike and Jockie poured through the open doorway with Timber walking slowly behind, holding the fourteen pounder as though it was a simple pin hammer.

There were two others inside the flat. Both of which had their backs to the door playing a racing game on a computer console. They'd heard the bang as the door went in, but the speed of Paul's squad was such that neither of them had any time to react and their Uzi semi-automatic weapons were still on the big kitchen table with neatly rolled notes of every denomination and drugs of every type.

Paul and Jockie grabbed the guns up swiftly as they went past and with a fluid motion of many years' experience, primed and cocked them with expert hands, pointing them directly into the faces of the two racing car drivers.

'Who's in charge here?' Asked Paul, but the two game boys looked at each other and shrugged not understanding a word of anything he was saying.

'I guess the big fella's the spokesman for the group then.

Right Timber, drag large lad over here, then you and Mike outside by the van. I don't wanna get caught in here with no backup, quick as yeh like lads.'

Without what appeared to be any effort at all, the Timber dragged the semiconscious heavy lump of man mountain into the main room by his arms, picked up his Thor's hammer and with Mike, departed the flat.

Jockie had already started collecting all the money into a black plastic bin liner with the drugs and mobile phones into a second separate one. Paul stepped into the kitchen keeping the two foreign racing car drivers covered while he went and filled a pan with water from the cold tap. This he slowly poured onto the face of the man on the ground with a lump the size of a goose egg in the middle of his forehead. The other two remained kneeling on the floor with their fingers interlocked on top of their heads.

Gradually he started coming around spluttering and coughing, slowly and groggily he sat up against the wall.

'What fuck you want,' he said rubbing the lump on his forehead.

'We have everything we want,' said Paul, 'just tell your boss, that we are from out of town and we are moving in. Tell him to watch his back cos were coming to get him, understand?'

'I understand plenty. I understand you a fucking dead man.'

'Right all three of yeh up against the wall, now and quick about it.'

The big man passed on Paul's instructions to the two kneeling gamers and all three stood backs against the wall, hands on their heads. Paul switched off the automatic fire on the gun he was holding and rapidly fired a single shot through each one of the three's right foot.

'That should slow the fuckers down a bit,' said Paul as he watched them all writhing around on the floor swearing and cursing in some foreign language he didn't understand. Paul and Jockie quickly departed the flat with the guns, the money and the drugs.

The four of them all went back to the van and headed out of the city to Paul and Mikes place. Once there, they unloaded the van, bringing all the bags inside.

'Best to park the van 'round the corner Timber, just in case the house is being watched. We've already had a visit from them the other day while we were out.'

'Okay Vicker, back in a very short while.'

'So now then, what the fuck do we do wi' this lot?' Said Mike to his big brother.

'Right, pile all the money over on the kitchen worktop and you start countin' Mike. Let's see just how much those bastards 'ave fuckin' lost tonight. Jockie mate, you put all the drugs in one big bin liner. We got some large cooler boxes out the back yard from the boat, we can stash it out there in one of them fuckers for the time being. Keep the weapons handy though, we might just have need of them. Saves us usin' our own.'

Just then Timber walked back inside.

'Anyone fancy a nice cup of tea and a packet of biscuits or two, my treat?' With that he walked into the kitchen and put the kettle on.

'Right lads, let's get this stuff outta the way and grab a few hours shut eye. Mike have yeh done a tally yet?'

'Aye boss, a few quid under fifty three thou', five hundred,'

'Ouch! That's gonna hurt someone's fuckin' pocket, especially when yeh add the junk in the yard to it as well.

There's gonna be some very unhappy little fuckin' Albanians wakin' up, spittin' their dummies out this fuckin' mornin'.'

CHAPTER FIFTY-THREE

'Sorry to bother you so early Mr Demaci, but there seems to have been trouble through the night at a few of the drops.'

Donika Demaci pulled himself up before looking at the gold Patek Philippe wrist watch on the cabinet by the side of the bed. The time was just coming up to half past six.

'What kind of trouble are we talking about Bashkim?'

'Well, it would seem that some of our men have been attacked in the streets and one of the drop houses also raided. Each of the men inside received a bullet through the foot. Some of the street pushers seem to have been attacked as well, with all the drugs and money taken off them.'

'How much have we lost in revenue then?'

'Based on what the men have told me, it's over fifty thousand pounds in cash. But if you consider the drugs that were taken as well, you can at least double that figure.'

'And do we have any idea who is responsible for this atrocity?'

'No, not really sir, one of the men said he recognised a Scottish accent and another said they mentioned coming from out of town to take over.'

'Outrageous! Taking over! Fucking outsiders. Who the fuck do they think they are? Right Bashkim get straight onto it. I want this matter resolved immediately and it might be worth your while doubling security on the streets.'

'Yes sir, straight away, but Mr Demaci, this is not the act of amateurs, these men appear to be quite professional and military in their actions.'

'Even more reason for our people to be more vigilant then Bashkim.'

With that Donika Demaci hung up. Swung his legs out of bed and walked straight into the shower. The day had only just begun and already Donika Demaci was in a fierce mood. 'Fucking outsiders, who did they think they were fucking dealing with?'

CHAPTER FIFTY-FOUR

Sally woke with a smile on her pretty face, stretched her long lean body and reached over to tickle the hairs on Dave's chest. After a few second's he seemed to stir and scratch with irritation.

Sally started to giggle quietly watching his annoyance slowly building up. Eventually his eyes opened and once he realised the cause of his discomfort, he grabbed Sally under her arms and started to tickle, making her squirm and wriggle like an eel.

'Stop it, stop it, you'll wake the bairns. It's too early for them to get up. Let them sleep for a while longer.'

'Excuse me lady, but if I remember correctly, it was you that woke me up. I was havin' a great dream as well. I dreamt I was in bed with this long legged beauty who kept forcing me to have my evil way with her.'

'That wasn't a dream, yeh kept wakin' up through the night an 'avin' a quick grope. Then rollin' over and goin' back to sleep again yeh mucky pup.'

Dave put his arm around Sally's shoulder and she snuggled into him,

'What time is it Sal?'

'Just after seven, we're okay for a few minutes. Then I'll get up and make breckies.'

'When we get the kids off to school Im gonna hafta go to my place and get some clean clothes if I'm stayin' here a while.'

'Oh, so yeh intend stayin' a while do yeh? Well we'll need to do a food shop then.'

'Okay, so you come with us, we drop the kids off, go to my place then do a shop, be back before lunch. Oh! Then what can we do?'

Sally giggled again, 'whatever comes up lover, whatever comes up.'

With that Sally jumped naked out of bed and climbed straight into the shower. Back after a few minutes fresh faced and squeaky clean.

CHAPTER FIFTY-FIVE

Paul was also up and dressed early. Eating the first of his two slices of toast and drinking his big mug of tea. Mike was upstairs fast asleep, with the Timber sleeping in his room on an air bed and sleeping bag. Jockie had shared Paul's room, also on an air bed.

Paul just started on his second slice when his phone came alive, he answered it on the fourth ring.

'Ya, who is it?'

'Alright mate. It's me Jacko, from the Ship and Anchor, remember?'

'Aye, course I remember. Mornin' Jacko best mate, how you doin' this fine fuckin' mornin'?'

'Fuckin' good mate, fuckin' good, thanks for askin' though. Hey listen, I think I may have got summit. Summit what's maybe of interest to yeh. Can we have a meet somewhere?'

'Why not Jacko, where and when?'

'We could meet at the pub again, say around eleven if that's alright wi' you.'

'Excellent idea, see yeh later then, cheers.'

The only thing that Paul could think of was that friend Jacko had either some more news for him, or friend Jacko was selling him out to a higher bidder. Whichever way Paul would be there, but so would his back up in a white van. No point in taking any unnecessary chances with scum like Jacko.

The others came down in dribs and drabs, helping themselves to the tea, coffee and toast. Timber fried a full half pound of smoked bacon and ate the whole thing in a large stotty with HP sauce, not even thinking of offering any of it to anyone else.

Paul explained that he had a meeting and the lads would need to wait outside the pub in case of uninvited guests, there was an agreement by everyone on that. They further agreed that they wouldn't raid during daylight hours as there were too many potential eye witnesses about and the Albanians were bound to be jittery, putting extra security on after last night.

At half past ten, Paul and Mike got into the Mondeo with Jockie and Timber following close behind in the white transit. They all pulled into the car park of the Ship and Anchor and while Paul and Mike went inside, the other's waited outside and watched.

Paul ordered a pint of orange and Mike a pint of best bitter with a glass of coke. They wished Dougie a good morning and went out the back into the pool room. The room was empty apart from the skinny, dirty, skank playing pool by himself.

'Now then Jacko mate, here yeh go, brought yeh a nice refreshing pint just for good fuckin' measure, come an' sit down and let's hear what's on yeh mind.'

'Cheers mate. Listen, this is from a friend of a friend okay? But I think it's pretty accurate. It seems that there's been a ship arrived in port within the last few days with a mega

231

shipment of fuckin' uncut heroin on board for your Albanian fuckin' friends.

'Where'd you get this info from then Jacko?'

'Well I know this pretty boy. His names Simon, smashin' lad, works for one of them fuckin' escort agencies and he's gorra rich sugar daddy who likes 'im a lot and works from home mostly and this was overheard the other evening when the fuckin' rich guy was on the phone in his office.'

'And the rich guy's name is?'

'Only fuckin' Donika Demaci, mate.'

Paul and Mike leaned over the table, closer to Jacko.

'Are you sayin' Donika Demaci the fuckin' Albanian is gay.'

'No, what I'm sayin' is, Donika Demaci the Albanian is not so much fuckin' bent as he is fuckin' twisted. He likes hurting young boys yeh see and young Simon feels he's probably suffered enough and would maybe like to be in a position whereby he could inflict a little bit of fuckin' pain hisself.'

'Okay, but I need to speak with this fuckin' Simon as soon as you can arrange it?'

'Give us five minute's mate and consider it done.'

Jacko walked to the other side of the room taking his pint with him, returning a few minutes later with a big black and yellow toothy grin on his ugly spotty face.

'He'll be 'ere in fifteen minutes if yeh wanna fuckin' wait.'

'Ya, we'll stay,' Said Paul'

While they were waiting, Mike decided to go outside and tell the lads in the van what was happening and that they should keep their eyes open for any other big lads in white vans that may just follow young Simon into the bar. Mike then returned to the pool room.

Almost to the minute, a tall, slim, very well dressed young man in a light grey suit walked in. Looked around and made a beeline to Jacko. After a few words together Jacko walked over and introduced Simon to the brothers.

'Right guys, this is the lad I was tellin' yeh about. His name's Simon, I'll leave 'im wi' yeh cos I'm gonna practice over on the fuckin' pool table for a while outta the way. Shout us if yeh fuckin' need us.'

Jacko walked over to the other end of the pool room as Simon sat down at the table opposite Paul and Mike. It was difficult for the brothers not to see how beautiful Simon was and they both felt somewhat confused by their feelings. It was almost like looking at a pretty, vulnerable young lass in lads clothing and they felt that they should somehow be protecting him.

'Hi Simon. I'm not gonna tell yeh our names for obvious reasons, but we understand that yeh have some news about stuff comin' in by boat for the Albanians?'

'You're not undercover cops or owt are yeh? Cos don't yeh 'ave to tell us if yeh are?'

'No mate, we're not cops.'

'Right, okay then, well it's like this. I work for an agency owned by a Mr Donika Demaci and I was told the other day that if I wanted the job then I had to be interviewed personally by Mr Demaci at his apartment in the Tower Flats. Anyway, I got the job, but it seems that he's taken rather a shine to me. At least he has for now and I've been up to his place nearly every day this week. So, as I said to Jacko earlier, Mr Demaci does a lot of his business from home and yeh get to hear all sorts of weird stuff. Apparently he was bollocking his right hand man Bashkim for doin' summit stupid the other night at some elderly couple's house. Mr Demaci was goin' mad sayin it had better not compromise the big shipment that arrived earlier in the week on board a container ship called the Rangoon Princess. I don't know all the little fiddly stuff, but he said it could have a street value of more than four and a half million and it was goin' to be hidden in bags of cement arriving from Karachi.'

'Was that everything?'

'No, they talked for a little while longer, but I couldn't hear everything they said. I did make out that it was waiting for customs clearance, then it was gonna be delivered to building sites in the area and that one of the containers was specially marked. I think this Bashkim was gonna follow the container that was marked and pick up the stuff from the building site after it was delivered.'

'Right Simon, you've been a massive fuckin' help mate. Would it be too much to ask yeh to keep in touch if yeh hear owt else?'

'No love, that's fine. Do yeh want us to call yeh direct or should I call via Jacko.'

'Call me direct son, that way it will be quicker when the time comes. It also cuts out any middle man, so less chance of the wrong ears hearin' owt.'

Simon gave Paul his mobile number and Paul called it straight back leaving his number on Simons phone. They all shook hands and Paul gave Simon a hundred quid out of the drug haul money for the information, letting him know he would be well rewarded if it all went through as planned. Simon waved to them both in his gentle effeminate way and left.

'What the fuck do we do now bro, this is too fuckin' big for us to take on.'

Paul nodded to his younger brother in acknowledgement.

'Aye, I know. We may hafta get Dave's crew onta this fuckin' one mate. Come on we'll pop around to Sally's place and have a word.'

Paul and Mike got up to leave and Jacko came back over.

'So, gentlemen was that worth a visit? Did Jacko deliver the goods then?'

'Ya, ya, yeh did well Jacko lad, but keep your ears to the ground and if yeh hear owt else let us know. Right here's another hundred to tide yeh over. We'll be in touch soon okay?'

With a quick wave, the lads walked out, saying tarah to Dougie behind the bar as they left.

CHAPTER FIFTY-SIX

Sally and Dave walked hand in hand from the car and climbed the two flights of stairs leading to Dave's flat.

They'd all had breakfast together earlier and neither of the two bairns seemed to be showing any undue signs of stress or sorrow from having been told that their nana and grandad had passed away.

Dave drove both kids to school, then after, Sally and him did a bit of a shop at the local supermarket.

While they were out and had plenty of time, Dave figured they might as well drive around to his flat and pick up some clothes and any few bits and pieces he might need.

While Dave had been washing the breakfast pots earlier that morning, Sally had gone through all the drawers and cupboards emptying the last vestiges of Charlie ever having lived in the house. Putting everything in black bags ready to give to the next charity bag collection that came through the door, or failing that, put it all in the bin.

They'd both decided that if Charlie did come back, he would be asked to leave and Dave would stand Sally's corner with her. We all know that was never going to happen though, don't we?

Dave opened the door to the flat and asked Sally to excuse any mess. She must take into account him being a bachelor and as a rule didn't get too many visitors if any.

The whole place, although minimalistic, was furnished very modern and in good taste. Immaculate throughout with not a thing out of place. It was a two bedroom flat overlooking a park in a nice residential neighbourhood.

The flat had a small but fully functional kitchen, a large lounge cum dining area, one double bedroom with fitted wardrobes, dressing unit and a large king size divan bed against the only spare wall. The second bedroom was nearly as big but only contained a cheap Ikea desk with a computer on it and strewn around were various body building paraphernalia plus a weight bench.

'Make yourself at home sweetheart, I'll go empty the fridge and pack my gear into me holdall.'

'Can I 'ave a nose 'round then, or are yeh hidin' summit I shouldn't maybe see?'

'Help yourself Sal, I got nowt to hide from you.'

Dave went and emptied the contents of the fridge into a carrier bag to take back to Sally's place, then took his wash bag into the bathroom and filled it with his shower gel, razors and deodorants, finally he went to pack some clothes.

It was as he entered the master bedroom, that Sally began to shout breathlessly.

'Dave! Dave! Hurry up man, quickly.'

Dave ran into the spare bedroom and there laid on the weight bench was Sally with a thirty kilo bar in her hands, laid across crushing her chest.

'How the hell did yeh do that lass?' He asked lifting it easily off the recumbent form of his new lady love.

'I just saw it and figured I can do that, it looks easy on the telly,'

'Well it's easy liftin' them off, the hard part's puttin' them back up again. Besides them on the telly practice for hours every day, I wouldn't want you to have muscles like them, I quite like yeh just the size yeh are.'

'Well I know that now don't I? Besides I don't need a bloomin' lecture officer Riley, I need a kiss to make me feel better.'

Dave put his arm around her and as their lips locked, his doorbell rang.

'Who the hells that? They must 'ave been watching for us coming in.'

Dave pressed the intercom connected to the downstairs front door.

'Hello, who is it?'

'It's yeh mam and sister, aren't yeh gonna lerrus in then pet?'

Dave gave Sally a look of total frustration and shrugged his shoulders while pressing the electric catch to open downstairs door.

After a few minutes a middle aged lady and a pretty blond woman of around thirty walked through the door Dave was stood holding open. As they passed him, they both kissed him on the cheek.

'Oh, we didn't know yeh had company our Davey,' said his mam'

'Mam, Kate, this is Sally, Sally me mam and big sister Kate.'

Sally felt suddenly very vulnerable and quite speechless in front of the two older women.

'Hello Mrs Riley, nice to meet yeh and you Kate.'

The two women smiled. They were genuinely friendly

smiles and Sally began to relax. The women both made themselves comfy on Dave's big sofa in the lounge.

'So where are you two off to then? Anywhere nice? I can see you've got yeh bags packed our Davey,' said mam Riley

'I'm staying over at Sally's place for a while Mam, took a stint off work, so we can spend some time together.'

'Oh how lovely, have yeh known each other very long then?'

'We went to school together. I was in the same year as Sally's older brother Mike, but we lost touch for a little while, anyway I found her again.'

'Sally and Mike? Don't tell me yeh played netball and have an older brother called Paul as well?' Kate spoke for the first time.

'Aye, I do,' said Sally, 'why?'

'Well, if it's who I think it is, then your last name should be Vickers.'

'Ya, Sally Vickers, how on earth did yeh know all that?'

'I was in the same class as Paul Vickers, at the same school you's two went to. I had the biggest crush on him. Tall long dark hair past his shoulders, all the girls fancied big Paul Vickers, played rugby for the school team.'

Sally and Dave laughed out loud and looked at each other in disbelief, what a small world.

'Oh dear, I think maybe I should shut up, but was that your mam and dad we heard about on the telly last night in the fire Sally love?'

Sally nodded and mam Riley and Kate came over to her, together putting their arms around her. This of course set Sally off sobbing again and it took several minutes for her to regain her composure.

'That's one of the reasons, I'm goin' round to stay at

239

Sally's place. The other one is yeh couldn't keep me away if yeh tried, she's gorgeous.'

'She's most certainly that our Davey. Such a bonny young lass. You make sure yeh take good care of her me lad. You let me know Sally love if he misbehaves at all and I'll sort him straight out for yeh pet.'

'I was sorta hopin' he was goin' to misbehave a little bit Mrs Riley,' said Sally wiping her eyes on a tissue.

They all laughed. Small talking up in the flat for a few more minutes, then Dave ushered them all out saying they had to be on their way.

Dave locked up and all four descended the stairs together, with mam Riley and Kate getting in their car and Sally and Dave getting in theirs, they all waved, then drove off in opposite directions.

CHAPTER FIFTY-SEVEN

Mike was driving the Mondeo and pulled up outside Sally's house with Dave in the Golf pulling up directly behind.

'Oh bollocks,' said Dave.

'What's the matter Dave love?' Sally questioned.

'Why, I was plannin' on spendin' the afternoon 'avin' nookie with you Sal, that's bloody all.'

Sally laughed and laid her hand on his arm, 'don't worry lover, you'll get your share of nookie before the day's out, I promise.'

They all said their hello's whilst Sally unlocked the front door letting Paul and Mike in. Then went back to give Dave a hand with the shopping and his bag of clothes. When they all got inside, Mike had already put the kettle on.

'Now then,' said Paul, 'how you two doin'?'

'We're fine thanks, I keep havin' a few tears every now and again but otherwise we're all okay.'

'You settled in Dave? Sal and the kids drivin' yeh fuckin' nuts yet?'

'No, actually we've just been to my place and picked up some clean clothes and bathroom gear. Don't tell Sal but I'm slowly moving in bit by bit. Sally met me mam and older sister. Oh! And by the way, our Kate sends her love.'

'Kate, I don't think I know any Kate?'

'I hope yeh do, cos she remembers all about you apparently. Her and her mates thought you were quite hot with your long hair out on the rugby playin' fields. She was in your class, Kate Riley.'

'Fuckin' 'ell, aye. Excuse me mate but your sister was quite fanciable herself if I remember. Shit Kate Riley, who'd of thought.'

'Well if yeh want her number, I can give it to yeh. She's single, divorced actually, with a young lass of ten, Gina. Kate's ex was Italian, couldn't live without his momma though and Kate couldn't cook pasta to save her life by all accounts.'

'You know Dave, I may just fuckin' take you up on that. Your Kate was a right cracker. Okay, right, do yeh both wanna hear about what we got up to last night then?'

Sally brought the tea's over and sat next to Dave at the little kitchen table, while between Paul and Mike they verbally revisited the sorties of the night before. Excluding the shootings and violence that may have otherwise been frowned upon by the new family member of the law enforcement fraternity.

'So, you were all busy then. Where's Jockey and the Timber now?'

'They've gone for another look 'round, but I'm not sure we're gonna do anything more for the moment.'

'Why? Do yeh think you've maybe hurt them badly enough?'

'Nowhere near Dave lad. We're just gettin' fuckin' started. No, but I got some news this morning that may have changed things a little bit. That's why we needed to see you and get your thoughts on the subject.'

Paul explained to both Sally and Dave what had been said by Simon and Jacko at the Ship and Anchor. Dave listened attentively without saying anything until Paul and Mike had completely finished.

'So lads what is it yeh want me to do?'

'To be fuckin' honest Dave, this is a bit too big for us to handle. We don't 'ave the expertise to deal with it properly. This is gonna hurt the Albanians far more than anything we could do by ourselves, but we don't 'ave either the manpower or organisation skills required for summit of this fuckin' size. I think we may need the big bobbies.'

'Okay, so let's get this straight. Yeh want me to have a word with someone back at the shop? You know there gonna wanna speak with yeh about it don't yeh? You're probably gonna hafta confess to a few issues about last night and hand in the money and drugs yeh took once I let the cat out of the bag.'

'Ya I figured that much, but we didn't do it for the money or the drugs. We did it to hurt those fuckin' Albanian bastards and this'll hurt them much more. Besides we didn't know what to do with the drugs anyway and if there's a few fuckin' quid gone missin', who's to know?'

Dave and Sally both agreed this could be the best way forward and it gave them all a good chance of staying a little bit closer to the right side of the law. While Sally went to put the kettle on, Dave went into the living room to make some calls, returning just as the kettle boiled.

'Right lady and gentlemen. I've spoken to my desk Sergeant and he put me straight through to the guys in the National Crime Agency who are sending someone 'round within the next hour or so to have a little chat. Apparently, they're all fully aware of your escapades from last night and are well impressed. For them to have got that far in such a

243

short time would have meant cutting so much red tape, albeit they would have done it legally, they'd never have managed to get away with what you guys did. So you lot are up there in hero worship land with the lads on the front line. They said it seemed to have been well executed and they were particularly impressed cos no civvies had been involved or injured. Hopefully that will stand you guys in good stead with the law.'

The happy family talked around the kitchen table for a while longer, then Dave got up and went upstairs to unpack his bag while Sally came and sat on the bed chatting to him about her past life in general.

Nothing was mentioned about the beatings and the abuse that Sally had received at the hands of Charlie. She was worried that this might inflame a resentment and anger in Dave that there was no possibility of him ever being able to extinguish. Maybe when and if their relationship grew, there might be a time at a later date when she would tell him, but for now with everything else going on, this was not it.

Sally and Dave heard the knock at the front door and both came downstairs together. Paul had already opened it to two very casually dressed plainclothes officers. He let them in and everyone entered the living room, with Mike and Dave carrying the bench seats from the kitchen so there would be enough for everyone to sit on.

'Hello folks, my name is Detective Chief Inspector John Turner and this is my associate Detective Sergeant Barry Whitmore. We are NCA officers and at this moment in time we have been assigned to the drug enforcement department. We understand from Constable Riley here that you were personally responsible for the raids carried out last night on the drug drops in the Seaborough city centre is that correct Mr Vickers?'

Paul nodded his head in acknowledgement.

'Right, can you please explain to me the purpose behind those incidents?'

Paul went into an extremely edited version of the events leading up to the raids. Explaining that Charlie may have had dealings with Oggy and then done a runner with some goods. Oggy in turn had dealings with the Albanians and then the Albanians turned up looking for Charlie.

Paul explained that it was his belief, the Albanians were solely responsible for their parent's deaths and the fire that had been started around the corner was the result of an incident between Mike and Hamiti and it had been the fire and death of his parents that had instigated his retaliation against the drug lord Donika Demaci and his henchman Bashkim Hamiti.

Paul further explained, without giving out any names or too many details, that information had come into his possession of a large shipment of heroin with a street value of around four point five million pounds being delivered within the next few days.

'So, at no time Mr Vickers did you ever consider notifying the police of any of this information?'

'I just did mate, that's why your fuckin' sat in my sister's house now.'

'What about the fire? You could have come forward with information appertaining to that.'

'Aye I could 'ave and I'm sure you'd 'ave said you were all goin' to look into it. Listen mate, in case you 'aven't noticed yet, we live in Westernside. The police don't come here unless they really 'ave to and when they do, they don't investigate crimes with any enthusiasm, cos they all fuckin' believe this is where all the fuckin' criminals live in the first place and we all probably deserve whatever we get.'

'Mr Vickers, you could be charged with an obstruction of justice and with criminal intent out on the streets last night.'

'Yeh I could and I really don't give a fuck mate. I have no police record, I served my country, what's the worst that could happen to me? I go down for a few fuckin' months? Who gives a fuck. Look around the area mate, what do yeh really think I'd be giving up? However, you on the other hand Inspector, you're gonna look like a right fuckin' ploncket when the press hear that you were more eager to nail someone from Westernside for not tellin' fuckin' tales, rather than apprehending a very powerful drug lord who's maybe just put four and a half million pounds worth of illegal drugs on the street. So Inspector, who do you thinks gonna look like a daft twat? Cos I'm not sayin another word now. Not without some sort of fuckin' assurances from you, that me, my family and my friends are gonna be exempt from any fuckin' prosecution.'

Inspector Turner and sergeant Whitmore looked at each other and smiled, then the smile broadened and they both laughed out loud.

'Sorry Mr Vickers, Paul, isn't it? We had to be sure we were dealing with the right person and I think you just showed us all, yeh might just be the right person.'

'Well guys, yeh fuckin' lost me. Do I 'ave your fuckin' assurances or not?'

'Yes, yes of course you do Paul. We've been trying to apprehend and put Danika Demaci behind bars for years and without any success as you may well know. We have a file on him and his operations nearly a foot thick. Damn right we want him and at any cost I might add.'

Inspector Turner then asked Paul to go over all the information he'd been given that morning. Not once asking for any details or the names of any of his informants.

Paul was forthcoming with most of the information, but

was adamant that he and his team must be part of the final skirmish. Paul further insisted to inspector Turner that when the time came and the police were unable, for whatever reason, to apprehend or hold either Danika Demaci or Bashkim Hamiti, then the officers of the law would turn a blind eye so Paul could enforce his own law, with his own people.

Inspector Turner said he was not in a position to agree to those quite illegal terms. However after he'd advised against any vigilantly heroics, he further assured Paul that there were times with any operation of this magnitude when things become somewhat chaotic and all the tactics which had been so scrupulously planned on paper, can sometimes go horribly wrong. Then, it was just a matter of picking up the pieces later and doing what needed to be done. In other words don't worry mate, you'll get your chance.

Paul was somewhat placated and told the Inspector to be ready, it was now just a matter of waiting for the cargo offloaded from Rangoon Princess to be released and delivered.

CHAPTER FIFTY-EIGHT

Donika Demaci hung up from the call he'd just made to the shipping agents local office. Having been advised that the goods being held in the customs clearance warehouse should be released by the following afternoon.

All Bills of Lading had been produced and as the cargo was not of any significant health risk, any danger to the public or to their knowledge, flagged for x-ray, then there should be no further hold ups.

The agent had also advised that he had made arrangements for the containers to be loaded onto the back of flat trucks for delivery to the various sites the morning after, as stipulated on his instruction sheet. However the pallets must be lifted off at the sites by forklift as they would not be permitted to lift containers off the back of the wagons for any reason. Any delays to the three hours unloading fee would incur extra costs.

Demaci had agreed to all the instructions letting the agent know that he was fully conversant with the agreement and contract and that he would have his people standing by waiting, ready to unload the containers immediately upon their arrival. If the agent would be so kind as to advise what time the trucks would be leaving the warehouse area and a reasonable expected delivery time.

Bashkim Hamiti had been present throughout the conversation and had made mental notes of all that was being said. He had also been on his own phone during the conversation with the agent, organising the white van and a couple of strong lads to load it.

'We're all ready to go Mr Demaci, everything's set up at our end,'

'Good, good and do they know where to take the bags once they have them on the van,'

'No, not yet sir. I will be there and direct them to the laboratory where the heroin will be broken down. They will have no use of that knowledge just yet.'

'As you wish Bashkim. You do know I won't be with you so please ensure there are no problems from our end.'

'Yes of course Mr Demaci.'

'Okay, so what is the latest with that fiasco from the other night? Are we any further ahead in finding out who was responsible?'

'I have spoken to all our associates sir and nobody has a clue. There are no rumours or allegations circulating from anybody, it's almost as though it never happened. Except we are a considerable amount short on profits.'

'Well this must be resolved Bashkim otherwise it may happen again and we can't allow that. We will become a laughing stock. First the Oggy incident then this the other night. I don't believe them to be related, however once we get this shipment secured I want you to give it your full attention, do you understand? If we give anything else away, we're going to start looking like a fucking charity.'

CHAPTER FIFTY-NINE

'Right, quiet, all of you, please pay attention.'

DCI Turner was addressing the full crew that would be attending the raid at the building site.

'The gentlemen sat at the back of the room, are two of the four civilians personally responsible for the attack and taking down of the drug drops the other night.'

There was a huge cheer went up from the plain clothes officers and a round of applause reverberated throughout the large incident room. Paul and Mike gave a nod in confirmation of the accolades being bestowed upon them and Dave who was sat next to them smiled at the uncomfortable embarrassment they were both feeling.

'Right, now listen up. These gentlemen have been given information appertaining to a serious import of heroin to be delivered to a building site nearby and have come to us with that information. We have already been in touch with our dear friends at Her Majesties Customs and Excise over at the container terminal warehouse and they've assured us that they will also be making a presence on the raid and will be adding their own charges to those we will be issuing. We further understand, that the goods will be released by customs tomorrow afternoon and delivered by road truck the morning after. We will have our own drivers attending the trucks and some of you will be placed on the various sites as building employees, so please wear your big boots cos your all gonna get mucky. At this present moment in time we do not know which of the containers is carrying the heroin, however we do know from sources that there is a total of twenty kilos with a kilo in each of twenty bags of cement imported to our fair city from Karachi. These twenty bags will be picked up at the building site by a white transit van, which will be following a marked container, any questions?'

No one had their hands up, so the Chief Inspector carried on.

'You might also like to know that the goods we are going after, belong to our long standing friendly Albanian, Danika Demaci and company. I would be very surprised if he was to make an appearance, however I'm sure his good friend Bashkim Hamiti is going to be there. As you are all aware these people carry weapons and have been tooled up in the past therefore we will have armed officers with us. You must also be advised that Hamiti is one evil little shit and do not be taken in by his outward appearance. He is without doubt a fucking hard, nasty, vicious, little bastard. To those of you who do not understand the political implications. Because the border patrol are involved, they have access and can confiscate anything they believe to be involved in the import of illegal substances, bought into the country by illegal means. This indicates that we will all have the legal access we need to Demaci and his business records if he is so implicated. That being said, I want all of you here at thirteen hundred tomorrow and we will issue any further updates we might have.'

Turner walked over to Paul and Mike as the other officers filed out of the room.

'So Paul, Mike is that about everything? Do you have any questions at this time?'

'No thanks Boss, we're good. Do yeh want us here tomorrow afternoon?'

'No, I don't think that will be necessary Paul. We can let you know what's happening by phone and I'm sure you will have your own sources advising you. What I would say to you is lay low and keep off the streets until this is over. We don't want to spook anybody, capisce?'

'Understood, we're gonna go back home and we'll be in touch if we hear owt.'

Turner then faced Dave.

'Constable, you have been seconded to this department for the period of this operation. Your main objective is to attend with the Vickers crew and keep them out of any mischief. You will not be involved with any of the operation directly, but indirectly you may be drawn in as and if required, are you okay with that?'

'Yes sir, thank you sir.'

'Good, if this works out and we get what we're after, I might even be able to put in a request that you join us on a more permanent basis. How would that suit you?'

'Suits me very well sir, thanks.'

'Right, now if there's nothing else then I'm off and would suggest you all make yourselves scarce. Oh! by the way Paul, the drugs you picked up the other night, we would appreciate them being put into our lock up at your earliest convenience, as they'll probably be used as evidence in any forthcoming prosecutions. As for the money, I would anticipate at least, what can we say, maybe twenty thousand you would have confiscated. Give or take a pound here or there of course, does that sound about right to you?'

    'Yes inspector, twenty thousand to the penny we found.'

    'Good. Good night then gentlemen.'

CHAPTER SIXTY

Dave left the two Vickers lads at the police station and drove himself back to Sally's house. Paul and Mike were going to drive back to their own place taking the Mondeo, then relax and have an early night after having been up most of the night before. They were also going to have to explain to both Jockie and Timber what had been said during the police briefing.

Sally was sat on the sofa in her pyjamas with her bare feet tucked up underneath watching the telly when Dave let himself in through the front door. He walked over and kissed her before sitting down and kicking his old trainers off.

'Where's the kids?'

'The kids are upstairs in bed Mr Riley. Bathed and storied. I told them that maybe you would pop up and say night, night, if yeh got back early enough, but that was a long while ago and they're probably both fast asleep by now.'

'I'll go up and check, won't be a mo.'

Dave ran quietly up the stairs and poked his head around the door whispering,

'Is anybody in here still awake?'

He heard a little giggle from the top bunk, where little

Charlie slept. Dave walked over and leant against the top rail.

'You still awake then mate?' He whispered.

'Ya, I was tryin to stay awake teh say g'night.'

'Why yeh must be shattered man. Away tuck yeh self in and get some kip, up early for you in the mornin' school day yeh know.'

'Dave, can I ask yeh summit?'

'Course yeh can mate, yeh can ask me anything yeh like.'

'Do yeh like our mam lots? I mean do yeh maybe love our mam?'

'Aye I do sunna, I love yeh mam loads, why?'

'Cos if yeh love her, does that mean you'll stay with us.'

'Well no one can be a hundred percent certain our kid, but as far as I'm concerned, I really want us all to stay together. I think you and me are becomin' really good mate's, don't you?'

'Ya. Me and our Georgia like yeh bein here and we like to see me mam happy and laughin' all the time too. She didn't used to, you won't never hurt me mam will yeh?

'How do yeh mean Charlie son, hurt her?'

'Well, me dad used to shout at Mam and swear a lot. Then he'd bray her for no reason and she would have bruised black eyes and bust lips and stuff on a mornin'. You'd never do that to our mam would yeh.'

'No son, I would never do that to yeh mam. She's far too precious to me.'

'Good! Night, night, then Dave and thanks.'

'Night, night, Charlie son and there's no need to thank me man. I'm always here if yeh wanna talk about owt, okay?'

There was no answer this time, the heavy breathing from the top bunk indicated that Charlie was already in the land of nod.

Dave took several deep breaths before he went down

the stairs. He needed to clear his head and get rid of the anger that had so quickly manifest itself inside him. The idea that someone could or would lay a hand on Sally was in his mind so unbelievable and yet how many times as a police officer had he been called on to attend a domestic disturbance. This was different though, this was him and Sally, the others were strangers, people he would never really get to know.

'You were a long time. Thought maybe yeh'd gone to bed without us.'

'No, Charlie was still awake, so we had a bit of a man to man talk.'

'Oh aye, and what may I ask are you two getting' up to?'

Dave put his arm around her and pulled her to him, Sally in turn snuggled in closer.

'Excuse me lady, this was guy stuff. I would be breaking a serious ethical code of conduct and regulations if I was to divulge to a lass that which was talked about between two lads.'

'Okay, I guess yeh don't want any of that nookie stuff yeh was so keen on havin' earlier then.'

'Away man, yeh can't do that Sal. Yeh not allowed to blackmail officers of the law with nookie yeh know. There's a rule against it in a law book I read somewhere, I'm sure I've seen it.'

Dave bent over and kissed Sally a long lingering kiss on the lips, mouths parted and tongues entangled with each other's and as they kissed. Dave's hand undid a button on Sally's pyjama top and he slipped his hand in, finding and cupping a naked breast, he then gently rolled the erect nipple in between his thumb and forefinger.

'About that nookie Sal. I am prepared to beg yeh know.'

'Good. I quite fancy the idea of yeh down on your knees in front of me. Away upstairs and turn the lights off on your way officer Riley.'

CHAPTER SIXTY-ONE

Paul and Mike arrived back at the house. Everything was quiet as they entered the front door. The two other squaddies were sat watching the football on the television each drinking a can of coke and munching on salt and vinegar crisps.

'Listen lads, things 'ave changed a little bit and it doesn't look as though we'll be goin out on anymore raids tonight. So relax and if yeh wanna have a beer, there's plenty in the fridge, go and help yeh selves.'

'So, what's happened then Vicker? Why the change of heart?' Asked the Timber.

'Circumstances mate. We had a long discussion at the cop shop with that DCI Turner. He seems like a decent sort, anyway, he's given us quite a lot of leeway with this whole fuckin' thing, so Mike and I have had to give certain assurances that we would hold off with any more raids until at least after delivery of the heroin. We figured it was only fair, we don't wanna fuck owt up now do we?'

'So, are yeh meanin', that wee Timber and yours truly here are fuckin' redundant then? Surplus to fuckin' requirements so to speak Vicker?'

'No, not at all Jockie lad. We're still gonna be fuckin' operational, but we'll just have to wait and see how this police operation pans out before we can make our next move. Don't worry Jockie, there's still plenty of fuckin' violence for yeh, but yeh may have to wait a little while to get yer next fix. Maybe a day or two, that's all.'

'Right,' said Mike, 'the beers are on me,' as he passed out four cold ones from the fridge.

Jockie and the Timber continued watching the football while Paul took Mike back into the kitchen area.

'Listen mate, I need to talk to yeh about summit that's been buggin' us since the fire. Mam and Dad owned their house outright didn't they?'

'Aye, as far as I know they did bro, I remember while you was away in Afghanistan, Sally and the fat fuck came 'round to Mam and Dads place for champagne to celebrate, why you askin'?'

'Okay, but did Dad ever sign over to you the ownership of the Bonny Doris?'

'No mate, not a chance. She was Dads pride and joy man.'

'Well, the point I'm makin' is. If dad never upgraded his fuckin' will or signed the Bonny Doris over to yeh, then there's a possibility she's gonna hafta be sold as part of the estate and we may end up losin' her.'

'Well that can't be right. Can't we just buy her back then?'

'I don't know kidda, I don't know a lot about this kinda stuff. It's just summit that's been on me mind is all.'

'We can always go and see their solicitors and ask, can't we?'

'I'm not sure Mikey. Will they give us that kind of

259

information? I mean, theoretically they worked for Mam and Dad not us.'

'Well let's get all this shit out of the way first and then we can start to concentrate on our mam and dads business. We owe it to them to give em both a good send off as well bro. No expense spared eh?'

'Damn fuckin' right our lad. The biggest fuckin' party this towns ever fuckin' seen.'

The two brothers lifted their cans and in unison toasted, 'Mam and Dad.'

CHAPTER SIXTY-TWO

'Come on up Simon, I've been waiting for you.'

Donika Demaci pressed the buzzer for the downstairs doors to open, allowing young Simon to enter and come up to the eleventh floor.

Simon had been engaged in the entertainment of an out of town businessman when he'd received the call from the agency telling him to literally drop whatever he was holding on to and get around to the boss's apartment. So here he was.

His last client was not a very happy camper, having to complete the job in hand all by himself.

Simon entered the flat by the front door that had been left open purposely. Demaci waved him in whilst still on the phone, making last minute preparations for the dropping off of the heroin.

'Yes, I know the drops at the fucking new Hidden Valley housing estate but you tell that fucking site foreman he had better be there to receive the shipment. He's being paid enough fucking money. The least he can fucking do is turn up. I do not give a flying fuck that his scrawny kid has been taken into fucking hospital. I do not want a single fucking thing to go wrong Bashkim, do you understand me, not a single fucking thing.'

Demaci stormed around the apartment in his silk kimono, going from room to room ranting and raving until he gradually started to calm down. Simon poured him a large glass of the expensive 1966 Dalmore Constellation single malt and he swallowed it in one gulp, holding his empty glass out for a refill.

With his glass replenished, Demaci sat down on the big leather sofa and put his head back while Simon walked behind and massaged his shoulders and temples.

'There, there, Donika darling, relax. None of this is worth the heart attack you're going to end up having if you don't calm yourself down. Come into the bedroom and let me make you more comfortable and remove some of those nasty, ugly, anxieties you're feeling, come on.'

As Simon spoke, he'd been stripping out of his clothes and had just thrown off the silk trunks, the last item before being totally naked. Wiggling his tight butt in Demaci's face he then turned and tempted him with his semi hard erection into the bedroom, Demaci followed like a lost puppy.

As was Demaci's way, Simon was asked to leave after he'd been used. Demaci lay naked on the bed totally exhausted watching him dress.

'Simon a question for you. If I were to ask you to move in with me, would you? You would be well provided for and have a very comfortable life style.'

'Yes, Mr Demaci darling, I'm sure I would. For a while that is, or at least until you became bored with me, or I put on too much weight, or a wrinkle or two appeared, or maybe even my hair began to thin and then you would be looking for someone much younger and I would be out on the street. No thank you my lovely man, this suits me fine, but a very kind offer nonetheless.'

Simon let himself out of the flat and as he went down in the lift he sent a text message to Paul's phone.

'Delivery to be at the new Hidden Valley housing estate. Site foreman trying to back out. Lotsa love bigboy. Simon xXx.'

CHAPTER SIXTY-THREE

Dave woke before Sally this morning and jumped in the shower without disturbing her. He'd showered and dressed and she was still breathing heavily, a slight smile across her beautiful porcelain face. 'Why would anyone want to harm that?' He thought.

Leaving her tucked up in bed, he went downstairs to the kitchen flicking the kettle switch on while he made toast in the electric toaster. He even managed to find the margarine and some strawberry jam and took that together with her coffee and his tea back upstairs.

'Away Lady Muck, let's be 'avin yeh, wakie, wakie, time.'

Dave stood at the end of the bed and watched the smile on Sally's face broaden as she stretched, then her bleary eyes eventually opened and she looked back at him.

'What you doin' up so early man? And dressed as well.'

'Ya, and made you coffee and toast in bed. How's that for service then?'

'Well officer Riley, I really don't know what to say. I've never had breckie's in bed before.'

'Well young lady, there's a first time for everything.'

Sally sat up with a pillow behind her and Dave laid on top of the bed next to her in his t-shirt and boxers, with his own mug of tea, helping himself to a couple of pieces of toast and jam.

'Hey mister, yeh can't just nick a lasses breckie's yeh know. I don't know, your takin' advantage of me officer Riley, nookie of a night, toast and jam of a mornin'. I'll never get rid of yeh.'

'Good cos I had no intention of leavin' anyway. Hey listen Sal, I never told yeh this last night, but that DCI Turner may be able to offer us a promotion to his crew if this job goes as planned.'

'Is that what yer wantin' then Dave, a promotion?'

'It'll be good for us Sal, more money, better prospects and all.'

'Ya, but that's your business Dave, it's nowt to do wi' us, is it?'

'Well I'm hopin' it has everything to do with us Sal, isn't it what yeh want like?'

'I'm not altogether sure what the offer is Dave.'

'Well I'm hopin' we're gonna be a team, a family, yeh know, what's mine is yours and vice versa. A relationship, or am I steppin' out o' line here?'

'No, my love, you're not steppin' out o' line. I was just thinkin' how well I was doin' getting coffee and toast in bed, now you're offerin' me a relationship too.'

'Well I know, we haven't been together very long and in that short time we've been together there's been so much goin' on. But during all of it and maybe it's just my imagination, but we've really been good together, or at least I thought we had.'

'I can't argue with any of that Dave my love. But miss

265

thicky nickers here, still isn't sure of what yeh sayin'.'

'I'm sayin I love yeh Sally and I want us to be together as a couple, as a family, properly, forever.'

'What, like married and everything?'

'Yes! Eventually anyway. But don't yeh hafta get a divorce first?'

'What kind of girl do yeh take me for David Riley? Nookie, coffee, jam on toast and a sort of proposal. Yeh must think I'm dead easy. If your proposin', which I'm assumin' that yeh might just be, then I'm gonna wanna nice ring with a real, not a fake, but a real shiny stone in the middle of it.'

'Then will it be official Sal?'

'Signed, sealed and delivered and I'll be yours. I was anyhow David Riley, I knew that not long after meetin' yeh. I was just waitin' for you to catch up. Do we 'ave time for some more of that there nookie stuff, before the kids wake up do yeh think?'

CHAPTER SIXTY-FOUR

Paul was the first down and made himself a fried egg on toast before any of the other lads had surfaced. It was the Timber who came down next, obviously having smelt the food.

'How many eggs mate?' Said Paul

'Just make it an even half dozen Vicker. Here, I'll do it if you like. I'm fairly good in the kitchen. Besides you go and enjoy your own breakfast, no need to wait on me.'

Paul sat and watched in amazement as the Timber made himself a six egg omelette with four slices of toast and a spiffing mug of tea.

The light on his mobile was flashing to show that he'd had a message and when he checked, he saw what Simon had left during the early hours. Paul would have been fast asleep at the time it arrived anyway and he didn't even think of taking his phone to bed with him. Not after four cans of lager.

The other three had stayed downstairs drinking beer, with the two ex servicemen reminiscing their war time stories with his kid brother until halfway through the night.

He looked at his watch and it was just coming up to

eight fifteen. May just catch DCI Turner on his way into the office. Paul dialled the inspectors number and waited.

'Turner here.'

'Mornin Chief, not gotcha out of bed, have I? Paul Vickers here.'

'No Paul not at all. A quiet night I trust?'

'Aye, very quiet thanks. I haven't actually been up too long meself, but I got a message on me phone through the night giving the drop address and thought yeh might be a wee bit interested.'

'Absolutely Paul, what is it please?'

'Well according to this, its goin' to be the new Hidden Valley housing estate and by all accounts the site foreman is tryin' to back out of his end of the deal.'

'Well that's good to know, a bit of bargaining power. Thanks very much for the update Paul, keep in touch and we'll let you know what time in the morning. Okay, cheers now.'

With that Inspector Turner hung up and Paul went to make himself another cup of tea.

Not long after that the others started to surface and when Paul had everyone's attention he shared Simon's message from the night before, letting them all know it was probably going to be a quiet day and night, so they should all chill out and relax. Tomorrow was going to be a busy day.

Mike and Paul also decided they would call around to Sally's place later in the day and have a bit of a chin wag with her and Dave. Letting them both know what was going on.

CHAPTER SIXTY-FIVE

'Okay ladies and gentlemen, if I can have your undivided attention please.'

It was thirteen hundred hours on the dot and Detective Chief Inspector John Turner was addressing the undercover officers of the National Crime Agency, together with officers from the Border Force, who had also been invited to the brief.

'We've all read the reports and you understand the people we are dealing with. Firstly I want no bloody heroics, there should be no need. We will be going in with team leaders in charge of small groups. You are all aware of who your team leaders are and they in turn have already been briefed with their own specific stratagems. Obviously, we know which wagon will contain the goods as per the manifest and consignment numbers and we know the site the goods will be delivered to, so that will be easy enough to follow. We are not after the drugs at this stage. We already have those so to speak, at least we know where they are. What we do want is as many as possible of those nasty little bastard villain's responsible for contaminating our Seaborough city limits with their filth. We mainly want the two at the top Mr Demaci and Mr Hamiti, they are our main targets. But unfortunately, we may only see one of them and that will have to suffice. Team alpha will be responsible for allowing the white van to load the bags and they will follow it out to wherever they may be storing or breaking it down. The weather is supposed to be clear and dry so we will be using the eyes in the skies to watch over us all and help pick up any stragglers who may have drifted or should we say legged it away from the scene. I'm anticipating that Hamiti will be there somewhere and probably not too far from the heroin's final destination. I cannot stress enough, be very fucking careful dealing with this man, he is extremely dangerous.

The good news is that we have the site foreman now on our side after persuading him that a long prison sentence was not in his best interests. He has no real details of Demaci's operation, his role was simply to turn a blind eye when the van came to collect the goods, after that he was surplus to any requirements and it wouldn't have surprised me to have found him at a later date face down in a corner of his own building site with a broken neck. The same as the illegal immigrant Mr Oghuz Galata who we found alongside the rail tracks last week. They won't want to keep any witnesses to their operations or their identities. That's it ladies and gentlemen, we will all re-convene here at zero seven hundred in the morning. The cargo will be released from the customs lockup at sixteen hundred today and will be loaded onto the trucks at zero eight hundred tomorrow ready to roll. Any questions? None? Good then let's all work together on this one and have a good afternoon.'

CHAPTER SIXTY-SIX

'Pour yourself some coffee Bashkim, you know where it is. What's the latest with these outsiders from the other night? Do we have any news yet?'

'No sir, as I said to you yesterday, there's not a word being spoken by anyone. There's nobody selling anything let alone at discount prices. It's as if it never happened.'

'You don't suppose our own people may have been responsible for this and pocketed the money, do you?'

'I thought of that sir, but it's highly unlikely they would have shot themselves in the foot to make it look good. No, whoever did this also took the automatic weapons and they knew how to use them.'

'They say there was four of them and one was Scottish is that correct? And have you doubled the security as I requested?'

'Yes sir. But the Scot wasn't the ring leader. They also said that there was a very big man with a sledge hammer. They think he may have been black, although they were all apparently wearing ski masks and gloves, except the Scottish one.'

'Okay Bashkim, we need to get this sorted out. I feel as though we're missing the obvious somewhere, but I don't know where.'

While they were talking, Demaci's phone rang and he walked over to his desk to answer it.

'Hello Demaci here. Ah yes. Fine thank you and your good self? Excellent, yes, yes, very good, yes that will be fine. Okay thank you for calling, and to you, goodbye.'

Demaci put the phone back on his desk and sat in the big executive chair, slowly spinning around.

'That Bashkim, was the shipping agent. Customs have released the containers and we will have them loaded onto the truck in the morning for delivery. They should arrive on site by around zero nine hundred hours.'

'Do you want me to follow the truck to the site?'

'No, I don't think that will be necessary. Let the others follow the truck, you can go directly to the site and wait for its arrival. You've had a word with the site foreman haven't you? He's back in line again is he?'

'Yes sir, he understands the alternatives. He won't give us any further problems and when this is over, he may just have to have a fall and break his neck at the bottom of a ladder somehow.'

'Yes, that would probably be the better solution. Right Bashkim if you will excuse me, I have some calls to make, then I'm going to take a long shower and maybe go for a nice meal out. You go home and relax and after tomorrow, we should be considerably wealthier people. Make sure you phone me when everything is completed, alright?'

'Yes sir Mr Demaci, have a good evening, enjoy your dinner.'

'Thank you, goodnight Bashkim.'

CHAPTER SIXTY-SEVEN

Paul knocked on Sally's door and walked in, closely followed by Mike, the downstairs was empty but muffled voices could be heard upstairs.

'Yeh don't suppose they're upstairs at it again do yeh Mike? It's getting fuckin' embarrassing to come 'round here nowadays man.'

Mike laughed then shouted upstairs,

'If you two are shaggin' can yeh please stop it for a minute and come fuckin' down for some fresh air?'

It was little Georgia who walked down on the brothers.

'Hi uncle Paulie, hya uncle Mikey, they're not shaggin' whatever that is. Me mam's tryin on her new dress what Dave's just bought for her and her new shoes and a bonny posh ring too. Me mams turnin' into a real bonny posh princess, you'll see.'

Sally walked down the stairs in a black off the shoulder mini dress, with four inch heels on her black ankle strapped platform shoes. She looked stunning.

'So what yeh think then lads?' As Sally made a twirl.

Both her male siblings were gob smacked, bongy eyed

and slack jawed,

'Fuck Sal yeh look absolutely gorgeous,' said Mike.

'Yeh can double that lass,' Paul replied proudly.

'Dave bought them for us and he's takin' us out for dinner somewhere really nice tonight. Oh and whatcha think of this then?'

Sally held out her left hand and the sparkle that shone off her ring finger blinded the pair of them.

'What's goin' on man?' Paul's face was a picture of pure confusion.

'I asked your sister if she would marry me,' said Dave coming down the stairs with little Charlie on his shoulders, 'and she's said yes.'

'Whoa! Hang about man, she's not even divorced yet. Yeh move fast Dave lad, I gotta give yeh credit for that, you've only bin together five fuckin' minutes man.'

'Well, we talked about it and decided we know that we can't get married yet. But there's nowt stoppin' us from gettin' engaged while we wait for Sal's divorce to come through is there? We're gonna see a solicitor next week to start proceedings.'

'Well fuck me. Congratulations then the pair of yeh, I really hope yeh both gonna be very happy. Honestly, fuck I'm fillin' up man.'

Paul walked over and hugged his baby sister kissing her on the cheek then went and gave Dave a big guy hug as well.

'Fuck man, Mam and Dad woulda been so chuffed with the two of yeh.'

'Mike gave them both a double hug and took a step back to look at them.

'I said from the beginning you two would make a great looking couple and I wasn't too far wrong was I?'

'So what yeh doin' with the bairns tonight then?' Asked Paul.

'We're droppin' them off at Jenny's for the night and I'll walk 'round in the mornin' to take them to school, while Dave here goes to work. Not before time I might add.'

'Well we only came 'round to give yeh both the heads up on what's been goin' on, but obviously yeh don't really give a fuck now, do yeh?'

'I had DCI Turner on the phone a little while before yeh got here Paul and he's given me my instructions. I'm to shadow you guys and stay with yeh to give yeh some sort of credence for yeh bein' there. So, I'll come 'round to your place in the morning say about half six if that's alright.'

'Brill Dave lad, that works for me. We'll see yeh in the morning then, bright eyed and bushy tailed as they say. Try not to wear 'im out tonight Sal, he's got work tomorra.'

CHAPTER SIXTY-EIGHT

Demaci was dressed in a light grey pinstripe suit with a black shirt and silver grey tie. On his feet, he was wearing grey silk socks and his black, very highly polished brogues. A second glance in the full length mirror in the bedroom impressed him enough to make him smile, he then gave himself a wink and nod of approval.

Earlier that afternoon he'd phoned the escort agency and told them he would like to take Simon out to dinner at the La Parisienne restaurant in downtown Seaborough and for him to meet him there at twenty hundred hours, eight o'clock in the evening to the rest of us.

The restaurant was only a ten minutes' walk from the Tower Flats and as it was a pleasant evening he decided to take a relaxing stroll.

It was Thursday evening and the restaurant was not too full. Demaci had already made reservations and even if he hadn't, the Maitre'd knew him well enough to make an exception and find him a table regardless of how full they might have been.

Demaci decided to have a drink at the bar while waiting for Simon to arrive and as they poured him a large glass of the Johnny Walker blue label he quietly sat on a bar stool and perused the menu.

Outside he noticed a small yellow car pull up and a very handsome young man in his mid twenties exited the driver's side and chivalrously walked around to open the passenger side door to a stunning young woman wearing a very short cut black dress, with high heeled black shoes. Her sandy coloured hair was also cut short and her very slim figure almost boyish. Although in general terms Demaci had no interest whatsoever in the female of the species, he found both the man and the young woman altogether incredibly attractive.

They both entered the restaurant holding hands and smiling into each other's eyes and for a split second Demaci felt a twinge of absolute jealousy. The idea of being in love and having someone loving you back for no reason other than they wanted to, was something that he realised all the money in the world was unable to buy. He'd even offered what he considered to be a very good deal to Simon and had it refused. Was Demaci himself so shallow that nobody could love him for himself? There was a question not worth considering if he intended to enjoy his evening.

Simon entered a few minutes later and stood awkwardly in front of Demaci. Did they kiss, shake hands or just manly slap each other on the back. Surprisingly it was Demaci who took the initiative by walking over and kissing Simon on both cheeks in a very European, cosmopolitan sort of way, whereby no offence could be taken. Even in the northeast of England where men were men and so were some of the women.

The Maitre'd showed them to their table tucked

privately in a secluded corner of the dining room, unobserved by anybody casually walking past.

Demaci had already decided upon what he would be ordering, but gave Simon the opportunity to catch up and while doing so, Demaci ordered a bottle of the Moet & Chandon Vintage. Food orders placed, they both settled back to enjoy their meal and hopefully each other's company.

Tomorrow was going to be a very busy day and Demaci had needed something to distract him whilst waiting. Maybe there could be further distractions with Simon back in the apartment after they'd finished their meal. Anything was possible, if you have the money that is.

CHAPTER SIXTY-NINE

After the lads had left, Sally still glowing with youthful exuberance had run upstairs, slipping out of the new dress and shoes she'd been trying on and into the bathroom. She showered, dried her hair and even filed and painted her nails a bright crimson red, before putting on her makeup, with lipstick to match her fingers and toes.

Dave was busy with the kids helping them to get their overnight bags packed with pyjamas, school clothes, tooth brushes and teddy bears. Ready for yet another sleep over at Jenny's house.

Then it was Dave's turn in the shower. He then shaved and dressed in his designer jeans, navy blue shirt with polished black shoes. Sally was all ready by the time he was, so there was no waiting around.

The kids were bundled into the back seats of the Golf and delivered directly to Jenny's front door two minutes later. A quick kiss on Mams cheek so as not to disturb the lipstick with a 'love ya, see yeh's tomorra,' a quick wave, then they were gone.

Jenny came over and congratulated the newly engaged

couple, telling them how gorgeous they both looked and like the matronly aunt she seemed to have become, waved them both off as they drove away down the road.

Dave had phoned the restaurant earlier to make a reservation, but was told there was no need they were not so busy tonight. There would be plenty of tables for two still available when they arrived.

Dave had never been to this restaurant before, but had been told by several of the lads at the station this was the place to be seen. Anyone who was anyone went here and it was normally frequented by the cities football stars and their wag's.

As they pulled up outside, Sally got a case of the nervous jitters, having never been to anywhere posher than a MacDonald's burger bar before. Dave held her hand and put her right at ease explaining that every man in there, was going to be so jealous of him walking in with her and every woman, was just going to be so envious of how beautiful Sally looked. Thankfully it wasn't too full, nor was Dave's prediction very far off the mark.

They were placed at a prime table by the side window overlooking the riverside, out of the way of constantly passing waiters and patrons. The staff were extremely friendly and maybe even aware of Sally's insecurities, but they all made her feel very welcome and very special and when she was asked if they were there for a special occasion, she was able to show off her ring and say they'd just got engaged. Even the manager came over to offer his most sincere congratulations shaking Dave's hand and kissing Sally's making her feel even more special than she already did.

Sally let Dave order for both of them, so they started with the Terrine Forestier of wild champignon on toast, followed by the Escalope de Puolet au Pest Citronne and for

281

dessert a Mousse au Chocolat, et voila!

The food was delicious if not a bit strange to Sally's palate. So much garlic in the sauce as is the French way, but totally delicious, something they both thoroughly enjoyed, deciding they would like to do it all over again and very soon.

Neither of the two were drinking alcohol, sticking to the Perrier water with a slice of lemon. Dave being the driver and needing to be up early. Sally, a non drinker anyway. However when the manager came over with two glasses of Champagne to toast the couple, they both obliged by taking a sip and thanking him for his kindness and generosity.

The meal over, the two of them had their coffees and finally waved to the staff thanking them all for helping to make their day so very special, promising to come back soon.

Dave paid the Bill and again they both walked out hand in hand. The smile that had been on Sally's face as she first entered the restaurant was still there as she walked out and her jaw was starting to ache.

Dave unlocked and opened the passenger door for Sally to get in the car, but before she did, she put her arms around her fiancé's neck and kissed him in a very French fashion stood by the side of the road.

Sally and Dave told each other how much they loved one another, before jumping back in the yellow Golf and heading out of town to Sally's house in the Westernside housing estate, Eastscar by the Sea. Where for the next hour after arriving, they made tender love before falling asleep in each other's arms.

CHAPTER SEVENTY

Paul and Mike arrived home after leaving both Sally and Dave and as they entered the small terraced house they could hear the sound of a football match coming from the big, wide screen television in the lounge and smell the sweet sickly aroma of Chinese food.

Both Jockey and the Timber were sat watching the game with a disarray of half empty takeaway cartons cluttering the kitchen worktop space.

'We ordered in from the local chinkie's lad's, help yerselve's there's plenty left over.' Jockie shouted over the noise of the telly.

Paul and Mike walked over to the remaining food and although they hadn't eaten anything since breakfast, the sight of the congealed noodles and greasy chicken inside the slimy oil filled cartons was enough to put them off food for life.

The last thing any of them needed the following day would be a bad case of the squidgie's, so the boys declined the generous offer and Mike put all the remaining cartons of food into a plastic bag and placed it in the outside black wheelie bin, taking both the sight and the smell out of the house.

Paul looked into the sink and there piled high were the plates from the mornings breakfast together with all that had been used throughout the day. Mugs with dregs of coffee and tea, grease covered knives and forks, plates with solidified food covering the surfaces. The brothers looked at each other before Paul bellowed.

'And who the fuck do yeh thinks gonna clean this fuckin' mess up then? Yeh fuckin' Mam does not live here lads and I'm not gonna fuckin' run around cleanin' up after two grown fuckin' men. Get yeh arses in here and tidy my fuckin' house up now.'

Both Jockie and the Timber lifted off the sofa in unison, grabbing all the remaining plates and cutlery from the coffee table and commenced cleaning down workspace, removing dishes and pots from the sink and stacking them neatly to be washed.

Timber rolled his sleeves up and started to run hot water into the washing up bowl while Jockie found a clean tea towel to do the drying. Within a few short minutes, the whole kitchen was spotless and tidy without a thing out of place.

'Right, gentlemen as I now have your full fuckin' attention, we will be leaving here at zero six thirty hours, so please be ready, no fire arms to be carried, we are working with the local fuckin' constabulary and Dave will be with us as our official nanny. It would be seriously frowned upon should we be carrying bigger fuckin' guns than these professionals. We will be taking instruction from Dave, however, be ready within any given second to act upon my orders, understood?'

Both squaddies nodded their heads in understanding, looking rather sheepish at having been spoken to in the manner that Paul had deemed fit.

'Well if there's nowt else lads, then I'm off to my fuckin' pit and I shall see all your happy, fuckin' smilin' faces first thing in the morning. Enjoy the rest of your evening but I would suggest not stayin' up too late, goodnight.'

Dave was outside knocking on Paul and Mikes front door at exactly zero six fifteen. The door was eventually opened by Mike, dressed in jeans, t-shirt and a navy hoody.

'Away in mate, help yeh self to tea, coffee, whatever yeh fuckin' fancy. We should be ready to go in the next few minutes.'

'Morning everyone,' said Dave to the rest of them sat at the kitchen breakfast bar finishing their coffees and toast.

'Have yeh had owt to eat Dave lad?' Said Paul finishing his tea.

'Aye thanks mate, Sal was up bright and early and we had our breakfast together before I left.'

'Wow! Lucky you, someone up making breckies for yeh, it must be true love then eh?'

'Ya, it was my turn yesterday. Besides she was awake most of the night with nerves about today and couldn't sleep.'

'Aye, and what about you? How're you feelin'?'

'Truthfully? I'm a bit nervy too. I'll be all right once we get started, I think it's mainly the waiting.'

'Your right there mate. Once that adrenalin kicks in you'll be fuckin' fine. We're all the same and don't let any fucker tell yeh different. Right you lot, are we all ready to rock and roll?'

They all nodded their heads in agreement as Paul stood up. The three ex servicemen all wearing their old green fatigues, minus any rank or insignia markings. Dave was dressed the same as Mike in jeans, t-shirt and a hoody.

'Right lads, it's maybe best if we all pile into the van and leave the car, that way we'll all be together, and Dave can keep an eye on us. We'll go 'round to the cop shop first for the final briefing and see what the big boss has to say. Okay lads, let's be 'avin yeh.'

At that they all walked out of the house in single file, climbing into the van parked round the corner. There was very few people around at that time of the morning, so nobody to witness anything strange about three squaddies and two civvies exiting a small terrace house and climbing into a white van first thing in the morning.

At that time of the day, there was also very little traffic on the roads, so the drive to the Seaborough police station took less than twenty minutes and the white van, driven by the Timber pulled into the large, almost empty car park at exactly zero six fifty hours.

Again, in single file, but this time with Dave leading, they all entered the police building and made their way to briefing room number four which was already filling with plainclothes officers, all in different garb, some dressed as site workmen, while others with just overalls and hard hats.

They were all as far from looking like police officers as you could possibly get. The one thing they all did have in common however was, they were all drinking coffee from the same Styrofoam cups served at the station canteen. That is, all except Paul's crew.

Within a very short length of time DCI Turner simply seemed to appear at the dais and began addressing the assembly.

'Good morning ladies and gentlemen. This is it, the day many of us have waited a seriously long time for. Today we will either apprehend the two main villains of this fair city, or we will have frightened them so far underground they may never see the light of day again. Either way, I think we might just win out here. Team alpha you will be following the van out and make the arrests after they leave the site. All others will be placed en route to the site and within the site area. You all know your positions so please proceed. For the sake of good order, Constable David Riley will be attending with Mr Paul Vickers and his crew. They are all civilians and an observation only group. Please do not allow them to get either in the way or in any possible cross fire, they have been instructed and have signed disclaimers to say that they are responsible for their own safety and have been permitted to attend simply as a courtesy for their previous involvement the other night and the information supplied to us for this present operation. Okay folks let's go and all of you, please try and stay safe today.'

Paul and his team followed the others out of the police station to their respective vehicles, allowing them all to leave before driving out of the carpark themselves.

The day had started slightly overcast, but clear and dry. By the time they'd left the station carpark the sun was high and visibility was good. They continued to drive out of the city limits, through the country lanes until they came upon the entrance to the new Hidden Valley building site.

They entered the site and reversed the van in the site office car park near to the main entrance gate facing outwards.

The time was just coming up to zero seven fifty five, so they would have nearly an hour to wait before the container lorry and the white van should appear. They all made themselves comfortable with the Timber, Paul and Dave in the front bench seats and Mike and Jockie in the back, sat on the equipment holdalls from the earlier excursion into the city two nights before.

They hadn't been sat long before a black Range Rover drove slowly in through the site gates and parked over by the stores compound. Stepping out of the driver side was Bashkim Hamiti and from the passenger side one of the big lads that Paul had previously noticed parked in a white van opposite Sally's house.

'This is it,' said Paul, 'the parties about to begin, Dave that little man over by the Range Rover is our old friend Bashkim Hamiti. Be very fuckin' careful though and don't think because he looks like that, he isn't hard. He's as hard and as nasty as they fuckin' come, so be careful mate. That goes for the rest of yeh, do yeh hear me?'

CHAPTER SEVENTY-ONE

Hamiti had found the site foreman and together with the big man by his side, got the foreman to unlock the gates to the stores compound in readiness for the truck to be unloaded.

The foreman kept looking over his shoulder as though he was waiting for something or someone, he was nervous, that was obvious to see, but DCI Turner who was stood giving out instructions from a hand held VHF radio from scaffolding at the top of a half built house, was far more concerned that the foreman was going to bottle it and give the game away.

Turner could see that Hamiti was doing a lot of pointing into the foreman's face and was using what appeared from a distance, to be a considerably raised voice. Fortunately, whilst this was all in progress a large articulated lorry, with a big red container on board, pulled up outside the stores compound and the driver climbed down from the cab, walking over to the site office.

The truck driver was inside for less than ten minutes before he came back out looking for the site foreman, recognising him by the orange highvis jacket with foreman written in bold letters across the back. He walked over and presented the consignee documents for the unloading of the containers cargo.

The foreman showed him where to park, then walked over to the porta cabins, extracting the sites driver from the coffee machine room, who then started up the forklift to prepare and unload the container.

Whilst this was all going on, a white transit van with two more rather large lads pulled up in front of Hamiti where he pointed to the far side of the yard. Showing them the parking area where they could stay whilst waiting for the container to be unloaded.

The site was filling up now and it was becoming hard to distinguish between real site workmen and the local constabulary, there seemed to be so many people milling about.

Paul had raised a newspaper that he'd found under the vans seat to cover his face. He being the only one visible in the front that could have possibly been recognised by either Hamiti or one of his goons who were constantly walking past, conspicuous by the fact that they were the only ones not wearing any personal protective clothing. This was brought to their attention by the site foreman and they all returned to their respective vehicles whilst waiting for the container pallets to be unloaded, not wanting to draw any further undue attention to themselves.

The forklift driver began and with each pallet he was required to enter into the back of the compound where each of the pallets were unloaded into the dry storage area to keep the bags from deteriorating in the damp north east atmosphere.

There was a total of twenty pallets, each with twenty bags of dry powdered Portland cement. Wrapped in heavy duty sealing plastic to hold them all secure and restrict any pilfering.

These needed to be unloaded and Hamiti stood by inside the compound while they were unwrapped. The bags were then lifted off the pallets whilst searching for any that might have the red sealing on the top.

When he came across one, Hamiti would call to one of his deputies to carry it into the back of the white transit van, now parked directly outside of the compound alongside the truck. There was one red sealed bag on each of the pallets tucked in the middle of the other nineteen.

All of the arrival and unloading operation was being recorded on a digital camera by one of the specialist plain clothes officers halfway up the top of an electricity pylon over a kilometre away.

The images were relayed back to the station where a full record and inventory of the events could now be viewed as it happened and presented later as evidence in a court of law for the Crown Prosecution Services to scrutinise at their leisure, with the faces of each and every individual who took part crystal clear and in vivid colour.

The truck unloaded, the driver closed the doors of the container, got a signature from the site foreman to say the container was empty and swung the lorry around in a huge arc, facing the opposite direction and driving out of the gates.

Hamiti went over and spoke for a few minutes to the site foreman before handing him an envelope, presumably containing the thousand pounds for his part in the subterfuge. He then went over to the driver of his white transit van and had a few words with him before jumping into the driver seat of the black Range Rover and together with the companion who he'd arrived on site with earlier that morning, drove out of the gates followed by his own white transit van.

CHAPTER SEVENTY-TWO

'Right Timber follow that fuckin' van,' said Paul to his driver.

'Wait!' Interrupted Dave, 'let alpha team out first, they have to follow and apprehend.'

As he spoke a dark blue BMW M3 GTS flew out of the gates. Inside were four heavily armed Specialist Firearms Officers looking as though they were the real business and apparently, according to everyone that knew, they were the real business.

'GO! GO! GO!' shouted Paul, 'follow them and please Timber, try not to lose 'em.'

Timber had his foot hard down on the accelerator and was right behind the SFO car, managing to keep up through the tight turns of the narrow country lane.

As the white transit came into sight off in the distance, everyone eased off and sat well back, trying not to draw any undue attention to themselves. The eye in the sky had been instructed by Turner and was now following from high up, so it seemed as though everyone else was just dawdling along.

They followed the van who in turn was following the

Range Rover into a small industrial estate on the outskirts of the city and they stopped to watch from a short distance away, allowing both vehicles to pull up outside the lock up warehouse and unload the bags of cement.

While Hamiti and his crew were inside, the SFO drove their car slowly and quietly to the front of the building. One officer jumped out and heavily armed with a holstered Glock semi automatic pistol, carrying a Heckler and Koch G36 in his hands and wearing his KR1 body armoured vest, ran around to watch the back of the building. His colleague's equally armed covered the front of the building, slowly edging their way forward to the front door.

Crouched low, the three SFO team slowly turned the handle and finding the door unlocked, swung it wide open and entered, all running and shouting simultaneously, 'ARMED POLICE DROP YOUR WEAPONS.' There appeared to be a relay of several bursts of automatic fire, but from Paul's van nobody could determine who was actually doing the shooting.

Paul waited several minutes and nothing more happened, he then told everyone to stay where they were as he clambered over Dave who was sat next to the van door, to stand on the lockups forecourt.

Slowly Paul edged his way forward, drawing his own Glock 17 from a holster under his jacket at the back of his waistband and cautiously under cover of the police BMW, approached the front door. As he was about to open the door, it swung wide hitting him in the face, trapping him behind. He was slammed against the wall and Hamiti, blood running down his left arm holding an Israeli Uzi submachine gun in his right, fired towards the van with all the lads still inside.

Dave who was now stood out in the open by the side of the van, having followed Paul, took a direct hit to the chest standing stunned for a second then his eyes glazed over as he crumbled to the floor, blood flowing copiously from the large wound on the right side of his chest. There was another burst of automatic fire and everyone hit the floor inside the van again.

The Timber crawled across through the inside of the van making his way to Dave, trying his hardest to staunch the bleeding with field dressings he'd grabbed from Jockie who'd lifted them out from one of the holdalls in the back. Hamiti then jumped into the Range Rover and drove off.

Paul made his way inside the warehouse building and found it looking like the inside of an abattoir. Bodies and blood everywhere. The SFO officer who had gone to cover the back had now made his way around to the front and was on his radio asking for assistance and ambulances. His colleagues were starting to come around, their body armour having taken the brunt of the bullets, all other injuries being superficial.

First inspection indicated that all of Hamiti's men were dead, with several bullets in each. The SFO group appeared to be okay but they were advised that there had been a major incident out on the motorway and ambulances would be delayed in coming.

Paul took charge and told them to bring down the helicopter and get Dave straight to the hospital. The officer with the radio immediately transmitted the request and within a few minutes the chopper had landed out on the roadside, with rotors still turning. Timber picked Dave up unconscious in his arms, as though he were but a small child and bundled him into the helicopter, crouching low to the side as it instantly lifted off again.

While the SFO team now fully conscious and functional started to dissect what had happened inside the small warehouse, Paul checked that everyone outside was okay.

There were no other injuries although there were several bullet holes in the side of the van, for whatever reason, they'd all managed to miss everyone inside.

Paul took Mike to one side.

'We gotta let our Sal know about Dave mate, watcha reckon, we go pick her up or phone her?'

'We gotta pick her up bro, she's gonna be fuckin' heart broken, Sal's gonna need us, what with Mam and Dad less than a week ago, she needs us mate.'

'Aye yer right, away, let's go.'

With that they all jumped back into the van and headed for the Westernside housing estate.

CHAPTER SEVENTY-THREE

Sally was just changing the bedding when there was a loud knock at the door and Paul's voice booming up the stairs.

'Are yeh there Sal?'

'Aye, I'm upstairs our Paul, hang on I'll come down.'

Sally was barefoot, wearing her shorts and the t-shirt that Dave had taken off earlier. She had hardly any make up on and there were beads of sweat on her forehead.

'I'm knackered our Paul, I've never stopped since Dave went out early this mornin'. Just tryin' to keep busy, where is he by the way? I thought he was workin' with you lot today.'

'Listen sweetheart, he was with us, but he's been hurt and quite bad. They've flown him by helicopter to the hospital, but maybe you need to be there too.'

'Well, how bad?'

'Sal, he got shot in the chest sweetheart. We came straight here to get you, so we don't actually know how bad he is.'

Sally grabbed her hoody and slipped her pink flip flops on, grabbing her phone and purse.

'Away then, take us to wherever they got him.'

The drive to the hospital took forty minutes in the van and when they got there Dave had only just been properly admitted and was being seen in the emergency ward by a team of trauma specialists.

The two squaddies Jockie and Timber waited outside by the van while Paul and Mike went inside with their sister.

'I need to let his mam know and his sister. They'd wanna know, wouldn't they?'

'Ya Sal, do yeh have their numbers?'

'No, I don't even know where they live. Oh God Paul, I'm no good at this am I? We only got engaged yesterday. Shit I love 'im so much.'

Sally began to cry, she curled up into a little foetal ball on a chair in the waiting room and her heart broke yet again. It was while Sally was crying that DCI Turner came striding into the hospital and saw Paul and Mike.

'Right lads, what's the score? Have they said anything yet?'

'No, nothing yet Inspector. You wouldn't happen to know how to get in touch with his mam would yeh?' Asked Mike.

'Well they should have that information at the station why?'

'This is Sally you remember, our sister and Dave's fiancée. They only just got engaged yesterday, anyway Sal's concerned that his mam should be here.'

'Quite right too. I'll get straight onto it. A pleasure to meet you again miss. I can see young David is not only very brave but also has an excellent taste in beautiful women.'

Inspector Turner shook Sally's hand gently then turned and got straight onto his phone to the station.

'Right, the station will sort out David's mother. Do we

have any update from anybody here?'

'No the trauma team were with him, but no one's spoken to us yet.'

'Right, let's find out who's in charge then shall we?'

Inspector Turner walked over to the main desk and pulled rank on a senior doctor. Talking for quite a while before returning back and sitting next to Sally.

'Okay Sally my dear. They're saying that the bullet went straight through David. Entered in the front, exited out the back. It managed to crack a rib or two and double puncture a lung. He will require surgery to repair the lung, but whoever had administered the first aid apparently knew exactly what they were doing and excuse my medical jargon, managed to bung up the holes. He's going to require staying in for a small while but should be fine. Apparently, he's super fit and strong, but keeps asking for you. So young lady, are you up to seeing him before they knock him back out?'

'Yes please and thank you Inspector.'

'Come on then my dear. Let's go and find your brave young man.'

A nurse took them to a cubicle with a screen across, pulling the curtain back to let Sally through. Dave was sat up with tubes and blood connected to his arms and another sticking out of his chest, he had on an oxygen mask and his eyes were shut, but when Sally walked in his eyes opened and a huge smile covered his face.

'Here she is, here's my beautiful Sal,' Dave whispered weakly

'What the bloody hell have you been doin' David Riley? Goin off and getting' yeh self shot at like that.'

Sally ran to him and threw herself across his chest crying and making him gasp with the pain.

'Oh sorry babe, did I hurt yeh?'

'No sweetheart. It only hurts when you're not here.'

Dave put his arm around Sally's shoulder so she could climb up onto his good side of the bed and snuggle into him.

'Oh Dave, I was so frightened when the lads told me yeh'd been shot. I couldn't bear the thought of owt 'appenin' to yeh.'

'Well it was all stupid the way it happened. But that's a story for another day sweetheart.'

'I got the inspector to call yeh mam. I didn't 'ave her phone number or her address, or I'd 'ave done it meself.'

'That's alright sweetheart. Mams got built in radar, she'd 'ave found out anyway, one way or another.'

Just then a nurse came in and asked Sally if she wouldn't mind stepping outside while the surgeon had a quick word with Dave. Dave on the other hand asked if Sally could stay. She needed to hear whatever was going to be said.

The surgeon entered the cubical.

'Mr Riley? My name is Donald Simpson and I will be operating on you this afternoon. Looking at your pictures we shouldn't be down there too long, it's a relatively simple repair job and we should have you back on your feet very soon. So, if you're ready then I'm going to go down and start to scrub up. We should have you back in the recovery room in a couple of hours from now.'

Dave and Sally thanked the surgeon. Dave's mam and sister had arrived and wanted to see him. Sally stood to one side to let mam Riley in with his sister Kate standing back out of the way as there was so very little space remaining in the cubicle.

The nurses then ushered everyone out and Sally kissed Dave before she left saying she would be here when he came out of surgery and then she told him how much she loved him and that he must behave and do everything he was told. They then all went over to the lounge area to make themselves comfortable and wait.

'So, what happened Sally love? How's our Dave managed to go off and get hiself shot like that?'

'I really don't know the ins and outs of it Mrs Riley. All I know is he went out early this morning with me brothers over there. They were all on some sort of police operation and that's about it really.'

'Is that Paul Vickers over there then?' Asked Kate.

'Ya, the big bonny one with the beard, that's our Paul.'

'I'll just go over and ask him what happened then Sally, leave you and our mam to have a chat for a while.'

Kate made her way over to where Paul, Mike and DCI Turner were busy talking, making a direct bee-line to stand directly in front of Paul.

Paul stared at her for a second or two, then asked.

'Excuse me love, can I help yeh?'

'Yeh don't remember us, do yeh Paul Vickers?'

'Sorry love, no I don't.'

'Kate, Kate Riley?'

'Oh my God, so it is, how yeh keepin'?'

'I'm in a bit better nick than me baby brother. What did yeh's do to 'im like?'

'Sorry love, we can't go inta any of the details, but we've been told he's gonna be alright, so that's a relief.'

'Aye, anyway just thought I'd say hello, give us a call sometime if yeh get a chance eh?'

'Definitely will Kate. It's great to see yeh again though.'

Detective Chief Inspector Turner turned to Paul.

'Okay gentlemen, I'm going to leave you all now, just to let you know Paul, we recovered all the heroin thanks to you. It's now just a matter of picking up Hamiti. He seems to have gone to ground, we lost him when the helicopter landed, but he'll surface again sooner or later. We can't touch Demaci at the moment, he'll just deny any knowledge and call his solicitor, but there again, we'll get him one day. Thanks for all your help lads, we'll be in touch.'

Turner waved goodbye then walked over to where Sally, mam Riley and Kate were sat and said goodbye to them all before leaving.

'Right Mike, let's get the lads together. There's no fuckin' way we're finished and those Albanian bastards are not gonna walk. We know where Demaci is, so he's no problem. We need to find that fuckin' Hamiti and there's only one person I know who can do that.'

'Yeh mean Jacko?'

'Aye, that's the very lad, I'll give 'im a call. You go say bye to Sal, tell her we'll be in touch later, we have unfinished business to attend to.'

CHAPTER SEVENTY-FOUR

Paul and Mike walked out into the hospital carpark while Paul took out his mobile from the breast pocket of his fatigues and dialled a number. It rang for a few seconds before being answered.

'Jacko speakin', who the fuck's this?'

'Hi Jacko, Paul Vickers here, we need a big favour mate.'

'Hya! Paul, what the fuck can I do for yeh?'

'We need to find Hamiti now, like as in fuckin' yesterday. He's gone to ground but I have every faith in your devious capabilities. listen Jacko lad, this is really very fuckin' personal and we're prepared to pay. Just fuckin' find him for us as quick as yeh can and let us know where he is, okay?'

'Right mate, give us a little while and I'll get back to yeh as soon as I can. Promise mate, I'll do me very best.'

Paul and Mike then walked to the van where Jockie and the Timber were sat in the front seats reading old newspapers and waiting patiently.

'So lads, how's the wee bobby? He gonna be alright?'

'Ya thanks Jockie. They've taken him down to theatre to patch 'im up and they seem to think he'll make a full recovery. I gotta commend you's two though, they reckon it was your patchwork skills that saved him Timber.'

'My pleasure gentlemen, that's what friends are for, besides, it's not like we haven't done it all on numerous occasions is it?'

'Right now lads, we have some decisions to make and they need to be unanimous. I've put out feelers to try and find Hamiti, whereas Demaci is probably sat upstairs in his penthouse. Well pissed off because he's just lost a considerable amount of money and drugs. Who do we go after first?'

They all sat contemplating the question when Mike came up with his interpretation of the situation.

'Hamiti has fucked off for now and it may take a bit of time to find him. As far as I'm concerned, they're both as bad as each other and the worlds gonna be a better fuckin' place without either of them. I say we round up Demaci and when Hamiti surfaces, which he'll have to eventually, then we fuckin' grab him as well.'

'Okay bro, so what your sayin' is we go for Demaci in case he wants to make a run for it, while we fuckin' wait for Hamiti's whereabouts?'

'That's exactly what I'm sayin' big bro. I really don't see the point of waitin' for the fuckin' grass to grow, do you?'

'Okay lads, any objections from anyone?'

There were no objections, so between them all they devised the best operational plan in an endeavour to remove the first of the towns two major villains.

Paul made another phone call, giving instructions to whoever he was talking to. Explaining in precise detail what was required of them, then he turned to the Timber and told him to drive into the centre of town and head for the Tower Flats apartment building and pull around the side by the underground carpark exit.

There they could wait for the departure of any vehicle and drive immediately into the underground parking area. They needed to be inside the building out of sight from any of the outside CCTV cameras.

CHAPTER SEVENTY-FIVE

Simon had been fast asleep at home when his telephone started playing Dancing Queen by ABBA. He answered it well into the chorus and sat up to take note of what the caller was saying.

He dressed hurriedly and swilled his face under the cold water tap to wake himself up, cleaning his teeth and applying a quick smear of moisturising cream all round.

It had been nearly three in the morning when Demaci had completed using Simons body. Not just for the sex but occasionally as a bit of a punch bag as well. The many bruises were starting to show now, 'sick bastard,' Simon thought. It's one thing to have plain dirty rough sex with someone but why they needed to inflict serious pain was beyond his comprehensive, effeminate mind. However, Demaci did pay exceptionally well and the meal earlier had been almost romantic, so we mustn't complain too much.

He grabbed his jacket from the back of the kitchen chair and left his small flat above a women's shoe shop in the centre of Seaborough fifteen minutes after receiving the call.

Simon then walked the short distance to the Tower Flats apartment block and pressed the buzzer of the eleventh floor flat of Donika Demaci. After a few seconds it was answered.

'Yes, who is it?'

'Hya Mr Demaci, it's only me Simon, I was just passing and thought maybe you'd maybe like a bit of company, that's all.'

'Well I don't, I'll call you when I want you.'

Simon stood perplexed, what to do now?

'Well, what it is Donika love, I've been thinking about that proposal you offered the other night and I've reconsidered.'

'What fucking proposal? I'm very busy Simon.'

'Well I fuckin' understand that Donika sweetheart, but I'd rather not stand here talking to a fuckin' metal box on the side of a wall about something so personal. Can't I just come up and see you for a few minutes please?'

The buzzer went and Simon entered the building, taking the lift to the eleventh floor. The door was open when he arrived and he entered the apartment, shutting the door over, but not locking it. As Simon entered he pressed the send button on his mobile phone and walked over to Demaci who was sat behind his desk and kissed him on the lips.

Demaci, pushed him impatiently away.

'So, what was this proposal you wish to discuss with me?'

Donika Demaci was agitated, that was plain to see. Something had seriously ruffled his feathers and Simon felt he should at least ask why, just as a simple courtesy.

'What's the matter Donika love, you look angry, not with me I hope.'

'No, not with you. A business deal has just gone terribly wrong and cost me a small fortune in both money and men.

This whole fucking week has gone fucking wrong come to think of it. Anyway, it's none of your fucking business, what was this proposal you were talking about?'

'Well obviously it's not that important if you can't remember. You'd asked me to move in with you, that was all.'

'Oh that. We'll have to discuss it another time Simon, I'm sorry but I must ask you to leave, I have other more important things to attend.'

Simon could see into the bedroom and there was an overnight bag on the bed already packed, Demaci was going somewhere fast by the looks of it.

On the desk, Simon could see an open leather briefcase containing a passport, numerous documents and several wads of cash. The safe behind the desk was also open and had been emptied and although Demaci was fully dressed, he looked as though he hadn't slept in a week.

'Are yeh going somewhere Mr Demaci? Yeh look all packed up and everything. Yeh never mentioned to me yesterday that yeh were off somewhere.'

'I'm just going out of town for a few days that's all. Now please Simon, you must leave.'

'Ya, but when will I see yeh again?'

'I don't fucking know, now go!' Demaci shouted.

Simon turned and was heading towards the door when it flew open and in burst three big men in green camouflage fatigues, each wearing ski masks, black leather gloves, carrying automatic weapons and a holdall.

CHAPTER SEVENTY-SIX

They'd all waited patiently in the van and after a short time, the up and over door eventually lifted and out drove a silver grey, Mercedes S class saloon. As it pulled out of the driveway, Timber whipped the van straight in through the exit, finding an empty parking bay and reversing ready for a fast get away.

'Right lads,' said Paul, 'Mike you stay with the van and keep the engine runnin', we may need to leave in a hurry. Jockie an' Timber your wi' me, masks and gloves on, they may have fuckin' camera's inside. Bring the holdall wi' the gear in it, we'll probably need that and the two guns we confiscated the other night. We shouldn't need 'em but they tend to keep people very fuckin' quiet when yeh point 'em. That's the lift over there.'

They all sat in the van for a few more minutes longer then Paul received a text message,

'That's it, apartment 511, eleventh floor, let's go, the front doors been unlocked.'

The three squaddies rode up to the eleventh floor, pulling their ski masks down over their faces. There was no camera's in the lift and up until now, they hadn't noticed any in the building.

They arrived on the eleventh floor and found flat number 511. With his ear to the door Paul could hear muffled voices, then someone shouting, they burst through the unlocked door with Paul drawing his pistol and both Jockie and Timber pointing the automatic Uzi rifles towards the person sat behind the desk, pushing Simon out of the line of fire.

Demaci never even had time to stand behind his desk. He did however have time to lift a small hand gun from the drawer and point it at Paul. Unfortunately, he just didn't do it fast enough, Paul pulled the trigger of his military issued Glock 17, shattering the glenohumeral joint of Demaci's right arm between the humerus and scapula. The arm holding the gun now hanging totally useless by his side. The agony across Demaci's face was enough to make Paul feel a lot happier about what they were doing.

'One of yeh, patch that fuckin' Albanian twat up. We don't wanna leave a fuckin' blood trail everywhere and while yeh at it, give 'im a double shot of fuckin' morphine before he starts blubberin' like a fuckin' baby. Amazin' how they can dish it out, but they can't fuckin' take it themselves.'

Timber walked over with the first aid bag and started to carry out Paul's instructions. Demaci had gone glassy eyed and was on the brink of passing out, but they gagged him regardless, just in case he managed to find a voice to scream with.

The morphine took hold immediately and Demaci sat quietly, while Timber put a wad of packing across the bleeding hole in his shoulder. Strapping the now useless right arm across Demaci's chest and tying the left wrist to his belt with a length of nylon cord, rendering him totally armless.

309

It was Simon who spoke next to Paul.

'He's got a load of money in his brief case love, I don't know if yeh want it or not.'

'How much?' replied Paul

'Don't know sweety, soon tell yeh though.'

Simon opened the case and counted the money.

'Two bundles, ten thousand in each. But wait a mo' cos he's got a bag packed in the bedroom too.'

Simon went into the bedroom and tipped the contents of the holdall onto the bed. At the bottom of the bag were eight more bundles of money.

'Looks to me as though there's around a hundred thousand in total.'

'Okay Simon lad, you keep twenty and give us the rest, is that fair?'

'More than fair darling. Ooh! Look out Ibiza, here I cum.'

'Right Simon, throw everything else back into drawers and throw that fuckin' holdall in a wardrobe out of the way. Put this fuckin' briefcase in with it too, but remove the passport. I want it to look as though our Albanian friends already fucked off if anyone comes lookin' for 'im.'

They glanced around and the flat looked spotless. It was as though Demaci had indeed left and tidied before he went.

'Right Simon, do you have any police record?'

'No, why?'

'Cos your finger prints are all over this fuckin' place, that's why.'

'Ya, but everyone knows I come up here quite a lot, so if I'm questioned, that's all I'll say. He called, I came, actually no, he called, he came, not me, yeh know what I mean though.'

Paul and the other two smiled at the humour from the pretty young Simon. He couldn't see it though because of the masks they all still wore.

'Last job for you, bonny lad. Go and get the fuckin' lift. When the doors open, hold it for us and we'll be straight out. You stay up here until we're fuckin' gone and then you leave by the front door and Simon, thanks for all your help mate, you take care now and go get the lift.'

Simon did as he was told and Jockie together with the Timber lifted the limp body of the once drug Baron of Seaborough city between them while Paul carried the holdall with the weapons and the money.

As Simon called and held the lift door open, the three ran out holding Demaci between them. As they entered the lift Simon lifted Paul's mask up and kissed him on his bearded cheek,

'Maybe in a different lifetime, eh?'

'Ya, maybe,' Paul smiled and winked.

They rode the lift down to the underground car park and Paul got out first to make sure the coast was clear. There was nobody to be seen and the others dragged the limp body of Demaci across the concrete floor to the back of the van and threw him unceremoniously inside, climbing in after him with Paul in the front passenger seat and Mike driving.

'Okay bro, let's get the fuck outta here,' said Paul

CHAPTER SEVENTY-SEVEN

After the shootout at the lock up, Hamiti had driven out of town and headed towards a cheap holiday bedsit that he paid for monthly, as a just in case place. He kept extra clothes there, a spare passport and his money in a metal safe box under the floorboards. No banks for our friend Bashkim Hamiti, he tried never to leave a trail and only kept the day to day essentials at his flat in the city.

His arm had now stopped bleeding, but the bullet was still lodged in the bicep muscle at the top and would need to be removed soon. He'd done this kind of thing before so was conversant with the requirements. He also had a first aid kit at the bedsit, however it was a very basic one and a sticky plaster would not quite suffice on this occasion.

In the back of the Range Rover there was a padded high visibility jacket used in case of breakdowns, so Hamiti drove out of the way and stopped at a chemist's open late for evening prescriptions, putting on the jacket to hide the wound and blood on his arm.

Upon entering he found a single young Indian pharmacist in attendance. He turned the sign on the inside of the door to closed and dropped the latch. Walking to the pharmacy counter, he pulled the Uzi from under his coat and told the pharmacist to go into the back room used for making up the prescriptions.

Hamiti then forced the young Asian to clean the wound and find needle and sutures together with antibiotics and antiseptics. Then with the gun pointed directly at his chest, Hamiti explained to the young pharmacist the elementary basics of removing a bullet, cleaning the wound and sewing it all back up before applying a dressing.

All the lights in the front of the shop had been turned off and with extremely shaking hands young Sonny Oomen completed the first and only operation of his young life. He would be found the following morning by the day staff, with his neck broken.

Hamiti left the pharmacy and continued on his way to some waste ground where he dumped the Range Rover.

Hamiti then walked the short distance to the main road wearing the sports jacket borrowed from the young pharmacist and with the Uzi tucked under his arm inside the jacket, he hailed a passing taxi asking him to drive out of town to the bedsit in the opposite direction from which he'd just come.

Hamiti paid the taxi and got out three streets before his destination. He walked into the local pub and ordered a large brandy, sitting quietly at the bar, watching the door for anything suspicious. He had a second brandy and after downing the dregs of the glass, walked the short distance to the bedsit, always checking behind, to his satisfaction finding nothing untoward.

Bashkim Hamiti then entered the big downstairs front doors and climbed three flights of stairs to the top floor and his

313

tiny room.

The key was where he'd left it in the opaque glass shade of the wall light on the landing and after opening the door and smelling the always damp, musty atmosphere, he walked to the window and checked outside for any unusual movement.

Everything inside was as he remembered it from a few days before, but he pulled back the rug and lifted the floorboards to check the metal box hidden below. Again, all seemed to be in order, his passport and three hundred thousand pounds, all his worldly possessions.

He would spend the night here and be gone in the morning, maybe to Spain or Portugal at least somewhere where the weather was warm and the sun shone.

CHAPTER SEVENTY-EIGHT

Paul had told Mike to drive straight to the Ship and Anchor. They needed to talk with Jacko immediately and see if he'd found any information as to the whereabouts of Bashkim Hamiti.

They pulled into the carpark and it was heaving with the usual Friday night revellers. They told Jockie and Timber to remain in the back and keep an eye on their parcel, they would be out as soon as they possibly could. Leaving instructions that should said parcel start to get noisy give it another shot of morphine.

As the brothers walked in there was an almighty cheer went up. Neither of them were dressed for a night out with Mike in his old jeans and hoody and Paul still in his green fatigues, they seemed to stand out like sore thumbs, but it didn't seem to matter to their fan club. Over at the other side of the bar was Chrissy and Julie making hand gestures asking if the lads wanted a drink. Paul gave them the no sign across his neck and made his way over to Julie shouting above the noise that they were working and had only just called in to see someone. If they got a chance later then they'd call back, both girls looked genuinely heart broken.

They found Jacko in his usual office out the back of the pub, near the pool table, looking amazingly more disgusting than he normally did. He'd obviously spent a lot of time and effort into looking this repulsive, it just wasn't humanly possible by natural development. Paul wondered if Jacko had ever been laid and if he had, then what the fuck had she looked like.

Jacko pulled the brothers to one side out of earshot of the local inhabitants and over the noise of the music and the pubs incandescent white volume, he explained that he had some information, but he hadn't called them because at this time it was all unsubstantiated.

Paul explained that he was prepared to go with that if there was any reasonable possibility of Hamiti's whereabouts and based on that Jacko explained that someone fitting Hamiti's description was drinking brandy in the Jack and Jill pub out on the outskirts of Eastscar at the far end of the Esplanade earlier this evening. He was only using his right arm, the left was either injured or he was carrying something under his jacket and didn't want it to be seen. Jacko's source had followed this person to a block of private rundown bedsits and after waiting outside for several minutes he'd watched a light come on in the loft. Unfortunately, at this time, there was no definite confirmation that this was Bashkim Hamiti, it was only a possible maybe.

Paul asked for the address and let Jacko know that he was prepared to go with a possible maybe, which was better than an absolute nothing. If it's not Hamiti, then they'll apologise profusely on their way out and try to leave everything as they'd found it.

Paul and Mike said goodbye to everyone as they left the

bar and jumped back into the van, letting the two squaddies know what had been said and what their intentions were. They then set off to the other side of the Eastscar Esplanade.

It only took a few minutes to drive the van around the back alley of the address they'd been given by Jacko. They parked across the gate to prevent anyone from leaving that way.

As before, Paul told Mike to stay with the van and keep the engine running while he and the others went inside. Paul also told him that if Demaci was to start playing up, he was to give him another shot of morphine from the syringe in the first aid bag. It didn't really matter how much, just keep him quiet.

Paul, Jockie and Timber walked around to the front of the building with their ski masks and gloves on, weapons and everything else were contained in the holdall.

They entered the unlocked downstairs door and stopped at the bottom of the stairs, listening for any sounds coming from anywhere in the building.

They slowly ascended the first flight to the next level, again pausing and listening for any sounds. Paul had removed his hand gun from the holster on the back of his waist band, while Jockie and Timber had armed themselves with the Uzi's from the holdall the Timber carried.

Paul signalled for the others to wait, then he slowly climbed up to the next floor. After stopping and listening, he signalled for the others to follow whilst waiting and listening for any noises. A television or radio could be heard behind one of the doors on this level but otherwise everything else was in order.

The final flight of stairs reached to the attic rooms. There were two of them one at the front and one at the rear of the building. Jacko's informant had said the light came on at the front, so that was the one they were going for. Fingers crossed, otherwise big apologies all round.

Paul waited as quietly Jockie and Timber climbed the last flight and took up positions on either side of the door. Paul took a small step back and with all his force, raised a booted right foot and brought it heavily to bear near the handle of the door.

The cheap door almost disintegrated with the force used and it swung wide open on its broken lock and now very loose hinges. The body that had been laid on the bed, sprung up reaching for what appeared to be an automatic sub machine gun by his side, but for whatever reason his reactions were far too slow and a swift punch to the side of his head by Paul lay him crumpled on the floor, bleeding from his mouth.

This didn't stop him reaching behind and finding the flick knife he carried in his back pocket. He lifted himself quickly off the floor and went into a crouched fighting position, he was obviously going to go down taking someone with him.

It was Timber that grabbed the wrist holding the knife and raised the arm high above his own head while Jockie went in double fisted with several fierce rabbit punches to the exposed ribs and kidneys.

Bashkim Hamiti could do no more, he hung by his only good arm, totally limp as Timber still had him raised off the ground like a punch bag. The big squaddie slowly lowered him while Jockie grabbed a couple of plastic ties from the bag and secured Hamiti's hands tight behind his back.

Paul walked over and quietly shut the door, sitting on the side of the bed, looking down at Bashkim Hamiti laid on the dirty rug with the corner turned back. Paul out of curiosity, lifted the rug back and saw the loose floorboards, raising them easily out. There he found the metal box hidden below.

After replacing the boards and the rug, Paul tipped the

contents of the box onto the bed and whistled a low sound from between pursed lips.

'Jackpot lads, here's our fuckin' bonus for clearing this scum from the face of the fuckin' earth.'

Then Paul removed his mask and raised Hamiti's chin so he could look him directly in the eyes.

'Fuckin' remember me yeh Albanian twat? Ya I'm the daft fucker who's nose yeh bust and who's mam and dad died as a result of your fuckin' actions. Yeh shoulda just fuckin' walked away mate and none of this woulda happened.'

'So, now what? You take me to the police station for a reward? I'll be out within a couple of hours, Mr Demaci and his solicitors will see to that.'

'I don't somehow fuckin' think so mate. Not this fuckin' time anyway.'

Jockie walked in front carrying the bag containing the guns, money and equipment with Paul and the Timber walking behind with Hamiti in between them, being dragged painfully down the three flights of stairs.

The three marines had replaced their ski masks, if nothing else it made them all look incredibly sinister to any passing busy bodies and they would be far less likely to be confronted by anyone whilst wearing them.

They all walked out the front door and around the back where Mike was sat in the driver's seat of the van, occasionally giving it a few extra revs to keep it warmed up.

They opened the back door and pushed Hamiti in to lay alongside his former employer on the floor of the van.

'Give 'im a dose of morphine will yeh Timber mate, it's not for the pain, couldn't give fuck how much he hurts, just want 'im to be fuckin' quiet. Right everyone in the van, I won't be long, just need to make a quick phone call.'

319

Paul walked to the other side of the alley way and phoned Sally.

'Hya Sal, how yeh doin sweetheart?'

'Hya our Paul, ya I'm good tah. Dave's back up from the operating theatre. The surgeon says he should make a full recovery, but he's got all these tubes in 'im to drain his lung and everything. He's still out cold but I'm gonna stay here tonight I think. His mam and sister 'ave gone home now and I phoned Jenny and explained what's 'appened and she's gonna keep the kids for another night, she said it was no bother.'

'Well that's all good news then Sal, I just wanted to check in and make sure everything was okay that's all. I'll tell the lads, they'll all be pleased. You try and get some rest as well sweetheart and I'll speak to yeh in the morning, right bye for now.'

Paul hung up, went over to the van and let them all know Dave was going to be alright. Then he told Mike to drive to the boatyard it was nearly midnight and it should all be quiet there.

CHAPTER SEVENTY-NINE

They pulled up in front of the big main gates, with Paul jumping out to unlock them, allowing Mike to drive through, then locking them again from the inside. Mike parked the van in front of the Bonny Doris and waited for Paul.

'Right lads, this is the deal. I need all the guns we've taken, puttin' in the boat. Mike, you take the money and put it together with all the other stuff we got back at the house and in the car and after we give the twenty grand to DCI Turner we should have around a hundred and ten grand a piece, split four ways. Does that sound about right to everyone?'

'Hang on Vicker,' said the Timber, 'we didn't come here for the money, we came here to help a friend and that's all we came for.'

'Aye I know that Timber mate and my whole family and I will always be greatly indebted to you and Jockie here. There's no way possible we could ever repay yeh both for what yeh did, the money just came along. I never expected it so it's like a bonus. It hasn't cost us owt so it's only right that you two take a fair share as well mate.'

'Well okay if you're sure, but then I think it needs to be split five ways to make it fair if that's the case.'

'How so mate?'

'Well Vicker, there's you, Mike, Dave and Sally, Jockie and myself.'

'Aye Timber mate, but I don't know that Dave will accept it 'cos he's a bobby.'

'Yes, but I'm sure Sally will, and she doesn't need to tell him just yet does she? Looks to me as though she's going to want a big wedding and they don't come cheap. Besides Jockie and I want an invite and you know how much that little fucker eats.'

The lads all shook their heads and laughed.

'Right,' said Mike, 'what do we do with these two fuckers bro?'

'We need to get them both into the boat kid. Then you need to launch me and take these two bonny lads back to our place for a couple of beers and a kip. I'll give yeh a call in the mornin' and yeh can come back out and give us a tow into the compound.'

'Hang on our Paul. If your gonna do what I think your gonna do, then yeh'll need my help.'

'Not gonna happen Mikey. If for any reason I get caught, I need to know you and our Sal are gonna be okay. We already lost Mam and Dad and Sal doesn't need to lose you and me as well. So please don't argue and for once in yeh fuckin' life do as I ask yeh best mate. Go on get the fuckin' tractor and get me fuckin' hitched up.'

Mike looked at Paul and shook his head, then he looked at Jockie and the Timber and they nodded their agreement with Paul.

Mike walked over to where the tractor was parked and started it up.

'Timber mate, is there any chance you can give us a fuckin' lift with these two into the boat?'

'No probs Vicker.'

They put the ladder up against the side of the boat and Timber threw the unconscious Demaci over his shoulder like lifting a bag of coal, climbed the ladder and threw him in a big heap over the gunwale. He then came down and did the same with Hamiti, all finished within five minutes.

Paul then climbed up carrying the holdall with the guns and medical supplies together with lengths of rope. The other bag was still in the van and he asked Timber if he wouldn't mind passing that one up as well. Timber lifted it but was quite surprised by the weight.

Mike backed the tractor up to the trailer of the Bonny Doris and hitched them together connecting lights and brakes, then both Jockie and Timber ran across the compound, unlocking and swinging the big gates wide open, allowing Mike to drive across the Esplanade down the ramp and onto the beach.

The tide was well out tonight, but that was no problem, the weather was good with only a very light south westerly breeze blowing. At least the wind would be behind Paul all the way out, he should make good time.

Mike swung round on the beach and backed the Bonny Doris into the water, Paul started the engine and put her in dead slow aft while Mike disconnected the boat from the trailer.

Within a few short minutes the boat was free. Paul swung her about, giving his younger brother a wave and putting her into full ahead, with a course set for outside of the deep water anchorage area.

CHAPTER EIGHTY

Paul sat on the tall stool they used in the standing shelter when the weather was calm. It wasn't possible to sit when the boat was rolling too much, but tonight was a good night and Paul found the slight gentle roll together with the steady throb from the big diesel engine quite soothing.

He was still heading for the deep water anchorage when Demaci started to come around, the gag from his mouth having slipped down to around his chin.

'Please sir I don't know who you are, but may I please have a small sip of water?'

'Not a chance pal.'

'Where are we? Where are you taking me? Have I offended you in some way? I don't even know who you are.'

'Well, that's what happens when yeh get daft twats to do all yeh dirty work for yeh fuck face. Yeh lose control of what's goin' on and in this case yeh seem to have lost total fuckin' control wouldn't yeh say?'

Paul left the wheel while he went over and checked the bindings on Demaci and Hamiti, finding them both well secured.

'What is it you want? I'm a wealthy man, I can make you

wealthy too, name your price.'

'Okay, I will and if you can match my price I promise yeh I'll turn this boat 'round and set you free, a deal?'

'Yes of course, anything.'

'I want me Mam and Dad back, there yeh go, fuckin' deliver that pal.'

'But I don't know who they are or where they are, I don't understand.'

'No, I bet you fuckin' don't pal. me Mam was Doris Vickers and my Dad was George Vickers and last week they both died in a fire set by someone from your organisation and because I don't know who it was, then you'll have to pay the consequences for their lives. You should have taken better fuckin' control of your personnel mate.'

'But that was Hamiti, you must speak to him about that.'

'Well Mr Demaci, if yeh look over your poorly fuckin' shoulder yeh'll see a big lump layin' near to yeh and that is Hamiti. So, if yeh wanna blame anyone, blame him. Personally, I blame the fuckin' lot of yeh and that's why me and me mates made a point of fuckin' with yeh.'

'It was you who destroyed the heroin drop this morning?'

'Partly yes and partly fuckin' no. We are the nasty twats that hurt your fuckin' drops last week. However, we received information about the heroin and passed it on to the police and they were the nasty fuckers that were waiting for yeh this morning. It was me little sister that was married to the fat fuck that started all of this. You may recall, his name was Charlie.'

'But he has gone and no one seems to know where.'

'Ah, but that's where your fuckin' wrong again fuck face, cos I know exactly where he is.'

'And that is?'

'And that is, twenty five fuckin' metres below us in a fuckin' lobster trap. Or to be more precise, in several fuckin' lobster traps.'

By this time, the Bonny Doris had passed through the anchorage area and was heading out past the steep shelf to the deep black outer waters.

Hamiti had started to come around and was also asking for a drink which Paul nonchalantly refused.

'So, you killed this Charlie?'

'More or less. He was a worthless piece of shit anyway. At least it was me that got rid of him and do yeh know what, you two are also worthless pieces of shit as well.'

'So, you have become the white knight cleaning up the town. You know that when we're gone, someone else will take our place?'

'Probably, but that's not my problem pal. Only you two were my problem and I'm dealin' with it.'

'But then you become as bad as you say we are.'

'If you wanna believe that, then that's okay with me, but I think I know different. I know the police's hands are tied by the law. I know what they would like to do with people like you. They say that justice is blind, she's only fuckin' blind when it suits the bitch. The police know when to turn a blind eye and tonight's one of those fuckin' nights.'

Paul looked around, there was no sign anymore of the lights along the Esplanade, they were way too far out. Even the big tankers with their deck lights were tiny little models in a big playing field, they were well passed the twelve mile port limits and into the international main shipping lanes.

The Bonny Doris was rolling steadily as Paul put the engine into stop and they started drifting. The depth in this area was deep and black, anything between fifty to a hundred metres.

Only really advanced professional divers came this far out and to be honest it wasn't worth their while. Even on a good day it was far too dark and the water too murky in this area to see much of anything down below.

Paul went straight to the big bag that Timber had lifted on board complaining of the weight inside and with good reason. Paul had stolen the weights from Mikes bedroom that he used every now and again to work out with. That together with several lengths of small diameter chain and some new combination locks that had all been bought at the boat chandlers earlier in the week when Mike and Paul had gone on their shopping expedition.

Paul went to Hamiti first. He was still semi incoherent and his hands were still tied behind his back by the strong plastic cable ties. He realised what Paul was about to do and started to kick out. That did him no good whatsoever. Paul drew his hand gun and shot him through both knee caps. Hamiti screamed with the pain and while he was busy screaming, Paul locked two twenty five kilo weights to a chain and fastened it securely around Hamiti's ankles. Paul then cut the ties securing Hamiti's hands behind his back and dropped the weights over the side of the boat. Hamiti by now was screaming like a banshee and if Paul could have understood Albanian he might have been quite offended, but he couldn't, so he wasn't.

He did however assist Hamiti over the side and watched as he quite rapidly sank below the surface, his white face slowly disappearing into the dark depths far below. After a short while the bubbles stopped and Paul restarted the engine and they moved farther offshore.

Demaci was now curled up and whimpering in the bottom of the boat. Realising that this large bearded young

327

man in green fatigues didn't give a fuck as to how Demaci felt about anything and Demaci didn't mean a thing to him.

Demaci then made one last attempt to save his now fragile skin.

'I'll make you very rich my friend, take me back ashore and I can offer you millions.'

'Yes, you possibly could mate, but you know what, some of us really don't give a fuck about that kind of money, power and all that other useless shit that goes with it. I wanna get laid occasionally with a consenting pretty lass. I wanna pint or two with me mates. I wanna play with me niece and nephew and when the time is right, I might wanna marry someone who loves me for who I am, not for what she can get from me. Now if you were to give me loads of fuckin' money how would I ever know I'd found the right girl eh? Let me ask you Demaci, how happy are you feelin' right at this very minute about bein' fuckin' rich, eh?'

Paul stopped the engine again and as the boat started drifting, Demaci commenced screaming like a young child that couldn't have its own way.

Paul opened the bags and threw the Uzi's overboard and anything else that had been a part of the Albanian organization. He wasn't worried about the noise, there was nobody for miles that could hear anything.

'Right mate, do yeh want the hard route? Or would yeh prefer the really hard route? It makes absolutely no fuckin' difference to me, you're a dead man either way and yeh know what? No one's gonna fuckin' miss yeh. For all yeh were a big roughy toughy hard bastard, nobody now gives a monkey's fuck.'

Paul got the remaining chain and weights from out of the holdall and fastened them around Demaci's ankles and not once did he move or try to fight, he just lay in the bottom of the

Bonny Doris and cried.

Paul threw the weights overboard and with one arm still strapped to his chest and the other still tied to his belt, Paul lifted Demaci over the side of the boat saying.

'Yeh wanted fuckin' Charlie and now yeh found fuckin' Charlie. I hope yeh both find lots to talk about.'

Paul then threw his side arm overboard and anything else that could incriminate either him or his family, swung the Bonny Doris around and headed back to shore.

CHAPTER EIGHTY-ONE

Mike was laid awake in bed, staring up at the ceiling when his mobile next to him rang. He grabbed it almost immediately.

'Ya hello.'

'Mornin' bro, yeh gonna come and get me? Should be landin' ashore within the next half hour or so.'

'On me way best mate.'

Mike was up and dressed within a few short minutes, leaving the other two snoring fast asleep while he went by himself to fetch his brother.

He drove the Mondeo through the not so busy streets of town on a Saturday morning, the time now creeping up to nearly eight o'clock and the drive taking him all of twenty minutes.

Mike parked the car outside the double gates, which were already open and when he looked inside, the tractor was already gone. Someone else was out and about this morning, he would just have to wait, then his phone rang again.

'Ya, hello.'

'Alright mate, where are yeh?'

'Up at the compound, someone's got the tractor out.'

'Yeh, it's old Albert, he picked up our trailer and he's bringin' me in now, just stay and hang tight, I'll be there in a mo'.'

Mike ran over the Esplanade and could see the tractor pulling the trailer with the Bonny Doris on the back. They were just coming up onto the slipway, so Mike walked out and stopped the traffic allowing them to drive straight cross the Esplanade into the compound with old Albert swinging it all around and reversing into their parking space like the true professional that he was. Mike disconnected the trailer and Albert the daytime watchman drove off with a friendly wave and a tenner in his pocket.

Paul didn't wait for the ladder, he jumped over the gunwale landing on his feet in front of Mike as though it was the most natural thing in the world to do.

'Away kid, let's go get some breckies somewhere, I could fuckin' murder a big bacon stottie and a pot of tea.'

'Are yeh okay our Paul?'

'Aye son, why?'

'Just with yeh bein' out there by yeh self and doin' what yeh did, that's all. Yeh sure yeh okay?'

Paul put his arm around his kid brothers shoulder as they walked to the car.

'Mikey, it was just a job that needed doin' mate. The worlds a far better place now and there's nobody gonna come lookin' for either us or them. As far as we know Demaci and Hamiti musta escaped and got outta the fuckin' country, back to where ever they fuckin' came from and if anyone asks that's all we need to say. We don't know fuck all else.'

Mike nodded his agreement, Paul was probably right, he usually was. They headed back to the house where there should be a couple of packs of smoked shoulder bacon left. So long as the Timber hadn't found them yet.

Jockie and the Timber were up when they got back and after the preliminary chit chat, Paul went up to the bathroom for a shower and a change of clothes, coming down to the beautiful aroma of bacon sandwiches that Mike had fried up for everyone.

They all sat around the kitchen worktop with the two bootneck's asking what was next on the agenda.

'That's it lads, it's all over, we can all get on with the rest of our fuckin' lives hopefully. I guess you two will be wanting to get on yeh way back home again?'

It was Jockie who replied.

'Aye lads, if you're no wantin' us to stay for owt, I may as well head back this mornin'. My missus will have a list of fuckin' jobs set out for us when I get back. Might even treat her to a night out in a posh hotel wi' the pennies yeh gave us. They'll definitely come in handy lads, tah very much.'

'Yes gents, I'll probably do the same and head home. It's been an absolute pleasure seeing you all again and if at any time you require a large black man for anything menial, then don't hesitate in calling me.'

With that, the two of them collected their belongings gave hugs all round and Timber drove Jockie around to pick up his car, still parked outside Sally's house.

'This place feels fuckin' empty Mike.'

'Aye, I know, nice innit?'

'We need to get tidied up and go see our Sal, make sure everything's all right at her end. Have yeh got her share of the loot?'

'Aye, it's in an envelope, why?'

'Bring it with us, we'll go 'round to her place for a cuppa.'

CHAPTER EIGHTY-TWO

Mike drove them both to Sally's house, with Paul dozing off in the passenger seat. The drive only took fifteen minutes.

'Anybody in,' shouted Paul opening the unlocked door.

'Away in lads, I just put the kettle on.'

'Why yeh musta known we were on our way pet.'

'I did. I got back through the night. Dave woke up and was all groggy from the anaesthetic but the nurses said he was gonna sleep for about the next twelve hours straight, so I grabbed a taxi and came home for a couple of hours kip. I just had a shower and spoke to his mam to let her know what was happenin' then I saw big Timber and Jockie pull up so I went out to say tarah and thanks for all their help. They told us they were all finished and headin' home, so is that it? Is it all over and done with now then?'

'Aye, that should be the fuckin' end of it.'

'Do I ask how or where or anything?'

'No!'

'Oh! Okay then, so what's next?'

'Well, unfortunately we gotta sort Mam and Dads stuff

out next. But that'll wait 'til after the weekend. Hey Sal, what you doin getting' fuckin' taxi's man, yeh must be well flush like?'

'No, actually I'm rock bottom skint our Paul. That was the last of me dosh, I might need a borra' if that's okay?'

'What? Go on Mike, give her it.'

'Here yeh go Sal love, summit to tide yeh over.'

Mike handed the big envelope he'd been carrying. Sally looked inside and her face lit up.

'What's all this? How much is there? Where'd yeh get it? Is it all ours?'

The lads laughed and explained it was a fifth of the proceeds from the escapades over the previous week. Together with what Charlie had left upstairs. They further explained that Dave might not be too keen on being a part of it, as most of it was gotten by illegal means.

'So, fuckin' hide it under yeh pillow me little petal,' said Paul, 'and say nowt.'

Sally ran straight upstairs and stashed her nest egg where nobody could find it, then came down and finished making the tea.

'So, when yeh goin' back to the hospital? We'll go with yeh and see young Dave if yeh like.'

'Soon as I'm ready. He'll be well pleased to see you two though, all me lads together eh?'

'Aye he's one of the lads now is our Dave. Away then, get yeh self ready hinny.'

Bye the time the lads had finished drinking their tea, Sally was dressed looking as good as she ever did. No bruises or cuts, no broken bones or threats of any kind of violence all she had to do now was get her kids and her new fella home.

This life thing might not turn out to be so bad after all she thought.

CHAPTER EIGHTY-THREE

Mike drove them all to the hospital and they walked straight into the recovery ward where the duty nurse told them that Dave had now been taken down to a normal ward.

She gave them all directions as to how to get there, but they still managed to get lost at least twice. Eventually there was Dave sat up in bed looking quite perky. When he saw Sally the smile on his face just widened as far as it could go.

'Now then lover how yeh feelin?'

'A lot better for seein' you sweetheart.'

Sally leaned over and gave him a big kiss on the lips, then sat on the bed next to him, so he could put his arm around her.

'Yeh lookin' a lot better than yeh did when yeh came out of surgery mind. I brought the lads to see yeh as well, they'd been askin' after yeh.'

'Hi Paul, hi Mike, thanks for comin' guys, how'd it all work out then?'

'Not so good mate,' said Paul, 'they managed to recover the drugs, but I haven't heard owt about what's happened with

Demaci and Bashkim. I think they may have fuckin' legged it. You'll have to check with yeh boss, he'll have a better idea than us, I'm sure.'

'Well we can ask him now, he's just walked through the door with me mam and our Kate, look.'

Paul and Mike looked at each other and it wouldn't have been too surprising to know they were probably thinking the same thing.'

'Dave,' said inspector Turner, 'looking much better, how are you feeling lad?'

'A lot better thank you sir. Should be up and about in a couple of days and all bein' well. Back at work pretty soon after.'

'Excellent news and when you return would you be so kind as to report to my office. Your transfer has already been stamped and approved, so you will be on my team upon your return. But take your time, I want you to be totally fit and well first.'

'Thank you sir, excuse me Inspector but what happened to Demaci and Hamiti? The lads here don't seem to know too much.'

'Ah, yes, Demaci and Hamiti. Well young man all I can say at this present time, because of course it is an ongoing investigation, but we think they may have possibly absconded back to Albania somehow. A search of both their apartments found nothing, so at this moment in time, we must just wait and see if they might pop up so to speak. Now, I'm sorry but I must break up this party and leave you surrounded by beautiful women. I'm glad to see you doing so well Dave. Take care everybody. Oh! Paul, might I have a word in private please.'

'Two minutes Inspector, I'll see yeh outside. Okay Sal are you alright to get home by yourself?'

'Ya, ya, you go off and I'll see yeh both later.'

Okay sweetheart. Dave mate, we'll pop in and see yeh tomorrow, do yeh need owt bringin' in?'

'No thanks lads I'm fine, got everything I need right here.'

'Kate have yeh got a mo?'

'Ya of course, what is it Paul?'

Paul took Kate by the elbow and steered her to the wards waiting area, looking around to see that they weren't being overheard.

'I was just wonderin' Kate if yeh weren't too busy tonight maybe yeh might fancy goin' out for a meal with us? give us chance to reminisce and maybe catch up like.'

'I'd like that very much Paul as long as we don't go Italian.'

'No, I'm not into pasta, pizza and such, maybe Chinese or Indian then?'

'Aye, that would be lovely, what time?'

'Say about eight. I'll pick yeh up at your place.'

They both swapped addresses and phone numbers. Paul then kissed Kate on the cheek and waved Mike over.

CHAPTER EIGHTY-FOUR

Paul and Mike followed Inspector Turner out of the ward and into the carpark. Outside there was another plain clothes officer waiting. All scrubbed up and fresh faced, wearing a smart suit and tie. A new guy Paul reckoned, he could tell them a mile away, he came over to join them standing alongside DCI Turner.

'Paul, there may come a time, when I might have need of your specialist services and I may call upon you and your friends to assist with a project that the police are maybe unable to complete. Let's just say within the fastidious realms of the law. A time when we might require an individual with certain talents, like yourself. Someone who doesn't mind bending the rules a bit. Can I rely on you and maybe your friends, do you think? I have put my recommendations to my more senior hierarchy, who are quite in favour of bringing a more brutal form of retribution to those who we feel are unable to be touched by successful lawful means.'

'But why me inspector? Me and our kid here are just a couple of local fishermen. We just go about quietly mindin' our own business.'

'Exactly, oh sorry, you have met DS John Lawson, haven't you?

'No sir, nice to meet yeh there John.'

'We've actually met several times before Paul. I'm nearly always undercover though. Most people just call me Jacko, I hang out in the back room of the Ship and Anchor.'

'Oh fuck! exclaimed Paul,

'Holy shit!' was Mikes considered reply.

'So, let me get this straight,' said Paul, 'you've known about us every step of the way Inspector and yeh just played us so yeh could get what yeh wanted, by-passin' the law a bit so to speak?'

'Our hands were tied Paul. We already knew about the drugs on the container, but we also knew we would have a very difficult time proving anything against Demaci. After the Sergeant and I came to your house, we realised we had an extremely valuable friend and you'd already proven to us that you were a more than capable ally by what you'd accomplished in one night out on the streets.

Needless to say, this conversation has never taken place. However, if we need you, we will call you. Have a very good day gentlemen.'

www.clive-barry.com

Front cover image © Rafael Ben-Ari

25252031R00202

Printed in Poland
by Amazon Fulfillment
Poland Sp. z o.o., Wrocław